INFATUATION

INFATUATION

Claire Lorrimer

This first world edition published in Great Britain 2007 by
SEVERN HOUSE PUBLISHERS LTD of
9–15 High Street, Sutton, Surrey SM1 1DF.
This first world edition published in the USA 2007 by
SEVERN HOUSE PUBLISHERS INC of
595 Madison Avenue, New York, N.Y. 10022.

British Library Cataloguing in Publication Data

Lorrimer, Claire
    Infatuation
    1.   Friendship - Fiction
    2.   Marital violence - Fiction
    I.   Title
    823.9'14 [F]

    ISBN-13: 978-0-7278-6488-8

All Severn House titles are printed on acid-free paper.

Typeset by Palimpsest Book Production Ltd.,
Grangemouth, Stirlingshire, Scotland.
Printed and bound in Great Britain by
MPG Books Ltd., Bodmin, Cornwall.

Acknowledgements

I would like to express my gratitude to Phaedra Neal of
Diabetes UK and Sheena Craig of Severn House for their
assistance with the medical information and Jan Cuevas
for taking so much trouble to supply me with Spanish
background.

CL 2006

One

It was on the afternoon the marquee arrived, four days before Lucy Godstow's wedding, that Vanessa realized there was a way after all that she could prevent it taking place. The idea, which came to her as Lucy's mother Bridget Godstow outlined her plans for the wedding rehearsal, fell far short of the drastic action Vanessa would have liked to take – to wipe Guy Weaver off the face of the earth.

She had realized following the night he had raped her so savagely that murder was out of the question. The repercussions on those she loved and who loved her would be too awful to contemplate were she to be caught. She had been too traumatized at the time to report the incident or have the tests taken which would prove Guy guilty. Instead she told everyone her bruises were the result of a fall from the ladder she had been using when decorating the ceiling of the flat she shared with Lucy. Had Lucy not been away on the last family holiday she would enjoy before she left home, the whole horrible incident would never have happened. Although Vanessa devoutly wished it had not, there had been the vital benefit of discovering exactly what Lucy's future husband was really like beneath the suave, man-of-the-world, caring individual he professed to be.

Vanessa now opened a new file on her laptop.

'All ready, Aunt Bridget!' she said. 'Shall I start with the list of people who will be at the rehearsal on Friday?'

Bridget Godstow was not really an aunt but ever since her daughter Lucy had become best friends with Vanessa at their boarding school, she had taken on the rôle of proxy mother to the orphaned girl. At the age of eleven, the poor child and her brother, Tom, only two years older, had lost both their parents in a car accident. At the time they were living in Australia where they had no relatives. Tom had been sent to Switzerland to live with his godfather and Vanessa to their great aunt, a Miss Joan Lyford who was by then in her seventies. Although she had never been unkind to the little girl, she was unused to children and lived almost entirely for her bridge games. As a consequence, Bridget's maternal instincts had quickly surfaced and Vanessa had become almost a fourth daughter. Lucy's two sisters, Jemma aged six and Julia two years younger, were equally happy to welcome the quiet, sad little girl into their midst, and Jonathan, Lucy's brother, ignored her just as he did the other three girls.

Bridget Godstow, a plump, matronly woman in her early fifties, looked admiringly at Vanessa who was proving a tremendous help with the wedding preparations.

'You're so clever, Vanessa dear, with that machine of yours,' she'd said repeatedly, grateful for the lists. Vanessa had been keeping for her lists of guests who would be at the little local church for the ceremony; lists of those who would be coming to the house for the reception in the afternoon; and now she was making a list of those who would be at the rehearsal on the afternoon prior to the wedding.

'The six of us, of course,' she dictated. 'You, Guy, the best man, who we've yet to meet; Guy's father – he's flying over from Spain on Friday morning and George is going to meet him.'

Vanessa looked up at Bridget's flushed cheeks.

'It's down here that a taxi will pick Mr Weaver up at Gatwick at twelve-thirty. You thought Uncle George would be too busy with all the drinks to organize.'

Bridget sighed.

'Which goes to show, wherever would I be without you and your little machine?' she said. Her face suddenly clouded. 'I wish we could have had the rehearsal in the morning, but the vicar said he simply couldn't fit it in. Unusually he has a Friday-morning christening. Why do people want their babies christened in August, for goodness sake?'

'So they don't catch cold in winter?' Vanessa suggested, smiling.

'Yes, well at least we must thank the good Lord for sending us such wonderful weather for the wedding,' Bridget conceded, 'but whatever shall I give everyone to eat on Friday if it stays as hot as this? We don't want smoked salmon as we'll be having that the next day. I suppose we could go Indian and have a chicken curry. Perhaps not everyone likes it,' she added doubtfully.

'Then we could have tarragon chicken as well, so they have a choice,' Vanessa recommended, her heart suddenly doubling its beat as Bridget voiced her suggestions for the meal. Here was the opportunity which she had been searching for and had failed to find until this eleventh hour, a way for her to put Guy Weaver very firmly out of action.

Vanessa was a newly diagnosed type 1 diabetic and had to inject herself with insulin four times a day – a tiresome routine but one which was necessary for her to stay alive. Her great aunt also suffered from diabetes, but the type 2 variety common in many elderly people, and she was able to control her blood sugar by using tablets and adjusting her diet. On one occasion, her aunt had forgotten she had already taken her daily dose and taken another. As a result she had suffered from a hypoglycaemic attack when her blood sugar level had dropped too low. Luckily her cleaner had been there and was able to telephone for medical help.

At that moment it flashed across Vanessa's mind that all she had to do to carry out her plan to incapacitate Guy was to steal some of her aunt's pills to crush into a powder and administer them to Guy mixed with some food on Friday. Hopefully they would make him ill enough for the wedding to be postponed. It was only a few weeks ago that she had read about a child being terribly sick after eating some of his mother's pills thinking they were sweets. She knew exactly where her aunt kept her medication – usually a month's supply in the bathroom cupboard. If she removed some her aunt would have plenty of time to replenish the medication and would just think she had miscounted the pills. She would have no reason to suspect that Vanessa had stolen them.

Yet again Vanessa found herself wishing she had the courage to tell Lucy outright that she was making the most terrible mistake! But Guy's threats to harm her or one of the family she loved, had been too realistic – a hit and run ending Julia's life as she walked back from school; a car accident such as her parents had suffered for her Aunt Bridget and Uncle George; a drug in Jemma's glass before she went to one of her gigs. And for her, a fire in their attic flat from which, contrary to regulations, there was no fire escape. Guy seemed to have thought of everything. Now, at last, she realized there was a way she could prevent the wedding taking place on Saturday.

'I've been thinking, Aunt Bridget,' she said in as casual a voice as she could manage, although inside she was trembling with excitement. 'Why don't I cook the supper for us all after the rehearsal? I love cooking and curry is one of my specialities. In fact, I think I have several recipes.'

This was the kind of unselfish gesture Bridget was well used to from Vanessa. 'But darling, you'll be tired and you're a bridesmaid. Maybe I can get one of the caterers . . .'

'I wouldn't dream of letting you go to any extra expense,' Vanessa interrupted. 'I heard Uncle George telling you this morning at breakfast that with the florist's bill which came with the flowers, you were way over budget as it was without any extras. Besides, I'd love to do it. My contribution to the Big Day!'

Bridget shook her head.

'You'll be doing more than your fair share tomorrow!' she said, aware that Vanessa had volunteered to help her arrange all the many bowls and vases of flowers now sitting in buckets of water in the shade of the big marquee. It had been erected very quickly and efficiently by the team of men who'd brought it together with enough chairs and tables for the hundred expected guests. The tent now stretched along the length of the lawn, its pretty gothic windows facing over the flowerbeds that were a mass of dahlias and gladioli. Lucy had opted for blue and white flowers inside the marquee and they had planned a little hedge of blue and white campanula to surround the small dance floor in the centre of the tent. Jonnie was going to act as the DJ and the younger members of the party would doubtless dance there until dawn.

Vanessa's thoughts were very far from flower arrangements. She was still wondering how many of her aunt's pills she would need to affect Guy badly enough for him to be taken to hospital – whether he would fall ill quickly or in the night. She did not want to give him so many that he actually died. Her purpose was only to get the wedding postponed. Enough crushed and concealed in a strongly flavoured dish like curry might just work. The effects would not be immediate – and when they did become apparent, he would in all probability be thought to be drunk if he was unsteady on his feet or his speech was slurred. It would be a viable assumption as Uncle George was planning Pimm's to drink after the rehearsal and there would be wine with the meal.

Bridget's voice brought Vanessa's thoughts back to the present.

'Do you think Tom will manage to come after all?' she asked. Bridget was very fond of Vanessa's brother, as were all the family, and before Guy had come on the scene, they had all supposed that one day he and Lucy might fall in love and get married. Although no one actually spoke of it, they all knew that Tom was already devoted to Lucy, and Vanessa had told them that he'd never had another serious girlfriend, although he was a good-looking young man with a great deal of charm. Lucy adored him, but openly, as she adored her sisters – especially young Julia to whom she was particularly close.

Bridget smiled, a warm feeling of affection flooding through her as she thought of her youngest. Plump, freckled, uncoordinated as a young puppy, Julia at fourteen was as outspoken as she was impulsive. She made no secret of the fact that she was madly in love with Tom and she had declared that if he would only wait for her to grow up, she was going to marry him if he didn't marry Lucy. When Guy arrived suddenly on the scene, she was gleeful at first; but when Tom next visited and she saw how depressed he was, her natural kind-heartedness came to the fore and she started to make unfavourable comparisons between the two men. Guy was too old for Lucy, she announced. Lucy had only just come down from uni and, at thirty-five, he was more than ten years older – old enough to earn the nickname 'Granddad'! Moreover, he lived in London in a flat and Lucy was a country girl who loved playing tennis and going fishing with Jonathan and Tom at Ardingly Reservoir and always had a mass of pets who needed gardens and walks. Besides that, Julia told her mother, Guy didn't have any sense of humour. In fact he'd objected quite strongly when she and Jemma had been telling silly jokes. One in particular had sparked a really sharp rejoinder from him. It was about a matador who had told the bull to stand still so he could put his dagger in the right place. Before Jemma could relate what the bull said in reply, Guy had emerged from behind the Sunday paper and announced in a cold, hard voice, 'If either of you had the slightest knowledge of the art of bull-fighting, you would know better than to joke about it. We may not approve of the sport in England, but those of us who have lived in Spain have learned to appreciate there are far greater art forms than football, and bullfighting is one of them.'

But Bridget knew that wasn't the only reason Julia disliked him, recalling the story she had heard. Julia and Jemma had taken the dogs for a walk one day. Lucy had gone shopping in Brighton with Vanessa, so Guy said he could do with some fresh air and he'd go with them. Suddenly, Widger found a myxomatosis rabbit. The dog brought it across the field and dropped the poor frightened animal at Guy's feet. It was obviously close to death and the girls had known it wouldn't get better if they took it home and nursed it because their dad had told them they always died once they got the disease.

'Don't worry, I'll soon put it out of its misery!' Guy had said.

He'd found a piece of wood on the side of the road and before Julia could look away he'd hit it. The blow wasn't hard enough and to Julia's horror, it had let out a heartbreaking scream. She had been appalled but Guy had just laughed and hit it again – and again, and went on hitting it long after it was dead. He hadn't stopped until it was just a squashed, bloody mess in the middle of the road.

When he'd seen the two girls staring at him, he'd said: 'Well, I had to do that – you can't leave a half-dead animal, can you?'

Jemma had defended Guy at the time, saying he was absolutely right to make sure the poor little thing would not suffer any more, and no wonder his face looked funny; so would Julia's if she had had to do the hitting.

'But it wasn't a sorry face!' Julia protested. 'I think he *liked* doing it, Jems.'

Bridget, despite this story, was completely won over by Guy's obvious adoration of Lucy. At first, Lucy had refused to take him seriously and announced that she and Vanessa had just got their flat together in Brighton and started their new jobs teaching foreign students, so she had not the slightest intention therefore of giving it all up and getting married. But Guy had persisted and both Lucy's parents considered that he would make an excellent husband for their somewhat wayward daughter. A partner in his father's property development company in Spain, he was clearly very well off and Lucy's life would not only be comfortable but luxurious. As George had reminded his wife, the couple would be well able to afford to have a family and Bridget would get the grandchildren she had craved ever since Julia, her baby, was school age.

It was of Bridget Vanessa was now thinking as together they planned the supper for rehearsal night. Melon with Parma ham for starters, followed by either the curry or tarragon chicken with rice and a green salad, and finishing with homemade raspberry ice cream flavoured with Cointreau. Having then decided upon the seating arrangements, Vanessa put away her laptop and tried not to think of Aunt Bridget's crushing disappointment if she were successful in having the wedding postponed. Aunt Bridget had put so much thought and effort into it. As for Lucy . . .

Deliberately Vanessa closed her mind to Lucy's feelings. Guy had arranged for them to have three glorious weeks in the Seychelles for their honeymoon and they were due to fly from Heathrow early on the morning after the wedding. If her plan went as she hoped, that, too, would be cancelled. Lucy's beautiful wedding dress – strapless, ivory silk with lovely delicate beaded embroidery on the train – was hanging in a cotton wedding-dress bag on the back of Lucy's old bedroom door. Her own bridesmaid's dress and those of Jemma and Julia were in the wardrobe in the spare room. Lucy had chosen a pretty aquamarine blue for her bridesmaids, partly to continue her blue and white theme but also because it would look good on Julia with her red hair.

I am truly sorry, Lucy, she thought as Bridget went out to talk to the caterers who had just arrived with crates of plates, cutlery and glasses. I wish there were some other way I could do this. If only . . . *if only* I could warn you what Guy's really like. I wish he had never come into our lives. We were all so happy before – you and the family and Tom and me. I wish I was brave enough to kill him so he can never, ever hurt you.

It was seldom any length of time went by when Vanessa

did not thank Providence for bringing her and Lucy together all those years ago. Well-meaning as her Great Aunt Joan was, there was a mutual respect but no real love between them. When she had been most bereft, most lonely, Lucy had offered her friendship, which had deepened and endured throughout their school and university days. Afterwards, sharing the tiny flat in Brighton had been Lucy's idea, like so many other good ideas she had for their joint pleasure, and with jobs in the same college, the future had looked quite wonderful – until Lucy had met Guy at a friend's graduation party. Even then, the knowledge of how much she would miss Lucy once she was Guy's wife had not been too distressing, believing as she did that Lucy was going to have an idyllic marriage. Lucy had promised Vanessa that she would be invited out to Spain where Guy's father had a beautiful villa overlooking Marbella and that they would go on seeing lots and lots of each other.

'You're as dear to me as my own sisters, Van,' she'd said. 'Being married to my darling Guy won't ever alter that.'

Remembering those words now, Vanessa shivered despite the heat of the August sun pouring in through the kitchen windows. As happened now so often at night, she relived the terrifying evening that had irrevocably changed her life.

Two

It was mid July and Lucy was on holiday in Ireland – the last family holiday the six of them would have. In a month's time, Lucy would be married to Guy Weaver. Vanessa as a matter of course had been invited to go with them but Tom had a week's holiday and was coming to stay with her. Vanessa had not seen her much-loved brother since the previous Easter so she had opted to remain in Brighton, despite the fact that the popular seaside town was usually crowded at the start of the summer holidays.

As Tom was not due to arrive until the weekend, Vanessa decided to spend the two days prior to his visit decorating the sitting room. She had barely finished applying the second coast of paint when the phone rang. She wondered if it was Tom phoning her from Switzerland with a sudden change of plan. After hurriedly replacing the lid on the can of paint she was using, she picked up the receiver.

'Is that you, Vanessa?' a male voice enquired. 'It's me, Guy!'

Surprised to hear from him but hoping nonetheless that he'd been in touch with Lucy and had up-to-date news of her, she waited for him to tell her the reason for his call.

'It's just that I'm missing Lucy so desperately and guessed you were, too. I'm at a loose end up here and I wondered if I popped down to Brighton whether we could have dinner together somewhere.'

Astonished by the invitation which, when she hesitated to give a reply, he again repeated, Vanessa guessed he just wanted someone to listen while he talked about his absent love. She didn't particularly feel like going out, still less with Guy. Although he seemed a nice enough person, it somehow seemed wrong for her to have dinner with Lucy's fiancé.

'It's kind of you to ask me,' she prevaricated. 'But if you're speaking from London, have you realized that it would take you over an hour at the very least to get here?'

She heard his chuckle before he said: 'Of course I know. I've done the trip often enough. Anyway, I'll enjoy the drive. It's bloody hot up here and it has to be a bit cooler by the sea. What say we go to that nice hotel, the Old Ship? I've made some enquiries and heard the food is really good there. I've booked a room there for the night in case you can make it.'

Vanessa was surprised he'd gone to so much trouble. When she'd first met him Lucy said how wonderfully attentive and thoughtful he was, but that was only to be expected whilst he was trying to get her to marry him! Not quite sure why such a cynical thought should have come to mind, Vanessa tried to make amends by agreeing to have dinner with him.

'I'll book a table. Eight o'clock, do you think? Oh, and by the way, I'll be phoning Lucy at seven so shall I give her your love? I can tell her you are going to stand in for her to cheer me up!'

Vanessa put down the phone and stood for a moment, wondering why she felt uneasy. Maybe she was being boring . . . old-fashioned, she told herself, but somehow it didn't really seem right to be going out with Lucy's fiancé. It was the kind of admonition Aunt Joan would make. Her aunt was very precise in the guidelines she had obviously felt obliged to make when Vanessa had reached eighteen. Her virginity was her most precious possession and no matter how attractive or appealing a boy might be, she must never, ever allow him to do more than kiss her or hold her hand. She must try always to go on dates in foursomes as chaperones were no longer fashionable. She must not flirt with men as inflaming their passions was most unfair since she had no intention of assuaging them. She must never, ever go out with a married man who would almost certainly try to seduce her. And so on! But as far as Vanessa could recall, she thought now with a smile, Aunt Joan's strictures had not envisaged the situation of dining out with someone's fiancé.

Suddenly, she wished Lucy were here to share the joke with her. It was what made their friendship so perfect – always seeing things the same way. She would have to tell her when she came home. Meanwhile, it was high time she stopped meditating and started to prepare for the evening ahead. She needed the bottle of white spirit to remove the paint on her hands – possibly even in her hair. She'd have a bath and wash her hair, which being quite long, would need time to dry. Then her one and only respectable dress needed a bit of the hem stitching and the whole thing ironing. She wasn't sure whether Guy would mind if she went in jeans and a nice top, but a dress would be cooler as well as being a safer bet. That was another of Aunt Joan's dictums – men much preferred feminine women in skirts rather than trousers. Still smiling, Vanessa went into the minuscule bathroom and forgot both Lucy and Aunt Joan as she turned on the shower.

The dinner did not go well. Although the food was delicious, Guy kept urging her to drink up and seemed not to take in the fact that as a diabetic, she really should not drink too much; and she'd already had one glass of wine when he called to pick her up at the flat. Not only was he drinking continuously, but also his conversational topics were very far from being to her liking.

At first, they both talked about Lucy, but after the main course had been eaten and cleared away, he began questioning her about their time at university; how many boyfriends they'd had? She thought this question a bit out of order however light-hearted his tone; but she laughed it off with a smile and a 'None-of-your business, Guy,' remark. But to her acute discomfort, he pursued it.

'Come on, Van! Don't be naïve. Everyone knows what you girls get up to these days. You're as keen on sex as we men are. Don't try telling me you're a virgin!'

Vanessa was suddenly very angry. Even allowing for the amount he'd been drinking, this kind of talk was totally inappropriate.

'I really don't think that's any of your business, Guy, and in any event, I can't think of any reason why you should want to know.'

He lent forward to tip the last of the bottle of red wine into his own glass and gave her a sardonic smile.

'So that's it! Or am I guessing wrongly and you're a lesbian? Yes, that would make sense the way you dote on Lucy. But I can tell you this much, my lady, you won't get much response from *her*. She really enjoys sex with me and . . .'

Vanessa stood up abruptly, nearly spilling Guy's glass of wine as she accidentally knocked against the table.

'Guy, I want to leave,' she said. 'Now, if you don't mind.'

'Well, I do, actually!' He mopped at the spilt wine with his napkin and then reached up with his other arm to put a hand on her wrist.

'Look here, old thing, sorry if I upset you. I was only joking, you know – just teasing. Do sit down again, please.'

He sounded contrite but that was no longer the point – she still wanted to go. More than ever, she wished she had not agreed to come out with him. It hadn't been too bad at first – he'd been polite, attentive, friendly. It was after the second bottle of wine he'd changed. She couldn't put a name to it. He was just different – and she didn't like the difference one bit.

Seeing that Vanessa had no intention of doing as he asked, he drained his glass, beckoned to the waiter and asked for the bill.

Ten minutes later, they were in Guy's silver TVR speeding along the Brighton promenade past the pier and the Metropole Hotel. Neither spoke until they were outside 26 Maddison Street. Guy hurried round to open the passenger door for her.

As he took her arm, he said: 'Honestly, Vanessa, I'm truly sorry I spoke out of turn. It was really stupid, rude, uncalled for. I do hope you'll accept my apology. Too much wine on top of that stiff gin you gave me before dinner, I expect. Am I forgiven?'

'Let's forget it, Guy,' Vanessa said. 'I dare say I should have realized you were just joking.'

The frown which had distorted his good looks, left his face as he smiled down at her.

'Lucy told me what a good sport you are. I shall have to confess to her what a fool I've made of myself and how cool you've been about it. Now we're friends again, can I come up for a coffee?'

'I am rather tired, Guy,' Vanessa said quickly, adding vaguely, 'all that painting today and I've got to go to work tomorrow morning. I don't want you to think I haven't – well, that it isn't all OK again between us. I'm just tired.'

'Of course! I wouldn't ask you again if it was only to prolong our evening. I think I probably need some coffee to sober me up a bit. I have the feeling I wouldn't pass the old breathalyser test if I got stopped on the way back to the Old Ship.'

Vanessa immediately felt churlish. He certainly did need some strong, black coffee and it wouldn't take him all that long to drink it.

'Come on then,' she said. 'I'll put the kettle on and make it really strong.'

As she climbed the three flights of stairs ahead of Guy, Vanessa couldn't see the triumphant smile on his face. She was hoping old Ma Parsons on the floor below would not come out on the landing as she was prone to do, partly to see what Lucy and she were up to and also to berate them for disturbing her. The Godstow children had run into her when they were visiting and had nicknamed her 'Mrs Nosey Parker', because it tied in with the parson's nose. The poor old girl lived alone and as far as Vanessa and Lucy had been able to ascertain, she never had a single visitor. She owned an obese ginger cat upon which she doted. Very occasionally, it found its way up to their flat, but as they never fed the overweight feline, it soon disappeared downstairs again.

As usual, there was a light under Mrs Parson's door despite the fact that it was a quarter to midnight. But she did not appear so Vanessa was able to let Guy into the upstairs flat undeterred. Guy did not speak whilst she made the coffee. She found his silence disturbing without quite knowing why. When she brought a steaming mug of black coffee to him from the kitchen, he had removed his jacket and was sprawled across the sofa bed they kept for the occasional visitor. He didn't stand up to take the mug from her so she put it on the small occasional table beside him. He looked completely at home and she found his relaxed attitude disconcerting. He gave a noisy, prolonged yawn.

The silence lengthened whilst Guy sipped his coffee.

'I don't want to rush you, Guy,' Vanessa said, 'but I'm really quite exhausted and it's time you were on your way, don't you think?'

Guy put down his now empty mug but made no move to get up. He looked up at her with a strange smile.

'Trying to get rid of me, eh?' He sprawled back against the backrest, his hands behind his head. 'I may have had a lot to drink but I'm not drunk, you know. All the same, I really don't want to risk getting breathalysed. What say I stay the night? Lucy's room is going spare, I imagine? Or I could doss down on this?'

Vanessa drew in her breath, her uneasiness increasing.

'I'm sorry, Guy, but Tom's coming to stay and I've just prepared Lucy's room for him and there are no more bedclothes,' she added lamely. 'If you don't drive too fast, you shouldn't get stopped. Or you could leave the car here and take a taxi.' She glanced at her watch and with an exaggerated gasp, exclaimed: 'Goodness me, it's half past midnight! It really is time for you to go.'

Had Guy been anyone else but Lucy's fiancé, she would have spoken a lot more sharply and simply told an unwelcome guest to get out.

When after a long pause he replied, there was an unexpected sharp edge to his voice although he was still smiling.

'I don't think I want to go, Vanessa,' he drawled. 'Now are you going to tell me why you don't want me to stay? I'm not stupid. It's perfectly obvious that preparing the room for your brother was simply an excuse to get rid of me, as we both well know. You're not frightened of me, are you?'

Yes, I am! Vanessa thought as she backed away from him.

Trying to keep her voice completely steady, she said quietly but firmly: 'I want you to leave, Guy. Now. If you don't, I shall . . .'

'Call the police? Don't be stupid!'

He swung his legs off the sofa bed and stood up. Before Vanessa realized what he was about to do, he took a step towards her and grabbed her arm. He held it so tightly she could not prevent herself crying out. With his other hand, he turned her face towards him in a rough gesture and stared into her eyes.

'You're scared, aren't you? Wondering how to get rid of me? Well, you won't.' He was breathing hurriedly and his handsome face was distorted by an emotion she could only identify as malevolent. The harder she struggled to free herself from his grasp, the tighter he held her. She was really frightened now and one thought went pounding through her head – she would have to tell Lucy she must never, ever marry this man. He was evil.

She felt herself pushed savagely back on to the sofa and realized as Guy threw himself on top of her that he was far, far stronger than she was and she could not possibly free herself. When he ripped the dress from her shoulders, she succeeded in hitting him but he ignored her flailing arm. Only when he removed one hand to unzip his trousers, did she manage to push him off her, her fear lending her strength she'd not known she had. She tried to reach her bedroom where she hoped to be able to lock the door against him, but her dress was now round her ankles and she fell with a painful thud to the floor. Within minutes, Guy was once more on top of her. She could feel his hot alcohol-fumed breath on her bare neck.

Her fear became terror as he tore off her bra and pants, leaving her in no doubt about his intended rape. He forced her legs apart and when she cried out in protest, he hit her, not once but several times, shouting at her in Spanish '*Puta, puta, puta!*'

She did not know what the word meant but from the viciousness of his tone, she guessed it was something horrible.

Her fear gave way to astonishment as she realized suddenly that he was unable to carry out his intentions. She supposed he had had too much to drink, which, she had heard, made it impossible for a man to have an erection. But her relief was short-lived. He began hitting her again, his blows so painful that she could hear herself screaming.

Then the blows stopped and whilst she was still trying to catch her breath, he suddenly rammed into her disregarding her gasps of pain as he brought himself to a climax. She was trembling violently when he lifted himself off her and disappeared into the tiny bathroom. Her horror at what had just taken place was equalled only by her fear of what he would do when he returned. Did she now have time to reach the sanctuary of her room before he emerged from the bathroom, she wondered as she covered herself quickly with the Indian shawl Lucy had bought to act as a throw for the back of the somewhat shabby sofa bed. But she was too frightened to risk Guy's emergence just as she passed the bathroom door. She heard the lavatory flush and a minute later, Guy came out of the bathroom. He looked entirely refreshed – and almost normal, although his voice as he approached her was threatening.

'Don't think you can get your own back on me by telling Lucy – or anyone else, come to that. I'm warning you now to keep that pretty mouth of yours shut or someone is going to get very badly hurt.'

Vanessa felt a surge of anger.

'If you ever touch a hair of Lucy's head, I'll kill you,' she said, and surprised herself by realizing that she meant it. It would be a pleasure to kill this man. Lucy must never, ever marry him.

Guy seemed unperturbed by her threat.

'I didn't say I was going to hurt your precious Lucy – *my* precious Lucy soon, I hope, so I definitely don't want to harm *her*, do I? But I gather your brother, Tom, will be here in a day or two, won't he? You read the papers, Vanessa, my dear. You've read stories about people getting knocked off railway platforms in front of trains; or getting run over and killed by fast cars; or falling off a cliff top. There are lots of ways, you know, to bump people off without being detected.' He continued for a further five-minute tirade, his threats horribly frightening.

Not wishing him to realize he had succeeded in terrifying her, Vanessa stared back at him.

'You don't frighten me with such silly threats,' she lied. 'You don't expect me to believe you'd risk getting caught if you murdered someone. I shall certainly tell Tom – and the police; and I'll most certainly tell Lucy. I'll . . .'

She broke off as Guy strode over to her and grabbed her wrists. He put his face so close to hers, she could see the stubble starting to grow on his chin. His grey eyes bored into hers.

'You'd better believe me, Vanessa. Don't delude yourself that I didn't mean what I said.' He drew away from her, a strange look of pride replacing the menace that had distorted it. 'It may surprise you to know that I've done it before,' he drawled. 'And I got away with it. Mind you it was a good many years ago.'

Why, he's bragging like a small boy, Vanessa thought. In total disbelief she shot back at him: 'If you did kill someone, which I very much doubt, it would have been before they found out about DNA. Today, if I go to the police and tell them you raped me, they'll do tests and they'd know from your DNA that you were guilty.'

To her dismay, Guy laughed.

'You don't honestly think anyone is going to believe I raped you? Why on earth should I have done? No, Vanessa, it would be your word against mine because I would say you asked me to fuck you; that you were jealous of Lucy and invited me up to your flat in her absence; that our little soirée was all *your* idea. Don't you think my version of events is far more believable than yours? It's not very likely I was overcome with desire for a girl like you. You're not exactly a sex bomb, are you?'

The tone of his voice chilled her. It was threatening but in a quiet, matter-of-fact way that made it horribly believable. If she couldn't prove he had raped her, he might carry out his threat and harm Tom or one of the Godstow children – even her great aunt. If, however unlikely it might seem, one of them met with a horrible accident, it would be her fault. Yet she couldn't stay silent and let Lucy go through with the marriage ignorant of Guy Weaver's true nature.

He was standing by the door now, his jacket slung casually over one arm, looking at her with an expression devoid of anxiety.

Opening the door, he even smiled as he said: 'And one more thing, not a word to Lucy. In fact I must insist you keep this little incident entirely to yourself, Vanessa, my dear. I really don't want to have to silence you myself.'

When the door closed behind him, she sat hunched and dry-eyed in the armchair hugging her bruised body. Rocking to and fro, moaning softly, she was horribly afraid that Guy was capable of carrying out his threats.

Three

Tom Lyford put down his wine glass, sat back in his chair and looked round the half-empty marquee. Tomorrow it would be packed with people, with little room to spare between the twenty circular tables at which the hundred wedding guests would be seated. At the far end of the marquee, there were three long trestle tables empty now but which tomorrow would display a lavish wedding lunch. For the present, a dozen places had been set round one of the tables for a simple evening meal for the Godstow family and their house guests.

It was typical of Bridget Godstow to include him in this family party, Tom told himself as she hurried past him with yet another artistically arranged centrepiece of flowers to go on one of the round tables. Her plump face was flushed with her exertions for she and his sister, Vanessa, had been hard at work turning the empty marquee into a festive ballroom.

'Doesn't it all look lovely, Tom?' Julia, the youngest of the four Godstow children, interrupted his thoughts. 'I can't wait for tomorrow!' Fourteen years old, she had followed him round like a puppy ever since he'd arrived at lunchtime.

'She's got a crush on you, Tom!' her sixteen-year-old sister Jemma had teased, causing the poor child to blush a deep pink.

With a sudden catch in his throat, he caught sight of Lucy. She was wearing a short, pretty blue skirt and white, cropped T-shirt, her long bare legs and arms displaying a pale coppery brown tan. Looking across the tent to where she stood helping her mother place a huge vase of delphiniums, lilies and white roses in one of the corners, he felt a pang of misery so acute it was like a sharp pain behind his eyes. Tomorrow Lucy was marrying Guy Weaver and there was absolutely nothing whatever he could do to prevent it.

As Julia moved away to talk to her father, Tom walked over

to the opening in the marquee and stood looking out at the Godstows' lovely garden. It was ablaze with brightly coloured flowers on this late August evening. It had rained almost continuously throughout the past two days and everyone had been on tenterhooks praying for a return of the good weather for the wedding. Now there was little doubt that tomorrow the sun would shine on the bride and groom.

Tom drew a deep breath as he tried to rid himself of the depression that had taken hold of him ever since Vanessa had e-mailed him to say that Lucy was getting married. He'd fallen in love with Lucy years ago when Vanessa had brought her best friend out to Switzerland for a skiing holiday at Easter. The girls were celebrating their seventeenth birthdays which fell within a week of each other in March. He lived with his godfather Charles Rowan who owned a large house on the edge of Lake Geneva. Like his godfather, whom he called Uncle Charles, Tom was an avid skier. It was a wonderful holiday, and at the airport where he'd gone to see the girls off on their way back to Gatwick, Lucy had suddenly flung her arms round his neck and kissed him. Tom was three years older than the girls so Lucy was by no means his first girl-friend. He had even had an affair with an Italian girl several years older than himself, whose apartment he visited in Lausanne whenever he could do so. But that had been purely sex, he realized when he fell in love with the seventeen year-old Lucy that holiday; and he'd never been seriously interested in anyone else since.

Uncle Charles, a banker who was his guardian as well as his godfather, had turned out to be enormous fun. He was a jolly, good-natured bachelor who was delighted to have a teenage ready-made son. He'd never married and with no children of his own to inherit his not inconsiderable wealth, Charles quickly realized that Tom's natural mathematical ability would qualify him to join the merchant bank when he left university. Meanwhile, he packed Tom off to the Lyceum Alpinum, the excellent international boarding school in Zuos, near St Moritz, where he'd quickly settled down. Good at sports, he soon made friends, became trilingual – learning German and French quickly – and enjoyed wonderful holidays with his uncle skiing at Christmas and Easter and yachting in the South of France in the summer. Uncle Charles's idea of life was that it should always be fun with never a dull moment, be it at work or play.

Lucy now came across the lawn to stand beside him. She was holding the empty bucket, which had contained the flowers she'd been helping Vanessa and her mother to arrange. Her face was flushed and her eyes were sparkling as she smiled up at him. Only five foot two tall, she often joked that she was obliged to stand on tiptoe in order to kiss him. Those kisses were bittersweet for Tom who knew they were sisterly, not lovers' kisses, and they made him more acutely aware of his loss.

'Aren't we lucky, Tom?' she said as she pointed up at the orange-pink streaking the sky behind the marquee. 'Looks like we'll have a beautiful sunset. Red sky at night, shepherds' delight,' she recited. 'It's going to be a glorious day tomorrow!' She tucked her arm through one of his and gave him a little hug. 'I'm so thrilled you could come, Tombo! When I was sending out the invitations, Van said you might not be able to make it, but I knew you wouldn't disappoint me.'

She gave a mischievous little laugh as she added: 'I've invited three ex-boyfriends but you're my first – and favourite! Do you remember the summer holiday we had when we booked that tent in the South of France? Pa would have had a fit if he'd realized you were sleeping in the same tent as Van and me. I thought I was in love with you and that one day, when I'd grown up a bit, we'd get married. Goodness, how juvenile I was – and you weren't much better, Tom. You actually proposed! Of course, we both knew it wasn't serious but it was fun, wasn't it?' She gave a deep sigh. 'Now I'm about to wed my beloved Guy who, I might add, is frightfully jealous of all my ex's, and of you most of all because I told him you would always be extra, extra special.'

She reached up and kissed him lightly on the cheek.

'Love you lots!' she said, and with a happy smile she danced away from him swinging the empty bucket as she disappeared into the house.

I shouldn't have come! Tom told himself miserably, and yet he knew he'd had to do so. Right up to the very last minute, he could still hope that something would go wrong and that Lucy would change her mind. He'd met Guy Weaver once, last spring at her engagement party, and tried very hard not to dislike him. He was a good-looking bloke – quite a bit older than Lucy or, indeed, than himself. In his mid-thirties, Vanessa had told him. His dark hair was long, straight and inclined to fall over his forehead. His eyes, a curious grey, struck Tom as being secretive – as if he was quietly sizing everyone up; except, of course, when he looked at Lucy and then his expression was intensely possessive.

Tom told himself for the hundredth time that he was being quite unfair; that his all-too-real jealousy was clouding his judgment. But Vanessa didn't like him either. Not that she'd ever said so despite his probing, but she never had anything good to say about the fellow, and the most he ever got from her was that she wished Lucy would wait a while before taking the plunge.

'I know you love her, Tom,' she'd said on several occasions. 'I always hoped so much that you and Lucy would get married. Then she and I would have been sisters as well as best friends.'

Maybe it's all this wedding hoo-ha that's depressing me, he told himself as he strolled into the rose garden. The Godstows' cream-coloured Siamese cat was lying curled up on the stone paving circling the sundial. It gave him a brief glance and went back to sleep. Needless to say, it was Lucy's cat, he thought wryly, aware that everything today was forcing him to remember happy moments he'd shared with Lucy which would never come again. He'd given Motty to her for her twenty-first birthday, having purchased the kitten from a pet shop in Brighton with the best part of his allowance. Motty had been tiny then and when he, Vanessa and Lucy had passed the shop window the day before Lucy's twenty-first birthday, she had fallen in love with it.

'Your mum wouldn't want another cat,' Vanessa had warned. 'Not with two dogs, Jonathan's ferret, Jemma's rabbit and Julia's tabby. After all, Lucy, she's the one who has to look after them when you lot are all at school.'

'Well, I've left school now,' Lucy had declared. 'And I could take it up to uni with me. Oh, Tom, I'd really, *really* love to have it.'

Vanessa had dragged her away from the shop window, but of course he'd gone back the next morning, and willing to

risk Mrs Godstow's censure, he'd bought the kitten, keeping
it until after lunch when he and Vanessa were going to the
Godstows' house for a birthday dinner. As Vanessa had
surmised, Mrs Godstow was appalled but Lucy was ecstatic,
of course, and her mother had finally weakened and allowed
her to keep it. As she had predicted, Motty joined the family's
collection of pets thereafter. Later that evening, when the
younger children had gone off to bed and he was alone with
Lucy for a moment in the old nursery which was now the
children's rumpus room, she had flung her arms round his
neck and hugged him.

'I shall love you for ever and ever, Thomas Lyford!' she
declared, her eyes shining. She stopped covering his face with
kisses to pick up the kitten she was calling 'Motty', and kissed
it instead.

'Why Motty, of all odd names?' he'd asked.

'Because it's Tom backwards!' Lucy answered and still
holding the kitten, managed to kiss him again.

Remembering, tears pricked the back of Tom's eyes. Could
he bear tomorrow? he asked himself. Could he bear seeing
Lucy walking up the aisle in the white wedding dress Vanessa
had told him had cost a fortune and was unbelievably beautiful? Could he bear to watch Lucy's father give the girl he
loved so much to another man? Worst of all, could he bear
to see her radiant face as she walked out of the church into
the sunshine another man's bride?

As Tom made his way slowly back towards the house where
he knew he would find his sister preparing the evening meal
in the kitchen, his depression was no longer centred on himself
but on Vanessa. She was going to miss Lucy quite dreadfully.
Lucy had already removed half of her belongings from the
flat – those she might need after her wedding, but the bulk
she had left for Vanessa – her bed, her chair, her duvet, her
pillows, even her coat hangers. He'd taken over her room
when he'd flown in from Geneva the previous day, and like
Vanessa, had had the uncanny feeling that Lucy would be
coming back to it. The faint smell of her scent, Ma Griffe,
which she always asked him for at Christmas, was still present
in the cupboard where she'd kept her clothes and where his
morning suit now hung ready for tomorrow's wedding, at
which he was to be an usher together with her brother Jonnie.

Her beanbag Kermit frog, which he'd once won for her on Brighton Pier, still lolled on top of the dressing table.

Julia, in skimpy cotton shorts and an orange sun top, came hurrying across the lawn. She was carrying a clipboard with a sheet of paper with names on it.

'Hi, Tom! I'm taking orders for supper,' she said, pushing aside with a bare foot one of the Godstows' springer spaniels who was trying to lick her scarlet painted toenails. 'Van's cooking a chicken curry or you can opt for tarragon chicken if you prefer. There are eleven of us altogether with Mrs Thingummy from next door.' She looked down at her list and added: 'Six want curry so far and three tarragon, so there's only you and next door to decide. You can have whichever you like.'

'I'll have the curry then, please,' Tom told her, adding with a smile: 'I hope you're not going to the wedding in that outfit tomorrow, JuJu.'

Her cheeks turned a bright pink and Tom silently chided himself about teasing the child. She hated the family nick-name for her, which she said sounded as if she was a wine gum or a fruit pastille. To make up for it, he told Julia he thought her mother was very lucky to have such a helpful daughter.

'I'm being waitress, too!' she said, beaming, delighted by his praise. 'I'll be laying the table in a minute. Who do you want to sit next to, Tom?'

'Well, you, of course, and . . .'

'Lucy?' she asked. 'You like her best of everyone, don't you?'

Unable to speak, he just nodded. Before Julia could run off, he told her that it would probably be more correct protocol to put Lucy next to Guy.

Julia frowned.

'Well she's going to be next to "Granddad" for ever after when she's married,' she exclaimed, 'so she can jolly well make the most of this time with you.' With which she marched off in the direction of the kitchen, her clipboard tucked under a bare arm.

Julia was right, he told himself. He must make the most of what time was left for him to enjoy Lucy's company, hear her laughter, watch her sudden smiles, look into her beautiful sparkling eyes and hear her soft voice – perhaps saying for the last time: '*Oh, I do love you, Tombo!*'

If only . . . if only she did.

As Bridget walked past Tom on the far side of the lawn carrying an empty pail, she waved to him.

'George is serving Pimm's up by the summer house,' she called. 'Do go and join them Tom, dear.'

She stood for a moment watching him as he wandered off before continuing her way towards the kitchen. Not only did she feel sad for Tom and Vanessa, but she also felt another brief pang of sadness, this time for her husband. Tom and Vanessa weren't the only ones who were probably wishing right now that Lucy had never met Guy.

George was going to have very mixed feelings when tomorrow he gave his eldest daughter to another man to love and care for. From then on, it would not be he, her father, but Guy who came first in her affections.

It wasn't proving easy – handing over your firstborn to someone else, Bridget thought as she stopped briefly to lift a frond of late-flowering clematis hanging over the kitchen door. Thank goodness none of the family disliked Guy, and it was clear that Lucy adored him.

Feeling a little happier, Bridget went into the kitchen where Vanessa was stirring a large casserole which was taking up space on the Rangemaster. Her face was flushed by the heat and her dark hair stuck to her forehead and one of her cheeks.

'Are you sure you don't want any help, darling?' Bridget asked.

'I'm absolutely fine, I promise,' Vanessa assured her, brushing her hair off her face with the back of a hand which was holding a large wooden spoon. 'Julia has laid the table and is going to be the waitress, so she's coming in at seven o'clock to start taking out salad dishes and such. I thought we'd eat early – seven thirty if that's all right with you?'

'It's perfect, my dear,' Bridget said. 'I really don't want us to be too late to bed this evening. We all need a good night's sleep if we're going to look our best tomorrow and you and Tom are driving back to Brighton this evening. I do wish you could stay here. But never mind. Now, if you're quite sure you can manage, I'll leave you to it, Vanessa. And thank you once again, darling, for all your help. The flowers are really beautiful and I would never have managed to do them all on my own.'

She gave the girl an affectionate tap on her shoulder and went back into the garden, pausing once more to inhale the sweet, enveloping scent of the stocks that she herself had planted in front of the red-brick walls of the old farmhouse. Bernard, their elderly gardener, had somehow managed to keep the whole garden flowering throughout the hot summer. It was even more his pride than theirs, Bridget thought, as she walked across the lawn towards the group of people sitting or standing outside the summer house in the shade of the massive copper beech. A dazzling blue-and-silver dragonfly danced ahead of her before dipping swiftly down into the goldfish pond. High up in one of the tall fir trees, two collared doves called softly to one another.

Lucy and Guy were standing side by side, each holding a glass of Pimm's, as they talked to Guy's father. Herbert Weaver, unlike his tall son, was a short, tubby man with a florid complexion, light blue eyes and a loud voice. Now in his sixties, he had all the self-assurance of a man who had made his way in life, in Herbert's case, by his own efforts. A property developer, he had made the bulk of his moderate fortune buying and selling land and building holiday villas in Spain, mainly on the Costa del Sol. He had started back in the seventies, with a small legacy from his father, and had bought a large ranch house and some land on a hill not far from Seville. Labour was relatively cheap and he'd turned the place into a five-star hotel, which he'd sold for a huge profit. He had then branched into buying rundown villas, refurbishing them and selling them at an even more advantageous profit. Not averse to greasing the palms of various Spanish officials, he had little difficulty in obtaining the all important *escrituras* needed to ensure the freehold sales were legal.

Later that night when Bridget was preparing for bed she thought it strange that Guy had refused to allow them to invite his mother, who must surely have wanted to attend her only son's wedding, but then she remembered what her daughter had told her about Guy's abandonment in childhood. Bending over to kiss her goodnight, George reminded her that all families were by no means as close as theirs. 'Mainly due to all the TLC you give them, my darling,' he said.

Within minutes of turning off the light, George fell asleep; only partly reassured by his words of comfort, Bridget's strange feeling of unease kept her awake. All was as it should be in the house – Lucy had been almost asleep in her old room when she'd called in to kiss her goodnight. Lucy had hugged her more closely than usual and thanked her not just for the lovely dress, but also for the marquee, the flowers, the effort her mother had put into the planning, but most of all for giving her such a wonderful childhood.

'Poor darling Guy had a pretty miserable time of it,' Lucy had confided. 'I don't know the details as he doesn't like to talk about it, but even the little he said made me realize how lucky I've been to have you and Dad for parents – and sisters like Julia and Jemma, and a brother like Jonnie. I know I'll be living with Guy from tomorrow, but I'll still come home, Mum, as often as I can. I'll still be your daughter!'

A little tearful but pleased, too, Bridget had looked in on the two younger girls. Jemma was asleep but Julia was wide awake.

'I just can't wait for tomorrow!' she'd whispered as Bridget bent over to kiss her. 'I really, really, really *love* my brides-maid's dress.' She hugged Bridget and suddenly sounded very sleepy as she added a contented sigh. 'When I tried it on yesterday, Dad said I looked so pretty I might outshine the bride!'

Bridget crossed the room and bent over her middle daughter's bed. Jemma appeared to be sound asleep. As she kissed her cheek, Bridget saw that there was a film of sweat on her forehead. Although the day's high temperature had dropped several degrees when night fell, it was still quite warm in the bedroom. She went over to the window and opened the curtains to allow the cooler night air easier access. Not only stars but also a full moon turned the night sky almost to daylight. It meant that the weather would be quite perfect for the garden wedding reception.

She knew better than to go into her son's bedroom. It was usually so untidy that there could even be a problem opening the door. Jonnie guarded his privacy as fiercely as if he were hiding a dead body, although he always kissed her goodnight

Four

As soon as her mother had closed the bedroom door, Julia opened her eyes, and sat up in bed. The room was filled with moonlight and through the uncurtained window she could see the shining white orb, its brilliance all but obliterating the sparkle of the hundreds of stars. Too excited to sleep, Julia glanced quickly at her sister and seeing that Jemma was lost to the world, she scrambled out of bed and pattered barefoot over to the window.

Taking large gulps of cool night air, she looked down to the lawn where the white shape of the marquee was outlined. So far in her life, she had never been to a wedding – anyone's wedding – least of all where the bride was one of her own family. Another wave of excitement engulfed her as she relived the rehearsal they'd had that afternoon. Of course, they had all been wearing ordinary clothes but Mum and Vanessa had already filled the church with flowers and even the ends of the pews had little posies on them with white satin ribbons reaching almost to the stone floor. It all looked quite different from when they went to Sunday services.

Darling Tom had stood in for Guy's best man – someone they still had not met as he was not putting in an appearance until Saturday morning, but who Guy said was an old school friend. When Tom was asked by Dad to take the best man's place, he hadn't wanted to. Julia wasn't sure why; not that he'd said so and probably no one else had noticed the look his face. But she could guess what he was feeling. She 't like Guy and she hadn't wanted Lucy to marry him st from the beginning. She had told Jemma who'd nded to know why – but she couldn't say – only that it feeling. Sometimes when she was looking at Guy, he turn and stare back at her and she was convinced he ow she felt.

when they were downstairs – even on special occasions, giving her a little hug.

Now, lying in the big four-poster she and George had inherited from his family when they were married nearly thirty years ago, she reflected with a feeling of gratitude how lucky she had been all her life. And today, not only was the weather quite perfect but the wedding rehearsal had gone without a hitch and this evening, darling Vanessa had cooked a delicious supper for them all before she and Tom had driven back to Brighton. Bridget had offered to make up camp beds for them but both insisted they would not mind the drive back to the flat – a mere half-hour journey at most. They would return immediately after breakfast, Vanessa had promised – in plenty of time for her to change into her bridesmaid's dress and to help Bridget to dress the bride.

Overcome suddenly by a hazy feeling of exhaustion, Bridget turned over so that she was closer to her husband's recumbent form, and promptly fell asleep.

Realizing she was almost asleep as well as being cold, Julia stood up and hurried back into bed. Snuggling under her duvet, her anxious mood gave way to a sudden glow of happiness. She might not have been able to do anything to stop Lucy marrying Guy but she had scored a tiny triumph tonight. When everyone was seated at the table, Van had given her the plates of food to hand round, two at a time. The last of the two, curry this time, not the tarragon chicken she and Tom were having, Van said she would carry out her own and Guy's plates; but when Julia insisted she was the waitress and that anyway, Van wanted to put on the coffee percolator before she sat down to eat, she had given in, albeit fussing. 'That one in your right hand is for Guy and the smaller one is for me,' she said twice and added, unnecessarily, to Julia's indignation: 'You're sure you've understood that, JuJu? The big one for Guy, the little one for me.'

Yes, she'd understood. She probably wouldn't have had the idea of swapping them over if Van hadn't made such a thing about them being different sizes. So she'd decided not to give Guy the larger portion; he could jolly well have the smaller one. With a bit of luck, she hoped Van wouldn't notice when she sat down and swapped the plates back. To that end, when she'd left the kitchen and made her way to the entrance at the back of the marquee, she'd used her middle finger to spread the heap of rice a little wider on the plate she was going to give Guy. Her luck was in because Dad had told everyone to 'get stuck in' before the food got cold and by the time Vanessa sat down, Guy had already eaten several mouthfuls so she had never noticed! Recalling her little subterfuge, Julia gave a sigh of satisfaction and promptly fell asleep.

Tom and Vanessa had left the party soon after coffee, neither one wishing to stay any longer witnessing Lucy's happy excitement as she contemplated her marriage to Guy the following day. The fact that they were both soon to lose her was too depressing and their nerves were strung to breaking point. Tom had driven over from Geneva in his old Fiat and Vanessa's fatigue was so acute, she was immensely glad she did not have to drive herself back to the flat.

'I'll make us a cup of tea!' Tom said as they went upstairs

to the tiny attic apartment. 'You sit down, Van. You look exhausted.'

Vanessa sat down but then remembered that she had been so anxious before dinner that she had forgotten to take her injection and promptly got up again.

'I *am* tired!' she admitted. 'But I don't think I could get to sleep.'

Her hands were visibly shaking as she held the syringe. Tom had told her once that he admired the way in which she was able to plunge the needle into herself at regular intervals.

'Sit down and relax, Van,' he urged her as she put away her equipment. 'I don't wonder you are exhausted after this week.'

'For goodness sake, Tom,' she said sharply. 'That's the second time you've told me I'm tired.' Immediately regretting her sharp tone, she added: 'Sorry! I didn't mean to bite your head off.' She crossed the room once more to open the window over the sink. The bright moonlight lit up the rooftops of the adjacent houses, and to the left, between two chimney pots, she could just see its silver pathway across the sea. It was possible at night to hear the repetitive sound of the waves as they hit the pebbled beach when the tide was in, but tonight it was quiet, only the regular hum of traffic to be heard as it travelled along the seafront. Being so close to the sea and the view over the rooftops were the main reasons she and Lucy had decided to rent the flat.

She felt the slightest of breezes wafting in through the window, sufficient to cool her skin which felt clammy and unpleasant. She realized her whole body was trembling, but she knew it had nothing to do with her exhaustion or the temperature of the air. It was because of the drastic steps she had taken this evening to save Lucy. Not that her plan, however successful, would put the wedding off indefinitely, but if it was only for a few days it would allow Lucy time to change her mind. Surely she would do so soon! Surely Guy would not be able to keep up his pretence at normality indefinitely and Lucy would realize that underneath the veneer, he was a cruel, loathsome sadist? So many times these past weeks she'd been on the point of warning Lucy, but at the last moment, she hadn't dared. However extreme Guy's threats had been, she was horribly afraid he could and might well carry them out.

She turned back from the window and stared at her brother where he sat dejectedly at the kitchen table, his cup of tea untouched.

'Lucy should be marrying you, Tom,' she said. 'Not Guy . . . *you!*' she repeated in a loud, angry voice.

Tom stared at the table, not altogether surprised at her vehemence although it was most unlike her to raise her voice. She was normally so quiet, so reserved.

Last month Tom had taken a week's holiday to coincide with the Godstows' family holiday. Unfortunately poor Vanessa had fallen off a ladder she'd used for painting and was badly bruised, so they couldn't go hill walking as they had planned. He had stayed on an extra week and when Vanessa felt better, they had spent most of it at the Godstows' house. By then Lucy had returned from Ireland but Guy had driven down from London both weekends, whisking her off in his opentopped TVR so he'd seen next to nothing of her. He had spent most of his time playing tennis with Jonnie and the girls or taking them all either to the beach at Lancing or to the cinema or bowling in Crawley depending on the weather. Some days Vanessa declined to go with them and he worried in case she had damaged herself in her fall and was not telling him. It had not been a happy holiday and he'd been glad to get back to Switzerland where his guardian, jovial as always, thought up different ways to cheer him up.

Tom leant back in his chair and turned to look at his sister, pointing to her cup of tea which, like his own, had grown cold. She really didn't look too good. As she walked back to the table, she stumbled.

'I suppose I should get to bed,' she said as she fell into the chair beside him. 'I'm feeling a bit dizzy.'

'Overdone it, I expect,' Tom said. 'You get into bed, Van. I'll make a fresh cup of tea and bring it to you.'

'I don't suppose I'll sleep – but thanks anyway.' Vanessa got out of the chair and stooped to kiss the top of his head. 'I'm so glad you could get here, after all. I'd have hated to be here on my own tonight.'

Vanessa went into her room, undressed and after a quick visit to the bathroom to wash and clean her teeth, she climbed into bed. Her body still felt clammy and despite the fact that she was now lying down, she still felt strange. There was no doubt about the fact that something was wrong with her. Could she be suffering delayed shock? It was only six weeks since Guy's horrifying attack. Fortunately everyone accepted the explanation for her bruises as having resulted from a fall from a ladder. She'd worried that her Aunt Joan, who she'd been due to meet next day, might suspect something less innocent. She'd telephoned to say she was unwell and followed it up with a letter saying she had a dose of flu but was on the mend and would see her aunt as soon as she had fully recovered.

Recovering from flu would have been simple but nothing had stopped the very real nightmares or, indeed, the doubts that plagued her waking moments – doubts as to whether she should risk Guy's threats being no more than bluff and come out with the truth. But no sooner had she made up her mind to speak out than pictures came into her mind of the harm Guy could so easily do – to Julia, Jemma, Tom – even Lucy, and each time she lost her nerve.

It was small wonder, therefore, that now she had finally acted her body was having this strange physical reaction. She hoped the result would have ensured there'd be no wedding tomorrow. Her nerves were strung so tightly she had difficulty in keeping her limbs still. She looked at the little travelling clock on her bedside table. It was half past eleven – four hours since Guy had eaten the curry. He must be back in his flat in London by now. He and his father, who was staying with him, would be driving down to Ferrybridge together tomorrow in time for the twelve o'clock wedding – except that if her plan was successful there wouldn't be a wedding to go to. Guy would hopefully be too ill to attend, and the wedding would have to be cancelled.

For the hundredth time, Vanessa tried not to think how dreadfully upset her darling Lucy would be – and poor Aunt Bridget and the girls who were so looking forward to wearing their bridesmaid dresses. Maybe Uncle George and Aunt Bridget would have the reception in the garden anyway because they would not have time to let the guests know the wedding was cancelled and so much food would otherwise be wasted. Then the girls – and Lucy – could still wear their beautiful dresses. Perhaps postponed would be a better word to use than cancelled.

Vanessa turned restlessly beneath the single sheet covering her. Although the day's high temperature had dropped a little, it was still much too warm for comfort and the possibility of sleep seemed remote. If only she had been able to think of some other way to stop Lucy from marrying Guy, she would not have had to leave it to the last minute to take such drastic action. Week after week she'd tried to devise a scheme that would force Lucy to change her mind, but none had occurred to her until the eleventh hour, when fate presented her with a risky way to postpone the wedding. It was not as if from the day Guy had raped her she had lacked sufficient determination to part Lucy and Guy. But when Lucy had returned from her family holiday in Ireland it was to announce that she and Guy were going to the Greek islands for the remaining three whole weeks of the summer break, where they would stay on Guy's father's yacht. She was bubbling with excitement about the holiday in Ireland and Vanessa had been unable to bring her back down to earth with warnings about marrying someone she did not really know very well.

She had wished desperately that she could have told Lucy what had actually transpired whilst she was away, but she was in no doubt that Guy would find a way to harm someone dear to her or the Godstow family if she did so.

She started now to doubt the efficiency of her plan to incapacitate Guy. Knowing so little about Gliclazide, she had only been able to guess how many of Aunt Joan's tablets to give Guy. She was not even sure if too many would kill him. Not that she would care if he did die were it not for the repercussions which would follow. But had she given him too few? She would not know the answer until the next day. Meanwhile she could derive a little hope from the fact that he had decided to go home early because, he had said, he had overindulged himself with too much good food and wine; so maybe the tablets had started to affect him already.

She had never had a hypoglycaemic attack herself, but she was aware of the symptoms and knew in Guy's case that no one would suspect the reason for his collapse.

Vanessa was comforted by this possibility but it was swiftly followed by another anxious concern. If she had given Guy too much Gliclazide and he had to go to hospital, the doctors might find it in his bloodstream and Guy would know she was the culprit. If that happened, Guy would certainly denounce her or might even kill her.

Vanessa smiled wryly as she recognized how truly dramatic that sounded, but at least she had ensured his depravity would not go unnoticed. She had written a letter to Tom on her computer to be read in the event of her death if Guy harmed her or which she could produce in her defence if she were arrested for harming him. It was a comprehensive one referring to the rape. Aware that Lucy had access to the computer, she had saved it on her memory stick and wiped it off the hard drive.

Vanessa became aware once more of how strange she was feeling. Although she was shivering quite violently, her face and body were wet with sweat, and despite the fact she was lying down, she felt dizzy. For a further minute she lay still and then she sat up suddenly as it occurred to her why she might be feeling so peculiar. She must have forgotten to take her insulin injection . . . or had she taken it when she got back to the flat? Try as she might, she couldn't remember. She knew if she hadn't taken it and her blood sugar ran too high, she could expect to feel ill – and sometimes aggressive. She had been sharp with Tom earlier. Poor darling Tom! At least he would be pleased when the wedding was called off.

Weary almost to the point of collapse, Vanessa climbed out of bed and went to her dressing table drawer. It was only then that she realized that she had left her blood testing kit in the Godstows' kitchen. Like an automaton, she gave herself the injection and then fell into bed, pulling the duvet around her. With the light turned off, moonlight flooded the room. She could see the two-sided picture frame on top of the chest of drawers holding her parents' photographs, but in the half darkness, they seemed to waver from side to side. Her head was swimming and without knowing why, she suddenly felt angry as well as restive. Men like Guy Weaver had no right to be on this earth. If God existed, He should surely have made sure Guy died when he was born.

Her head was still swimming and she realized she was feeling sleepy. Her thoughts were of how much Lucy would hate her if she knew her best friend was responsible for ruining her Big Day. But Lucy would thank her later when she found out what a dreadful mistake she'd made falling for a man like Guy. She, Vanessa, could bear the thought of Lucy's pain the next day knowing that it was ultimately for the best.

It was Vanessa's final thought before she drifted into a profound sleep from which she would never wake up again.

Five

B y nine o'clock on Saturday morning, the August sun was warm enough for Joan Lyford to consider wearing her thin green georgette dress for the wedding. As she took it from the wardrobe and laid it out carefully on her bed, she recalled the superstition that green was unlucky, but she had no intention of acceding to such nonsense, partly because she considered all superstitions were nonsense, but also because she had nothing else suitable to wear. Anyway, she reflected, who would be bothered by what *she* wore. Everyone's eyes would be on the bride and bridesmaids.

She lifted the dress with care over her head so as not to disturb the tight set of curls her hairdresser had fixed the previous day. It was the same more formal style she liked for special occasions such as her bridge competition days. Thinking of bridge reminded her that she'd had to forgo two extremely important games because of the Godstow child's wedding. She didn't like weddings anyway, but in this instance, she knew she could not get out of going. Not only was the bride Vanessa's best friend, but also the parents had always been exceptionally hospitable to her great niece which had enabled her to continue with her comfortable bridge routine without feeling that she was not doing her duty by her ward.

Opening her jewel case, she took out the double row of pearls she wore on festive occasions. When she'd reached seventy, she had decided she was too old to wear the matching drop ear rings and that her ageing face looked better with her hair covering her ears and the sides of her wrinkled cheeks. She was on the point of brushing a dusting of rouge on her sallow cheeks when the telephone rang.

Surely not one of those dreadful salesmen offering a cruise or something equally stupid? she thought. Nor, hopefully, was it her friend, Elsie, who could go on talking for hours if she didn't shut her up. Crossing the room, she padded in her stockinged feet into the hall and lifted the receiver. At first she didn't recognize the voice of her great-nephew, Tom.

'Are you there, Aunt Joan? I hope I haven't woken you but . . .'

'My dear boy, I'm hardly likely to be asleep at this time of the morning,' she interrupted him, a hint of reproach in her voice. She felt a tiny prick of anxiety since it really was a little early for a social call.

'Is something the matter, Tom?' she enquired.

There was a short silence before he said: 'Yes, I'm afraid so, Aunt Joan.' There was another pause and then he added: 'It's Vanessa! She . . . she . . .' His voice broke.

She asked anxiously: 'She's not ill, is she? Tell her she must pull herself together. Am I not right in thinking she is the chief bridesmaid?'

She could hear Tom coughing and then he spoke again in a voice that was quite definitely hoarse.

'It's very bad news, I'm afraid. I wish there were a better way to tell you . . . Vanessa . . . I'm afraid . . . she died last night!'

The elderly woman sat down heavily on the hall chair. Without being aware of it, she smoothed the skirt of her dress to prevent it creasing. Surely she could not have heard her great-nephew correctly? Vanessa . . . *dead*?

Before she could find her voice, Tom spoke again.

'Are you all right, Aunt Joan? I did wonder if I should ring you first but I just don't know how to tell the Godstows – it's so awful . . . the wedding. I mean, will they still have it? Ought I to ring Mr Godstow and tell him?'

There was a break in his voice and his aunt suddenly realized he was crying. What a terrible shock this must be for him as well as for her. Vanessa was his much-loved sister; they'd been very close ever since their parents died, and although they had always lived in different countries, they had visited and written to each other frequently. She could recall Vanessa as a young girl forever asking for suitable stamps to put on her letters to her brother.

'I really don't understand, Tom. Vanessa rang me yesterday and she didn't sound in the least bit ill.'

'That's exactly what I told the doctor!' Tom's voice was a

little steadier now. 'I took a cup of tea in to her at half past six because she'd asked me to wake her early as there was so much to do. At first I thought she was asleep, sound asleep, so I . . . I shook her arm and that's when I realized . . . I can't quite believe it either.' His voice broke again and then he cleared his throat and continued. 'The doctor was very good. He came at once and said she must have died in her sleep and she wouldn't have known anything about it. He said they'd find out what had happened when they do a post-mortem. He couldn't be sure but he suspected it could be something to do with her diabetes. Or else some damage she'd sustained when she fell off the ladder which suddenly manifested itself. I'm waiting for the ambulance to arrive. Aunt Joan, what *am* I going to say to the Godstows? Lucy will be beside herself – and . . . and Van . . .'

'I know, I know!' Joan said quickly, realizing that Tom was finding it difficult to stay calm. Her mind raced as she tried to calm her own feelings of distress. What *was* the boy to tell the Godstows? Lucy would be devastated and in no state to get married. The whole family would be in tears.

'No, Tom, you mustn't tell them – it would be too awful. There is no need to do so. I mean, you could ring Mrs Godstow and say Vanessa has food poisoning – yes, that would do; that she had been up all night and was still rushing to and from the bathroom, so you had called the doctor and you were staying to look after her.'

For a moment, Tom did not reply. Then he said: 'I don't know if I could say all that without . . . well, without breaking down. I mean, Mrs Godstow, Lucy . . . they'd be bound to ask questions and I'd have to make up things and Lucy would want to rush down and see Van . . . Couldn't you ring them, Aunt Joan? You could say I'd rung you first because the doctor wanted to know about her medication; that I was going to the chemist to get a prescription so I'd asked you to let them know Van and I wouldn't be able to go . . .'

His voice trailed away and Joan realized that he really was in no state to carry out this subterfuge. Subterfuge it must be, she decided as she told Tom to leave everything to her and to take his telephone off the hook so no one could ring him.

As she went slowly back into her bedroom, she caught sight of herself in her bedroom mirror – the green dress floating around her as she walked. She was really too old for this kind of shock, she thought, lighting one of the cigarettes she had never yet managed to give up despite all the warnings. After inhaling for a few minutes, she felt a little calmer. Vanessa wouldn't have wanted Lucy's wedding day ruined, which, were her death to be announced, it could not fail to be. Even the absence of her best friend would diminish Lucy's happiness. No, there was no way Lucy must know the truth nor, indeed, Bridget Godstow who she, Joan, knew to be almost as fond of Vanessa as she was of her own children.

I'll tell them the truth after the reception is over and everyone has left, she resolved. Meanwhile I shall have to let the family know Tom and Vanessa won't be attending.

Refusing to allow the unexpected tears to fall, she went back into the hall to pick up the telephone.

Jonathan Godstow answered it and replying to her request to speak to his mother, he said she was frantically busy and could he give her a message.

Joan took a deep breath to steady herself.

'I suppose you could. Yes, perhaps it would be best if you broke the news to her. It isn't good news, I'm afraid. I've just had a telephone call from Tom and it seems Vanessa has been very ill – the doctor thinks it may be food poisoning. He has asked the doctor to call. So you see, she can't possibly get to you today – or Tom. He's desperately sorry.'

Jonathan said he was sorry, too, and goodness only knew what his mother would do. 'Van was going to be the chief bridesmaid . . .'

'Maybe your Jemma could take her place,' Joan suggested. 'I'll have to go, Jonathan. I'm on my way to Brighton to help Tom look after Vanessa. Tell your mother I'm so sorry to miss the wedding but I'll be there in spirit.'

Joan was quite breathless when she put the receiver back on its rest. At the age of seventy-nine, she was far too old for this covert behaviour, or indeed for the shock of her poor young great-niece's death. Her heart was hammering so fast she wondered for a moment or two whether she herself might be about to have a heart attack and die.

Made of sterner stuff than she knew, Joan Lyford arrived at the flat in Brighton in time to be of some support to Tom as the ambulance called to take Vanessa's body away.

Down at The Willows, George Godstow was doing his best to stem his wife's tears.

'I know it's an awful disappointment for you, darling, and particularly for Lucy, but it's not the end of the world. Jemma can be chief bridesmaid now. It's poor old Vanessa I'm sorry for. She'll hate missing the wedding.'

Jonathan, who had been standing awkwardly at his mother's side, lifted his eyebrows.

'I wouldn't lose any sleep over that!' he said in a dry tone. 'Both Tom and I think she doesn't much like Guy and wishes Lucy wasn't marrying him.'

Bridget stopped weeping and stared at her son reproachfully.

'That's ridiculous, Jonnie. I've never heard Vanessa say a single word against Guy.' For a moment, she looked uncomfortable and then she added: 'I do realize that Vanessa may not awfully much want Lucy to get married – to anyone, I mean. She'll miss Lucy terribly. Then there's the flat. After Tom goes back to Switzerland next week, she'll have to find a new flat-mate – and that will be difficult for a start. But she has nothing against Guy. Why on earth should she?'

Jonathan was saved a reply by the advent of Julia who could not fasten the tiny pearl buttons on the back of her brides-maid's dress.

'Oh, Julia, darling!' Bridget protested. 'It's much too early to get dressed. Put on your jeans or shorts and go and eat something. Edith has arrived and she'll cook you some break-fast if you're hungry.'

Reluctantly Julia returned to her bedroom to change her clothes before going down to the kitchen, where she found Jemma eating a slice of Ryvita covered with a scraping of butter. Jemma was on a very strict diet and was determined to get down from a size 14 to 12 before the end of the summer holidays. Lucy was a delectable size 10 and Jemma had told Julia her aim was to emulate Lucy by the time she left school next year. Boys weren't attracted to fat girls, according to Jemma, and Julia did wonder if she ought to diet, too, and get rid of what her mother called her 'puppy fat'. She very much wanted Tom to think her attractive. On the other hand, she was ravenously hungry and Edith was cooking bacon and sausages and beans for Jonnie so she decided not to start dieting this morning. Wedding days were special, and anyway, her mother had said that the wedding lunch probably wouldn't begin until at least 3 o'clock by the time everyone had returned from the church and had drinks in the garden. She'd probably faint in church if she didn't have a proper breakfast, like Jonnie's, with perhaps just one sausage instead of two.

It was going to be a very exciting day, Julia reflected, inhaling the delicious smell of frying bacon. She simply *couldn't* wait much longer to put on her beautiful delphinium blue silk bridesmaid's dress. She would have a circlet of cream rosebuds in her hair and carry a darling little posy of blue campanula and cream roses, the stems tied with narrow trailing blue ribbons.

As she sat down happily at the kitchen table Jonnie came into the room. He was, as usual at this time of day, still in his pyjamas and unshaven.

'Better not let Van see you like that!' she told him. But for once, Jonnie did not react and instead of grinning, he looked concerned.

'Bad news, JuJu!' he said. 'Van's got food poisoning and so she can't get here today and Tom's not coming either because he's got to stay and look after her.'

Julia stopped buttering her piece of toast, her expression doleful. She had been really, *really* looking forward to Tom seeing how pretty she looked in her beautiful dress. At the wedding he wouldn't have gone rushing off somewhere with Vanessa, Jonnie and Lucy as he usually did when he came to stay in the holidays, so she would have seen him all day. She had already persuaded her mother to move the place settings so that she sat next to him at the lunch, and . . . she broke off this line of thinking as a new and unpleasant thought struck her. If Van had food poisoning, it was probably last night's supper that was responsible . . . probably the chicken. Everyone said chickens were very suspect these days if they weren't farm-reared. And she, Julia, had swapped the plates and given the bad one to Vanessa when it should have gone to Guy.

If she'd done as Van had asked, she thought, it would have been Guy who had got food poisoning and then Lucy's whole wonderful wedding would have had to be cancelled. Maybe Guy *did* have food poisoning, too, but nobody knew. Julia allowed her train of thought to progress further: *then* Mum would want to know *why* she'd swapped plates and she'd have to say it was because she didn't like Guy and then there would be more 'why's' and she wouldn't be able to say because she didn't altogether know why she felt as she did – except the rabbit thingummy and . . .

'What on earth's the matter with you, Julia?' Jemma asked as she saw that her younger sister was pouring tomato sauce over her bowl of Shreddies. 'For heaven's sake, Jonnie, why didn't you stop her? Whatever were you thinking of, you two?'

'We're thinking of Tom and Van!' Julia burst out, close to tears. 'They can't come. Van's got food poisoning. Isn't it awful?'

Jemma nodded.

'Yes, I heard. Ma just told me. She tried to telephone Tom but the number is engaged all the time. Dad said he's probably trying to keep the flat quiet so Van can sleep.'

'Has anyone told Lucy yet?' Jonathan asked. 'She's going to be really pissed off!'

'Jonathan!' His father voice was suitably angry as he sat down at the table, adding: 'You know very well I won't have that sort of language in this house – and with your sisters present.'

'I know much worse than that, Dad!' Julia boasted. 'We often say shit at my school though you get a black mark if the teachers hear you.'

'Well, don't let *me* hear you,' her father replied, 'or you'll get a lot worse than a black mark! Now cheer up the lot of you. Jonnie can borrow the car tomorrow morning and drive you both down to Brighton. Lucy is going to give you her bridal bouquet to take to Vanessa and some wedding cake for Tom. I don't suppose Vanessa will want any just yet, poor girl! Now eat your breakfast and Jonnie, *when* you have shaved and look a bit more respectable, take those two dogs for a walk. We'll have to shut them up when we get back from the church. As for you girls, go and paint your nails or frizz your hair or whatever it is you girls do these days.'

All three children were still smiling when they handed their empty plates to the long-suffering Edith, and made their way back upstairs.

Six

A month after she and Guy returned from their honeymoon in the Seychelles, Lucy was still too shocked to consider anything much beyond her darling Vanessa's suicide. Unexpectedly, she received a phone call from Tom saying he would be coming to England the following Sunday evening; would she be able to meet him at the flat?

Lucy had as yet not come to terms with the idea that Vanessa could have been so depressed she had actually wanted to end her life, and she welcomed the opportunity Tom's proposed visit would give her to discuss the verdict. She had not seen him since the funeral – a heartbreaking day she tried not to think about. Apart from wanting to see her, he told her he had decided to come by car as he knew Vanessa had a number of books and family photograph albums he would like to keep as well as an original watercolour painting of their family home in Australia.

Lucy had, of course, at once said 'yes'. She would meet him on the Monday without stopping to think that Guy might have other plans for the day. Guy had told her on their honeymoon that he didn't want her to go back to work as there would be frequent occasions when he would need her to join him at business lunches when clients brought their partners.

Just to talk about poor darling Vanessa would be a relief, Lucy thought, putting Guy's breakfast things in the dishwasher before going into the bedroom to get dressed. She was feeling uncomfortable because she had lied to him about Tom's phone call telling him she'd been speaking to a female friend who wanted to meet her for lunch in Brighton on Monday. Deceiving him was abhorrent to her, she had told herself looking down at the rumpled, unmade double bed where they'd made passionate love the previous night. She loved him so much and their honeymoon would have been utterly perfect if she had not been told before she and Guy went away that poor Vanessa was in hospital and couldn't be visited.

Guy had become a bit irritated when on the evening they arrived in the Seychelles, she'd wanted to telephone home twice a day to see how Vanessa was getting on; if she was feeling better. Thereafter, whenever she could she phoned when he was not around. The calls, usually on Guy's mobile, always ended with her asking whoever in the family was on the other end, to give Vanessa 'oodles and noodles' of love – an expression left over from their childhood days.

Twice Guy had interrupted the call, indicating he wanted her to cut it short as he was waiting to take her somewhere. She had begun to wonder if he was just the tiniest bit jealous because some of her love was going to Vanessa. He was very possessive but he'd denied being jealous when she'd gently teased him about it. Nevertheless, during the last week of their honeymoon, she had stopped talking about Vanessa in front of him.

Lucy took the express train down from Victoria to Brighton and from there a taxi to the flat where she knew Tom would be waiting for her. Guy was up in Manchester where he had gone to see a client and so she had a whole day to help Tom clear the flat. After paying the taxi driver, she mounted the stairs leading up to the third floor, memories flooding back to her of the eight months she and Vanessa had lived here. The sadness was like a hard stone in her chest, too deep for tears. Maybe, she thought, she would be able to cry later, with Tom.

On the second landing, the door of Mrs Parsons's flat opened suddenly and the old woman peered out at her.

'Oh, it's you!' she said. 'Wouldn't go up there if I was you . . . not safe. She's dead, you know. He killed her.' Her voice became a whine. 'Why doesn't anyone ever listen to me? Think they know best, don't they?'

With a sick feeling she realized this crazy old crone was fantasizing about Vanessa's death, and she hurried on past her and up the last flight of stairs.

Tom opened the door and Lucy was suddenly inside, crying and he put his arms round her. He didn't speak but held her for a few minutes before helping her into a chair. Drying her eyes, Lucy watched him as he crossed the kitchen to put on the kettle. When he had made coffee, he brought a mug to her and pulled up a chair next to hers.

'Drink it whilst it's hot,' he said. 'Then we'll talk.'

The enormous pleasure he felt in seeing her was tempered by the reason for their meeting. It was not simply just to clear the flat of all the girls' personal effects so that it could be sub-let to a stranger; but because Lucy was desperate to discover the reason for the coroner's verdict.

'I still can't make myself believe it. Guy thinks I'm being stupid; that it was suicide – how could it possibly have been anything else? Tom, Van wouldn't. I know she wouldn't.'

Lucy burst into tears again and only calmed down when he told her he would be at the flat for several more days as he'd come over from Geneva expressly for the purpose of arranging to re-let it; so he was entirely at her disposal and they would have all the time in the world to talk everything over.

Her tears drying, she looked at his concerned face and trying to smile, reached out a hand and touched his cheek.

'Darling Tom, you're always so kind to me!' she said.

Because I love you so much, Tom thought but could not say. He knew from her phone calls how utterly devastated Lucy had been on hearing that poor Vanessa had never been ill but had actually died before the wedding. She'd kept reiterating: 'But I should have been told when it happened.' Both he and her mother and father had tried to make her see that if she had been told on the morning of her wedding, she would have been so upset she might have called it off.

'Of course I would!' was Lucy's immediate reply. 'How could I have celebrated anything knowing that I'd never see Van again?'

Guy, of course, had supported her at the funeral – a quiet family affair in the church where he and Lucy were married. Great Aunt Joan had agreed that Vanessa should be cremated and her ashes buried in the same churchyard – because Lucy had said that was where all their relations were buried, so she would be too when she died and then Vanessa would be near her.

'Bloody maudlin, I call it!' Guy had said aside to Tom when the idea was mooted. 'Now Lucy will want to go and do her mourning there – as if she hadn't cried herself stupid already!'

Tom recalled Guy's remarks when Lucy told him haltingly that she thought Guy was jealous because he knew how close she and Van had been and he and she weren't as close as yet.

'It's so childish!' she said to Tom. 'He doesn't seem to understand that I *need* to talk about Van.'

'Perhaps it's because he was an only child and didn't grow up sharing feelings with someone else, so he doesn't understand you wanting to. I seem to remember you telling me that his mother left him when he was quite young. And Lucy, we should remember he'd not known Van for very long.'

'I suppose!' Lucy said sighing. Then her voice deepened as she said urgently: 'The suicide verdict, Tom. I know it looked like an overdose of that diabetic stuff she had to take, but I know Van, she *wouldn't* have done it – not just before my wedding. Knowing how I'd feel . . . and Mummy and Daddy and the awfulness for you of finding her and . . . Tom, I *can't* believe it. Surely you don't either?'

Tom leaned back in his chair, his face distorted by the indecision of his thoughts.

'I know what you are saying, Lucy, and I've had all the same doubts as you, but the post-mortem showed that Van had too much insulin in her blood: that she must have given herself another injection. Presumably after she had gone to bed. We found the syringe on the floor by her dressing table. They also found Gliclazide, which she is not prescribed. The doctor told me she would have gone into a coma. I did look in on her to make sure she was all right and thought she was asleep.'

His voice faltered and was husky with emotion as he added: 'I'll never come to terms with the fact that if I'd only realized she was comatose I could have saved her life. You see, I knew she was overwrought as well as exhausted and I should have looked more closely.'

Lucy reached up and gently touched his cheek.

'You musn't blame yourself, Tom. No matter what you or the doctors say, I still believe it was an accident or a plea for help. I don't believe she intended to kill herself.'

He turned to take her two hands in his.

'However much we don't like to think it, we've just got to accept it. Van was almost certainly over-tired; depressed because she wouldn't be seeing you very often once you were married; that she would have to find another flatmate . . .' His voice trailed into an unhappy silence.

Lucy's tears began anew.

'I told her we'd see each other lots and lots and that I'd come and stay with her whenever Guy had to go away – if I couldn't go with him, of course. And besides, she was always so pleased when you visited, Tom. I know she was worried you wouldn't come to the wedding, and after your phone call saying you could make it, she went out specially to buy another electric fan so it wouldn't be too hot for you in my room. I'll never believe she meant to kill herself – never.'

Tom put his arms round Lucy and painfully conscious of her proximity, he rocked her gently until she was a little calmer. Whatever beliefs made it easier for her to accept the fact that Vanessa was dead, he would happily go along with.

'I suppose it could have been an accidental overdose,' he said gently. 'Van wasn't all that much of an expert about her illness, was she?'

It was a very unlikely supposition but Lucy grabbed at it.

'Yes, yes, that's it!' she cried, wiping her eyes and returning to her own chair. 'Oh, I *am* glad you're here, Tom darling. You make me feel so much better. I expect it's because I know you loved her as much as I did but . . .' Her voice faltered and then she sighed. 'I'm afraid Guy doesn't understand. Can I write to you, Tom, when you go back? You'll be a sort of life-line for me when I just *have* to talk to someone. I could talk to Mum but she starts crying and then we both do and we end up even sadder. Dad won't talk about it at all. He sort of pretends it hasn't happened and last weekend it was awful, he forgot and asked if Van would be coming to lunch next Sunday. Julia burst into tears and Jemma went out of the room and then, because no one had answered him, Jonnie, who was down from uni for the weekend, tried to divert Dad by asking him if he wanted another beer and Dad was angry because he said Jonnie knew perfectly well that he only had one beer before lunch and anyway he was drinking whisky! It would have been funny if it hadn't been so sad.

'Then Guy said in a loud voice, "Have you forgotten, Mr Godstow? Vanessa's dead." It was so awful, Tom. It got worse because Julia turned on Guy and said: "You don't care, do you? You want things to be dead like the rabbit and I hate you!"'

'The rabbit?' Tom asked as he found a piece of kitchen towel to give Lucy who was mingling sobs with her words.

'Oh, some silly grudge Julia has against him because he once put a myxi rabbit out of its misery. Guy was furious with her and started telling her off and then Jonnie got up and shouted at Guy that we were all upset even if he wasn't, and because he was married to me it didn't give him the right to tell Julia off. So I thought it would be best if Guy and I left so I told him I wasn't feeling very well so could we go back to London – and that's what we did.'

'Poor Lucy!' Tom said. 'I have to say I'm glad I wasn't there. Anyway, of course you can write to me, or we can text each other if you prefer. As for Guy, I don't think you should be too cross with him. You and your family are quite a formidable obstacle for him, aren't you? Six of you all utterly devoted and unusually close to each other! I remember the first time Van brought me to The Willows with her that summer holiday not long after you and Van first met. You had taught her the egg language and all five of you kept talking to each other – he-egg-e hegg-as fegg-un-egg-y egg-eyes and I didn't know what you were talking about other than that it made you laugh and I knew it was something you were saying about me!'

Lucy's face broke into a smile.

'But Tom, you soon learned to speak it faster than any of us if I remember rightly. Mum and Dad never could get the hang of it. Guy can't, either. I tried to teach him when we were on our honeymoon because he'd heard Jemma and Julia jabbering away but in the end, he gave up because he said it was stupid and childish – which, of course, it is!'

They were both silent for a moment and then Tom stood up, pulling Lucy to her feet.

'I want you to help me go through Van's things,' he said gently, 'but only if it won't upset you too much. I've not touched anything yet – well, I didn't feel up to it but it's got to be done if we're re-letting. I thought most of her clothes could go to Oxfam unless you think Jemma might like to keep anything. Maybe if you could just put things in two piles? The police have returned her computer and papers so I'll deal

with them. Do you think Julia would like Van's laptop? It's
an old model but it still works.'

'She'll be thrilled!' Lucy said as she went into the kitchen
to make them both another mug of coffee. Tom stood watching
her as she poured boiling water into the mugs.

'I wrote and told you, didn't I, that the estate agent said
we'd get a higher rent if we leave the furniture, crockery –
that sort of thing?'

Their lease did not run out till next year, and if she, Lucy,
was not to be sadly out of pocket, assigning the lease to
someone else was necessary. The next quarter's rent was due
shortly, but as yet she hadn't felt able to tackle the paperwork or, indeed, the task they were about to do today. It was
a heart-breaking job for Lucy. Vanessa's clothes, kept far
more tidily then her own, still held a lingering vestige of
her scent. There was a photograph album, too, with dozens
of pictures of herself and Vanessa taken on various childhood outings. In every one, they were holding hands and
their arms were linked.

'I'll never, ever forget you, Van,' she whispered as she put
the album aside to take back to London when she left. When
they had first learned of Vanessa's suicide on their return from
their honeymoon, Guy had been far from sympathetic, pointing
out that for Vanessa to kill herself on the morning of Lucy's
wedding was an utterly cruel and selfish thing to do. Had Tom
and his great-aunt not thought fit to conceal the news, he
maintained, Lucy's big day would have been completely
ruined. If Vanessa had to kill herself, she should have chosen
some other time. It was several days – and only after Guy
had said he was sorry at least six times – that she had forgiven
him for even thinking unkind thoughts about her dead friend,
let alone voicing them. Loving him so much, Lucy could not
stay angry with him for long but she had not entirely forgotten
it. It was a warning, she told herself, to try and keep the extent
of her grief from him. Now, too, she must not fill their lovely
flat in Fulham with too much memorabilia in case Guy accused
her of turning their home into a shrine.

How much easier it would have been if Tom was her
husband, she told herself as she tipped Vanessa's dressing
gown and bedroom slippers into the big black dustbin bag
Tom had labelled for Oxfam. Loving his sister as he always

had, he understood how she, Lucy, felt. She must make herself less cross with poor, darling, Guy who, as Tom said, couldn't be expected to feel the way they did.

But for all her good intentions, Lucy was close to tears yet again when Tom came into the room to show her a letter he had found in the back of a drawer in the desk she and Vanessa had used to support their computer.

'It's addressed to great-aunt Joan,' he said uneasily. 'It must have been overlooked when that detective sergeant went through her papers.'

Lucy's face drained of colour as she took the envelope from him.

'The police never found a suicide note, did they?' she whispered. 'You don't think Van was writing to tell your great-aunt that . . . ?'

Her voice broke and Tom quickly put a comforting arm round her.

'No, I'm sure it isn't!' he said. 'It's probably just a perfectly ordinary letter, probably about me, telling Aunt Joan I'd be staying with Van for the wedding.'

Partially reassured, Lucy took a deep breath but her face clouded again as she said: 'If it's just news, Tom, she could have telephoned.'

Tom smiled as he interrupted her.

'You know as well as I do telephoning my aunt is always a total waste of time. She's either out somewhere at bridge or at home playing bridge and all you ever get is the answer-phone; and then she always goes for days without calling 1571 for her messages.' Seeing the look of relief on Lucy's face, he took the letter from her. 'We'll post it when we go out,' he suggested. 'If we can find a stamp!'

'You don't think we should open it, Tom, just in case . . . ?'

'No, I don't,' Tom said.

'If you're sure, Tom, we won't bother to post it. Your aunt is having lunch with Mum tomorrow and I am going down to Ferrybridge too, so I'll give it to her then.'

As she took the letter back, Tom looked at his watch.

'It's gone one o'clock, Lucy. High time we went out and had some lunch, and afterwards, you and I will go and have an hour putting pennies in those ridiculous machines on the pier – just to cheer ourselves up before we come back and finish what we're doing. You don't have to go back to London too early, do you?'

Lucy tucked her arm through his, her eyes shining as she responded to Tom's suggestion. Brighton Pier had been one of their favourite outings when they were children.

'No, I've got the whole day free,' she said happily. 'Guy won't be back until late so we've got the rest of the day to ourselves.'

As they locked up and made their way downstairs, Mrs Parsons's door opened. Her voluminous musty tweed skirt reached to the ground and the dirty green cardigan she wore over a once-white blouse was spotted with moth holes. The steel spectacles she wore were tilted unevenly on the end of her nose, and her lank white hair hung sparsely to her shoulders.

'You, is it?' she said peering over her glasses at Lucy. 'I remember you. Had the police here, we did – and the ambulance. Up to no good he was for all his airs and graces. Kicked my cat, he did.'

'Excuse us, we're in a bit of a hurry!' Tom interrupted, hurrying Lucy on downstairs where the old woman's voice followed them.

'Sounds as if they'll soon have to take her away and lock her up,' he said. 'I don't recall her being quite so batty previously.'

Lucy grinned, remembering how Mrs Parsons used to corner her and Vanessa whenever they'd returned late from a party. 'Up to no good!' she'd screech at them, especially if they'd brought friends back. Then they were 'wicked', and if they had brought back boys, they were 'no better than harlots, hussies, whores'.

Telling this to Tom as they went out of the main door into Maddison Street, Lucy told him also of the time Vanessa had had enough of it and shouted back at the old biddy that she was 'off her rocker'.

'We laughed so much we nearly fell downstairs!' she said.

Not only relieved but enormously glad that Lucy could laugh about one of her memories of Vanessa, Tom tucked his arm in hers and they walked in companionable silence to find a place for lunch.

Seven

Much later that night when Guy returned from Manchester, Lucy was already in bed as he came into the room. He smiled at her as he removed his overcoat and went over to the big double bed and kissed her. When Lucy drew away from him breathless, he pulled her roughly up against him demanding to know if she had missed him, and saying how much he had missed her all day. Lucy knew from the expression in his eyes that he was intending to make love to her.

'Time I joined you in bed, young lady,' he said huskily. 'You're not going to tell me you're too tired, I hope?'

Lucy felt a familiar rush of guilt. Ever since she learned of Vanessa's suicide, she had excused her unwillingness to respond to Guy as being due to fatigue, although the real reason was that it somehow felt wrong to be enjoying such heights of physical pleasure when it was so short a while ago that her friend had died. Tonight would be different. Somehow the day with Tom had cheered her up a little, despite the sadness of the tasks they had done.

'Love you, darling!' she called to him as he went towards the bathroom. He stopped suddenly in front of Lucy's dressing table mirror against which she had propped Vanessa's letter to her great aunt so she wouldn't forget to give it to her next day.

'Where has that come from?' Guy asked sharply. 'Who's it from?'

Surprised by his tone, Lucy confessed she had met Tom that morning in order to clear the flat in Brighton. Surprisingly, he seemed unperturbed that she'd told him earlier she was meeting a female friend.

'I thought the police had gone through the flat with a toothcomb when they were searching for a suicide note.'

'Yes, they did!' Lucy answered, sitting up in bed, 'but the

letter was right at the very back of the computer desk drawer. If . . . if it was . . . what you think . . . if Van wanted her aunt to know why she . . . what she was about to do, she would have posted it or left the letter where it could be seen. Suicide notes are meant to be seen – that's what Tom said. He thought it was just an ordinary letter she had forgotten to post. You don't think . . . ?'

'No, I'm sure Tom's right and it's not important.' Guy's voice had suddenly regained its loving tone. 'No need to worry about it, my darling.'

Lucy sighed as she lent back against the pillows.

'We were going to post it when we left the flat, but then I thought I'd give it to Aunt Joan tomorrow. She's going to lunch with Mum and I've said I'll be there if you don't need me for anything. I thought it might be less upsetting for her if . . .' Her voice faltered. 'Well, I thought it would be awful getting a letter from someone after they'd died – so if I gave it to her, she wouldn't be on her own when she read it.'

Guy stood silently for a minute staring at the envelope in his hands. His face was expressionless as he turned to look at Lucy.

'As a matter of fact, I don't agree with you. I should think Miss Lyford is the last person to want to show her emotions in public. It's my firm opinion she'd much prefer to read this in private. Trust me to know what's best for her and stop worrying about it, darling. I'll find a stamp and post it in the morning on my way to work. Now, would you like a hot drink? I'm just going to make myself a quick cup of coffee. Won't be long.'

He disappeared with the letter and as soon as he was in the kitchen, he switched on the kettle. As it started to boil, he held the back of the envelope over the steam until he was able to peel it open. It was handwritten but perfectly legible. His eyes quickly scanned the pages.

> Dear Aunt Joan,
>   I'm really sorry my last letter worried you so much and I promise I am making a good recovery. I think I told you Tom would be coming to stay for a few days as Lucy is away again with her fiancé so I shall have someone to look after me and you can rest assured nothing

else unpleasant will happen. I have only just realized it happened on Friday the 13th, so perhaps I should not make fun of superstitions again!

I did try to reach you on the phone to thank you for the lovely flowers, but I think you must have been playing bridge. I hope you got my message. I should not have told you in my last letter how awful I was feeling. Yes, it was a very nasty shock but I am equally to blame for not foreseeing what could happen. So you must please stop worrying about me. As I said in my last letter, I know I can trust you absolutely not to say a word to Lucy, Aunt Bridget or Uncle George when you see them; they would be so angry with me for not telling them.

I really appreciate your offer to visit me but I promise it isn't necessary. I will ring you when Tom arrives so we can arrange a time to come and see you.

With all my love,
Vanessa

Guy took a deep breath, his heart pounding as he took in the significance of Vanessa's unposted letter. It was not what it contained but its reference to what had been in the previous letter which unnerved him. He had banked on his threats to harm Lucy or one of her family to stop Vanessa telling anyone what he had done to her. It was not even as if he had wanted to risk everything by having sex with her, but when she had refused him, he'd lost control. Knowing it could happen, he should never have allowed himself to have so much to drink.

Now it looked as if she might have confided in that elderly aunt of hers. He'd only met the old lady once when he and Lucy had become engaged and Vanessa had taken them to see her. He doubted very much whether he would recognize her or she him although he did recall she talked of little else but bridge. Vanessa, mercifully, was no longer in the land of the living to give evidence against him. Now, suddenly, for the first time he wondered whether she had killed herself because of his attack. Or as everyone thought because she couldn't bear the fact that he had taken Lucy from her?

Not that it mattered, he told himself. What mattered was

whether Vanessa had told her aunt in a previous letter and whether the aunt had decided not to tell anyone else. The letter he was now holding referred to Friday the 13th, the evening he and Vanessa had been at the Old Ship. He remembered it specifically because the young waiter had spilt a few drops of claret on the tablecloth and Vanessa had made light of the superstition relating to the unlucky date. So as far as he knew Vanessa had told everyone she had fallen from a ladder but it was just possible she had told her aunt the truth. Would she have dared to name him despite his threats? It seemed highly unlikely but he would never feel entirely safe until he knew what information that letter contained.

An ambulance siren breaking the silence of the night brought Guy's thoughts back to the salient point. He needed to find out if the aunt still had that letter, but how? There was absolutely no way in the world he was going to risk losing Lucy's love. For most of his adult life, he had avoided any close involvement with women. He was good-looking as well as being well-heeled – women were frequently attracted to him and made themselves available. But although he'd used them, he'd previously never allowed himself to fall in love with them – until the day he met Lucy. Never normally fanciful, he saw her as a bright colourful butterfly, laughing as she danced from flower to flower; friendly, compliant, caring, but never at first responding to his overtures. He had slowly become besotted with her and realizing that he was seriously in love for the first time in his life, he had been determined to marry her. Now, since their wedding seven weeks ago he was even more deeply in love, their sexual closeness as important as her physical presence in his life.

For a brief moment, Guy felt panic rising in him. He had tried not to think about the evening with Vanessa and his loss of control. That night he had been dangerously stupid and it had been unnecessary, his only excuse being that rejection from a woman was one thing he could never tolerate, no matter how hard he tried to disregard it.

Rising to his feet, Guy crossed to the unit above the fridge and took down a bottle of whisky. Pouring himself a generous two fingers, he added some ice and sat back at the table. Tomorrow he was meeting a client for lunch in Birmingham.

He had planned to leave after breakfast but supposing he were to leave a lot earlier? Before Lucy woke up? Would he have time to drive down to Seaford where the aunt lived and demand to see the letter – if she still had it – and still make Birmingham by one o'clock? Taking a marker pen and the memo board, he worked out the mileages from the route planner he obtained from the AA's website on his computer. It could be done. Old people were usually up early so he could reasonably call on her at eight or eight thirty, stay a half hour at most and be back on the M25 by ten. It could be done but what possible excuse did he have to question her? To demand the letter? There was only one possibility – to present himself as a member of the police force still making enquiries about Vanessa's suicide; or, as a private detective. The woman might think it odd but then Vanessa's suicide was odd in that she had left no note. That in itself had been strange.

Guy now tried to recall the route Vanessa had taken to that seaside town where her aunt lived – Seaford. As far as he could recall, the bungalow was down a one-width lane with other small private residences set back behind fences and hedges. Assuming he could disguise himself sufficiently well to pass as a detective, how could he possibly disguise his state-of-the-art TVR Sagaris? Wherever he went, it brought admiring glances and if he stopped in a busy car park, other motorists invariably came up and asked him about its performance. He could borrow Lucy's little green Golf hatchback but were she to wake and need it in the morning how could he explain its absence? Nor, in any circumstances, did he want Lucy involved in his activities.

Guy had taken several large gulps of whisky before the unexpected moment of fear left him. Then a smile spread across his face as he recalled with complete clarity a Latin quotation he had had to write out five hundred times as a penance at school for not submitting his homework. '*Audentes fortuna juvat* – Fortune favours the daring.' (*Virgil, Aeneid X*). So if he had the courage, he had the means to borrow a friend's car to use for his purpose. Jeremy Hart-Pennant, his best man and erstwhile school friend who lived round the corner in Chelsea and with whom he played squash once a week, had gone on an eight-week safari to Africa. He had left the keys of his Volvo with Guy so that he could open up the garage when the dealer

came to collect it for servicing in a week's time. H-P was a bit
of a cynic to say the least, and had told Guy he didn't trust the
garage mechanics not to make use of the car whilst he was out
of the country.

A Volvo S80, Guy thought now, was not the latest model
so there would be many others about if it was sighted in
Seaford. No one would have reason to connect it to H-P or
to himself. Now all he needed to consider was how adequately
to disguise himself – some horn-rimmed spectacles . . . there
was a pair his father had left behind on his last visit as well
as the old Burberry he'd had to go out and buy to wear at the
races because of the appalling weather whilst he was in
England. He, Guy, might part his hair quite differently – grey
it down with some of Lucy's talcum powder.

Now keyed up with excitement, Guy went in search of his
wallet and extracted the security card he used for his London
office, and put it in an old leather wallet he had discarded
when Lucy had bought him a new one for his birthday. He'd
wave it in front of the old girl but not let her look at it long
enough to recognize the photo. There was a pair of old slip-
ons at the back of the wardrobe which he would replace with
his own handmade leather lace-ups before he got to
Birmingham. He'd take a notebook and pen – as if he were
intending to take official notes. He would disguise his voice,
which since he was bilingual would not be too difficult. Perhaps
he might pretend Tom Lyford's Swiss guardian had sent him
to make enquiries. He was, after all, in *loco parentis* to Tom
if not Vanessa.

Even more pleased with the plan he was devising, Guy
hurriedly scribbled a note for Lucy which he left on the kitchen
table for her to read in the morning. It said simply that he
had decided to leave earlier than he'd planned as he'd heard
on the radio there were hold-ups on the M40. Having done
so, he drained his glass and returning to the bedroom, he
slipped very quietly into bed beside Lucy's warm body. The
rush of love he felt for her as in her sleep, she flung her arm
round him, was so intense it all but took Guy's breath away.
He knew at that moment he would do anything – anything at
all – even murder, if he had to, to prevent her ever leaving
him as his mother had done.

Now that the low ebb of fear he'd felt when he'd read

Vanessa's letter had vanished, he decided that Fate had given him all the aces. There was still another reassuring aspect to the mess he had stupidly got himself into – so far at least the aunt had said nothing to Lucy. It was now over three months since the 13th of July and had the aunt thought fit to expose him, she would most certainly have done so by now or, even more likely, at the time of Vanessa's suicide.

Lucy had been sleeping deeply for over an hour when Guy climbed into bed beside her. Only half-wakened by his move-ments, she thought sleepily that she had somehow managed to slip into the habit of thinking him insensitive at times; that his emotions were on a totally different wavelength from her own. Tonight he had shown himself more sensitive than herself or Tom, neither of whom had stopped to think that poor Aunt Joan might find a post-death letter from her niece quite devas-tating, and that she would obviously not wish to read such a letter in the presence of the family, still less so if it turned out to be the suicide note the police had never found.

Lucy was too close to drifting back to sleep again to analyse why she should have begun to consider her adoring husband as lacking compassion, although she was vaguely aware that it had to do with his reactions to Vanessa's death. Perhaps, she told herself now, she had been quite unfair to expect him to mourn her friend just because she and Tom did. The fact was over the years she had become so accustomed to both Tom and Vanessa reacting to misfortunes and mishaps in the same way she did, that she had not made sufficient allowance for Guy's sudden introduction into her life.

Before they got engaged, her mother had said: 'Darling, the two of you have only known each other a few months. I have no doubt whatever that Guy worships you but are you absolutely sure you love him, my poppet? He is quite a persuasive character and your father and I have wondered if he has . . . well, pushed you into this engagement.'

At the time she had given no thought whatever to her mother's fears that she and Guy did not really know each other all that well. It was not until Bridget Godstow had added: 'It doesn't seem all that long ago, my darling, since you were telling me that you and Tom were twin souls.'

As she drifted back to sleep, there was a slight smile on

Lucy's face. Of course that was the way she had felt when she was a teenager. Tom was her first real boyfriend and although they never slept together, there had been plenty of snogging. They were a triumvirate – she, Van and Tom. Now those days were gone and she was the wife and lover of a husband who adored her. She had totally misjudged him, thinking him insensitive and wishing to be as close to him physically as in her thoughts, she shifted her body closer to his and put her arm around his waist.

By the time she awoke in the morning and went through to the kitchen to make tea for them both, Guy had already left the flat and was on his way to Whitegates in Seaford and his planned encounter with Vanessa's aunt.

Eight

When Guy slipped out of bed, taking care not to wake Lucy, the kitchen clock showed six a.m. He dressed as quickly and silently as he could and taking his brief case, the Burberry and the slip-ons, he made his way to the underground residents' car park beneath the block of flats to collect his Sagaris. The TVR model was an absurd extravagance, he was well aware, especially for someone living in a traffic-controlled city like London. But he had wanted to impress Lucy as well as her family; and with a generous cheque from his father, he was well able to afford the silver Sagaris. Today, he told himself wryly, he would have been a great deal better with a common-or-garden Ford. Well, H-P's Volvo would have to do and there were enough of them about for it not to be too remarkable. All he had to do was to avoid having an accident or his unsanctioned use of the car would become known to its owner.

As he crossed Chelsea Bridge and made his way south on to the A23, Guy ran through his mind yet again the day's timing. He had all the information he needed clear in his brain, which at this time of the morning was at its sharpest, despite the limited time he had slept. Sixty-odd miles to Seaford – two hours at most. Half an hour with the Lyford woman and another two hours back to Chelsea to return the car and pick up his own. Give or take a few miles, it was near enough one hundred and twenty miles from London to Birmingham, so he should arrive in the centre of the city where he was meeting his client with a good half hour to spare. He had a book of Sussex town centre street maps, which he had bought when he was first visiting Lucy at her home near Ferrybridge. From it, he had discovered Pepper Lane in Seaford so he knew exactly where he was going and would not lose precious time trying to find Miss Lyford's bungalow.

His thoughts turned to the letter burning a hole in his shirt pocket. He would give it to the old lady to read and provided she was prepared to come clean about whatever tales Vanessa had told her in that earlier letter and, if she still had it, gave it to him, he might not have to harm her. If, on the other hand, she refused to do so or she admitted that Vanessa had said he'd raped her, then he would have to shut her up. Even if she swore never to reveal the fact, she was too much of a loose cannon for him to feel safe. That incident had been an hour or two's madness, which had overcome him. He had reacted without thought of the possible repercussions. To have put his relationship with his beloved Lucy at risk for no reasonable purpose was little short of insanity. But there was something about Vanessa's attitude that evening which had stirred the latent memories of female scorn, rejections and ridicule which were always lurking at the back of his mind. From the first, she had barely troubled to conceal the fact that she did not think him good enough for Lucy. When he'd suggested he took her out for a meal, he'd had some stupid idea that if he behaved with adequate charm, he might win her over; make her change her mind about him. He was very conscious of the closeness of the bond between the two girls and he badly wanted Vanessa on his side. When she rejected him he had simply flipped.

For a brief moment, Guy's hands shook and he gripped the wheel more tightly. Now he was having to pay the price for that loss of control. And it was not for the first time. His mind went back to his teenage years in Spain when he had come very close to ruining his life forever. Since then, he had determined to show his father that he was an achiever. This he had done, choosing a life of dedication to work and only allowing passing pleasures that would not impinge on his time. He neither liked nor trusted women, but Lucy was different – so different. The day she had finally agreed to marry him was one of triumph because he had begun to doubt if she would ever give in to his persuasions. Now that she was his, nothing and no one would ever be allowed to take her from him.

It was eight o'clock when Guy parked the car in an overgrown gateway at the entrance to Pepper Lane. He was relieved to see that the road was deserted. Not a single soul was about as he walked down the dusty lane to Miss Lyford's house,

'Whitegates'. He was counting on the fact that elderly people were usually early risers and he was not mistaken.

Joan Lyford was in her kitchen at the back of the house making herself a cup of tea when she heard the doorbell. Since it was far too early for visitors, she supposed it must be the milkman and wondered why on earth he should have rung the bell of the front door. Usually, when she paid him it was at the back door where he left her milk.

'Good morning, Miss Lyford. May I come in?'

Rendered almost speechless with astonishment, she stared up at her visitor. He did not look like a salesman standing there in a somewhat crumpled mackintosh. Was he someone who had come to the wrong house, she wondered? But he had known her name.

'What was it you wanted?' she asked. 'I don't think we are acquainted, are we?'

Guy held out his hand and smiled reassuringly.

'My name is Pierre Duval,' he told her in accented English. 'I am from Switzerland where I have been employed by Monsieur Charles Rowan to make some enquiries on his behalf.'

At once familiar with the name of Tom's godfather, Joan decided to allow the man into the house. She judged him to be in his fifties, going grey and although he spoke excellent English, she assumed he was probably of Swiss origin.

'You're very early, Mr Duval,' she remarked as she led him into the living room. 'Would you like a cup of tea?'

'Thank you but no. I had a very early breakfast when I came off the ferry. I took the all-night crossing, you see. I should explain myself to you, Miss Lyford. Will you be seated?'

When she was seated opposite him, he continued in his phoney accent: 'Monsieur Rowan informed me that when the parents of your great-niece and nephew died, you and he were nominated as their executives.'

Joan nodded.

'That's quite right, Mr Duval, but that was fifteen years ago and I don't see what relevance that can have today.'

Anticipating the comment, Guy said smoothly: 'It is to do with your great niece's death, Miss Lyford. Monsieur Rowan is far from happy with the result of the inquest. He does not believe Miss Vanessa committed suicide. You see, he had had a very happy letter from her only a day before she died.'

Joan looked thoughtful.

'Then why didn't Mr Rowan attend the inquest – tell the coroner about my niece's letter?'

'Indeed, Miss Lyford, that is exactly what he is now regretting. He knows it is too late to change the verdict, if that is what it is called, but I am here to make enquiries that might put his mind at rest, so to speak. Monsieur Rowan thought it was quite possible that your niece might have confided in you if she had any problems . . .'

He paused briefly whilst he searched in his jacket pocket for Vanessa's letter which he had removed from its envelope.

'Your nephew found this amongst Miss Vanessa's belongings when he was sorting her effects. It seems the British police had overlooked it so he sent it to Monsieur Rowan to ask what he should do with it.' He lent forward and looked directly into Joan's face. 'As you will see, it refers to "recovering from something unpleasant"? Something your niece had told you about in a previous letter? Do you by any chance still have that letter, Miss Lyford?'

There was something vaguely menacing in the man's tone that caused the elderly woman to hesitate before she replied. The more she thought about it, the odder this whole encounter seemed. People – detectives even – did not arrive unannounced at so early an hour. Not everyone would be up and dressed by eight. As to Charles Rowan suddenly concerning himself with poor Vanessa when she was not his ward . . .

'Do you have a letter for me from Mr Rowan?' she asked, wondering suddenly if her visitor was far from being who he purported to be but was, in fact, a member of the press. Suicides were always newsworthy and they had managed to keep Vanessa's death more or less out of the papers on the grounds that it was accidental. She, herself, believed it to be so though Tom had told her at the funeral that his sister had been very depressed.

When Guy admitted he had no letter from his presumed employer, Joan decided that without such authorisation, she would say nothing more.

'I'm sorry, Mr Duval, but I have nothing more to say to

you. I'm afraid you have come here on a wild goose chase. You can tell Mr Rowan – if indeed you *are* here on his behalf – that I can't discuss my family's personal affairs with strangers. You . . .'

She got no further before Guy rose angrily to his feet. The speed with which he moved to his feet was sufficient to dislodge his horn-rimmed spectacles.

'Miss Lyford, I want that letter!' he said in a cold, hard voice. 'I shall not leave here until I have it, do you understand?'

She was not listening to him but was staring at him with a look of pure astonishment. Too surprised to keep her thoughts to herself, she blurted out:

'Why, it's Mr Weaver – you're Lucy Godstow's husband. You're not a private detective. Yes, you're Guy Weaver. I remember you now.'

Guy was momentarily too disconcerted to think clearly. He had counted on the fact that the old woman would not recognize him since he, himself, had almost no memory of her. He had been stupidly careless imagining that the heavy spectacles and greying his hair would add at least fifteen years to his age, might be enough together with his foreign accent to deceive her. Just for a second, he toyed with the idea of denying his real identity so she would think herself mistaken. But he knew a minute later that it would be far, far too risky. They would be bound to meet again sooner or later at the Godstows and she would recognize him at once as her early morning intruder. She had but to remark on it in front of Lucy for his involvement with Vanessa to be discovered by her.

Guy was quite suddenly consumed with rage – partly at his own stupidity but also with this woman who could so easily have handed Vanessa's letter to him – if indeed she still had it – and he could have been on his way without a hint of the danger he was now in.

He made no effort to keep the threat from his voice as he caught hold of the old lady's wrist.

'Well, do you have it or not?' he said through clenched teeth. 'I want that letter, Miss Lyford and I'm not leaving until I get it.'

Joan Lyford was now extremely frightened. For one thing, she had not the faintest idea why Lucy's husband should have come here demanding information about poor Vanessa. For another, she was beginning to wonder if he was in his right senses. There was a strange look in his eyes and a horrible, menacing tone to his voice. But pride would not permit her to let him see her fear. What this man did not know – nor, indeed, did any of her family or friends – was that she had been in the SOE during the last war and at the age of twenty-one, she had been dropped behind enemy lines in France as a wireless operator. Following the death at sea of her fiancé, she had not cared whether she lived or died and the latter was statistically the more likely. As it had transpired, she had survived but ever since she had always known that if she could brave capture by the Gestapo, she could face any other fear with impunity.

Guy's grip on her arm tightened.

'I asked you – do you have that letter or not, Miss Lyford?'

Staring straight back at him, she said: 'No, I have not kept any of Vanessa's letters and even if I had done so, I would not give them to you, Mr Weaver. Now please let go of my wrist and get out of my house or I shall have to call the police. You may be Lucy's husband but however distressing it might be for her, I shall feel obliged to inform her of your irrational behaviour.'

It was as much the mention of Lucy's name as the woman's resistance that undermined Guy's self control. He crossed the room to her desk where he had seen a roll of parcel tape and beside it a steel paper knife shaped like a dagger. As the old lady started to struggle weakly to her feet, he dragged her back into the chair and started to bind her arms tightly to her sides. Quite certain now that Guy was insane, she said in the tone a mother might use to a difficult child:

'I do assure you, Mr Weaver, I do not have any of my niece's letters. You have my word.'

But it was not enough for Guy.

'But Vanessa told you what I'd done to her, didn't she? *Didn't she?*' Guy's breath was hot on her cheeks. She tried to keep her reeling senses steady. He seemed to want her to tell him something – something about Vanessa. What had he done to her? Surely not physical harm? Why on earth should he have wanted to hurt Vanessa – Lucy's friend? And if he had, why would he want her to tell him that she knew what, if anything, he had done? And she knew nothing – only that Vanessa had fallen from a ladder whilst painting her living room ceiling. Was he there? Had he pushed her?

Her horrified gaze fell on the knife he now held in his right hand. He was pointing it in front of her face. Sweat was pouring down his cheeks which were now a florid purple. His eyes were not so much looking at her as through her.

His voice was almost unrecognizable as he shouted: 'Do you really think I'd let you tell Lucy – my precious Lucy? I warned Vanessa. I warned her if she ever told anyone I'd raped her, they would come to serious harm. So she disobeyed me and told you, her maiden aunt, for heaven's sake! Who'd have thought she'd use you as a confidante?' He gave a derisory laugh. 'Your bad luck, I fear, Miss Lyford. I wish I could believe you would keep your knowledge to yourself, but I simply can't risk it. Vanessa promised she'd never tell a soul yet she told you. So how can I believe you if you promise to keep silent?'

Finding her voice at last, Joan Lyford gasped out: 'I know nothing about a rape, I give you my word. I'll swear it on the Holy Bible. I do beg you to release me, Mr Weaver. I'm an old woman and I cannot possibly do you any harm.'

'Indeed you can!' Guy said fiercely. 'You could tell Lucy. No, I'm sorry but I'm not prepared to take any risks.'

Before she could reply, he took a step forward and quickly bound the sticky tape round her mouth. Her spectacles fell forward on to her chest and her eyes searched his in frantic appeal as he lifted his arm high above his head, the knife glinting as he brought it down towards her chest. The tip glanced off the cameo brooch which fastened her crêpe blouse and entered the base of her shoulder.

Aware she was now fighting for her life, Joan Lyford managed to use every last ounce of her strength, to twist her body so that the chair fell forward, nearly knocking her attacker over. He swore as her foot hit his shin causing him considerable pain, and now any tiny last remnant of pity he might have had for the trussed woman lying at his feet, vanished with his self-control. Without thought for the possible consequences of his actions, he pulled her chair upright and began systematically to stab her.

It was several minutes before Guy realized that Joan Lyford

must have died minutes ago. There was blood all over the Burberry and his shoes as well as on the victim herself.

The raincoat and shoes he could dispose of somewhere on his journey – the rubbish bin at a service station, he realized, as sanity returned, might be the answer. Stupidly, in his concern to leave the flat without waking Lucy, he had forgotten to take with him the bag containing his city lace-ups.

Meanwhile he'd have to remove the ones he was wearing lest he leave too many bloody footprints. He'd have to find a plastic bag in Miss Lyford's kitchen and barefooted carry the shoes back to his car. It would be no problem driving the automatic Volvo without shoes. His mind working furiously, he decided he would go into a shoe shop in the Birmingham suburbs – say he'd vomited on his old ones so he'd binned them. Lucy wouldn't notice he was wearing new shoes which wouldn't look all that new after a day's wear anyway.

Carefully avoiding the pools of blood on the carpet, he walked in his socks to the kitchen where, after locating a couple of bags for his slip-ons and raincoat, he carefully washed his hands and face. A quick glance at his watch confirmed that he had been there far too long but before leaving, he must do what he could to make it look as if there had been a burglary. In the room where his victim now lay slumped in her chair, he'd seen a small mahogany display cabinet containing some items of silver. They did not look particularly valuable but they would do, Guy decided as hurriedly he broke the glass doors and stuffed as many items as he could into another of Miss Lyford's plastic bags. One was from the Seaford Co-op he noticed with a wry smile. He was no longer in the grip of uncontrolled anger and his brain was working coolly and methodically as he sought to cover his tracks.

Looking at his watch, he felt a tiny frisson of fear. There was no time for him to take H-P's car back into London and retrieve his own. He would never make Birmingham by one o'clock. He did a rough calculation in his head. He should be able to get there in the Volvo, joining the M25 at the Reigate junction and from there on to the M40. He'd save an hour that way. The only risk would be if he was stopped for speeding or for an accident using H-P's car . . . and that risk was no more than losing a friend if he objected to his, Guy's, unauthorized use of his Volvo. That risk was insignificant against being late for his lunch appointment. His client was going to be his alibi.

He felt no remorse for having killed Miss Lyford. In a strange way, the repeated stabbing had been cathartic – helping him get rid of the build-up of anxieties he'd had about Lucy. With Miss Lyford dead, there was nothing now that could come between them.

Nevertheless, the elation he had felt when he was actually stabbing the woman had abated and he was acutely aware of the need to return to his car unobserved. Although he had replaced his hornrims, he did not wish to be recognized by an early postman or milkman who he might expect to meet at this time of the morning. Barefooted and now in his business suit, he would be far too memorable a sight once the old woman's body was discovered.

Only once did Guy have to dive quickly into an open gateway when a car drove by. He had heard it coming so was well concealed when it passed him. Just for a moment, his heartbeat had quickened but by the time he reached the Volvo and was on his way back towards Brighton to join the main London Road, he was completely calm.

Silencing Joan Lyford was the most sensible thing he could possibly have done, he told himself as he reached the M25 and headed west. Extreme though it had been, he felt he could congratulate himself for taking the action he had. To have committed a murder was no light matter but there was no reason for anyone in the whole wide world to connect him to the elderly spinster. He did not envisage that he was in any danger of discovery.

As he turned on to the M40 in the direction of Birmingham, Guy wondered if Lucy would be upset when she heard of Joan Lyford's death. He imagined how he would comfort her and show her how sympathetic he could be when they went together to choose a wreath. He had been genuinely shocked by Vanessa's suicide, so had not had to act the part. Nevertheless he'd found her suicide less hard to believe than Lucy, who tearfully insisted for weeks afterwards that Vanessa would never have done such a thing. Obviously, she *had* overdosed, Guy thought, despite Lucy's protestations to the police. Sometimes, he'd wondered how seriously Vanessa had been affected by him raping her. As far as he was concerned, Vanessa

Lyford would always have been a loose cannon – able to denounce him to Lucy at any time, and he could not have been more relieved when she saved him the trouble of despatching her.

As Guy passed the turn-offs to Banbury and then Worcester, he allowed his thoughts to return to Miss Lyford's bungalow. He needed to reassure himself that he had not left any clues. The road had been empty when he'd reached the house and in the hour he had spent there, he had not seen a soul. As to the old lady's silver now covered by a rug on the back seat, he'd take it up to the attic and put it in the old chest that was up there. There was no question of his trying to sell it when it might be traced back to him. It wasn't as if he needed the money. No doubt its failure to surface would baffle the police but that possibility was no threat to himself.

He was perfectly safe, Guy told himself, and putting the morning's events to the back of his mind, he drove happily through the more affluent part of Birmingham to meet his client.

Nine

When Lucy went into the old nursery she found Julia curled up in the ancient old armchair reading a book as it was half-term. She jumped up and running to her sister, gave her a huge hug.

'Oh, Lucy, I didn't know you were coming. What a lovely surprise! Jemma has gone riding with the Morrisons and I'm all on my own.'

Lucy tucked her arm through Julia's and drew her down on to the sofa bed under the window. It was quite cold this October morning and Julia had turned on the gas fire. A pair of her netball socks were drying on the old fender and Lucy was suddenly reminded of the carefree afternoons she had spent in this room as a child, her sisters sticking pictures into their scrapbooks, Jonnie making a model of an aeroplane, his ongoing passion in his teens, and she herself in charge of the record player, dreaming about falling in love. Sometimes Vanessa was with them and together they would practice the latest dance.

Afraid of the tears which seemed to threaten every time she thought of Vanessa, Lucy turned her attention to Julia. She seemed to have lost weight since the wedding and according to their mother, was by no means her jolly chatty self. Julia was now looking at her questioningly.

'I thought we weren't going to see you until the weekend. Mum said you and Guy were coming for Sunday lunch.'

'Well, we are. Today is an extra. Guy had to go to Birmingham of all places to meet a client.'

Julia looked down at her hands which were clasped tightly together.

'Can I ask you something, Lucy? About Guy, I mean . . . I mean, why doesn't he want you to have a job? Mum said Guy was quite rich and you didn't need the extra income, but Lucy, you must be terribly bored. I mean you were always going to have a career – you and Van. Remember you were going to start your own language school and . . .'

'JuJu, don't go on,' Lucy said gently. 'I wouldn't want to do any of that without Van. As to my being bored, well, there was a lot to do when we were first married – things to buy for Guy's flat which I showed you when you came up to London. And then there were all the thank-you letters I had to write for our wedding presents, and I've had to buy a lot of new clothes – Guy likes me to look fashionable when we entertain his clients.'

Her voice trailed away and, after giving a huge sigh, Julia said: 'But that's all so boring, Lucy. You hate shopping – you know you do! You used to make poor old Van go out and buy things for you . . .' She broke off aware that yet again she was treading on thin ice. Lucy had told the family she didn't want anyone to mention Vanessa – or at least not until she could do so without bursting into tears.

For several minutes, neither girl spoke, and then Julia clasped her hands together and gripping them tightly, said almost inaudibly: 'Lucy, there's something I've got to tell you. I should have said something before but . . . but I was too frightened. Now I can't sleep at night because of what I did and I think of it all the time and wonder if . . . if Van died because of me . . .'

She burst into a storm of tears which dripped on to Lucy's shirt front as she hugged her youngest sister. Julia's garbled words had both confused and frightened her. This was all so totally unlike her carefree, impulsive, mischievous little sister. Was it possible Vanessa's death had preyed on her adolescent mind to the point where she was imagining all sorts of weird things?

'Julia, stop crying. I want you to tell me exactly what it is that you are worrying about. Nothing that happened with Van had anything whatever to do with you. Vanessa . . .'

'No, that's the whole point. I think it was all my fault. It happened on the wedding rehearsal day. You see, I was helping Van and she gave me these two plates, one with a big helping and one with a small one. I – I didn't see why Guy should have the big one like Van said. She was the one who was working so hard, so . . . so I swapped them.' Julia was once more in tears but through them, she managed to say: 'I didn't dare tell anyone in case . . . in case . . .'

'Enough!' Lucy said firmly. Her relief was so great, she was close to smiling. 'You've got it all wrong, JuJu. It wasn't something in the curry which was responsible for what happened. If it *had* been, the verdict would have been death due to food poisoning, but it wasn't. Van just took too much insulin, JuJu. I'm sure she didn't mean to harm herself. I know she wouldn't have done that. It was an accident. Tom said she had been working really hard and was probably overtired and people do silly things when they are on the point of exhaustion. So you see, you've been worrying for nothing.'

Lucy said suddenly: 'You don't really like Guy, do you, JuJu?'

Julia turned a deep pink..

'It's just that I . . . well . . . all of us, really, hoped you'd marry Tom. I really, really wanted you to marry him and Van did, too! I mean, if you'd never met Guy, you probably would have married Tom, wouldn't you?'

Lucy drew a long sigh.

'It's really not quite as simple as you are imagining, JuJu. For one thing, when Van and I signed the lease of the flat in Brighton and took jobs together I'd never dreamed of turning my back on our plans and getting married to anyone. Of course, I loved Tom and I know he loves me but we're like brother and sister. It was the same as I felt that Van was my sister. I know it's what we planned when we were little – I'd marry Tom and then Van would be my sister-in-law; but it was all different once I met Guy. I didn't mean to fall in love but . . . well, he wouldn't take no for an answer, so in the end, I said yes, I'd marry him. He loves me very, very much and spoils me terribly. Sometimes I wonder if I deserve his adoration!'

'Of course you do, Lucy!' Julia cried hugging her. 'You're one of the nicest people in the whole world and I don't wonder Guy adores you.'

Nevertheless, that adoration could prove quite a weight round her neck, Lucy thought, as tucking her arm through Julia's, she led her downstairs to the kitchen where she knew her mother was busy making lunch in preparation for Joan

Lyford's visit. Guy could be excessively possessive at times. If he was home early and she was ten minutes late back from an afternoon hair appointment, he would be pacing the floor, wanting to know what had held her up; who she had been talking to; why she had disregarded the fact that she knew he'd be worried waiting for her when she could have phoned him. It was entirely against Lucy's nature to be punctual, let alone conscious of the time at all if she was enjoying herself. Vanessa had always been the one to drag her away from a party, saying they'd miss their train or warning her they would be late for work, and who would religiously record family birthdays and remind her to buy cards and post them in good time. Now, suddenly, she had to keep tabs on herself – not for her own benefit, but for Guy's.

'He'll quieten down once you've been married a bit longer,' one of her married friends had commented wryly. 'Before you know where you are, lover-boy will be forgetting your birthday, anniversary, whatever, and turning up late at a restaurant because he has so many more important things on his mind! Make the most of it whilst you can. And don't be too accommodating – let him sweat a bit from time to time. Does them good to realize you aren't on this earth just for their pleasure and convenience.'

Her thoughts having travelled in this direction caused Lucy to glance up at the kitchen clock as she and Julia went into the room. Guy had said he might get back from Birmingham in time for a drink before he took her to their favourite Italian restaurant for dinner. She would have to leave home no later than four o'clock. The thought was followed by a far less happy one – that she really didn't want to hurry back to London. She would have liked to stay until her father came home and have supper with the whole family instead of going to a restaurant.

Her mother, too, was looking anxiously at the kitchen clock.

'Joan Lyford hasn't turned up yet and it's nearly one o'clock,' she said to Lucy, a frown creasing her forehead. 'I've put the casserole back in the oven but it's the vegetables I'm worried about.'

'I'm sure they'll keep a bit longer,' Lucy said comfortingly. 'Shall I telephone to see if she's been delayed or forgotten the day or something?'

Bridget's frown deepened.

'I've done that already,' she said. 'There's no reply. 'I just hope she hasn't had an accident on the way here. Your father said she drove much too fast for a woman of her age when she gave him a lift into Ferrybridge that day last month.'

At this juncture, Jemma came in with three friends and half an hour later, having decided to wait no longer for their guest, they were all grouped happily round the big kitchen table making short work of Bridget Godstow's lunch. Everyone was talking at once and Julia had let the two springer spaniels in from the garden. They were charging round the table hoping for hand-outs which they were not really allowed but frequently enjoyed. Lucy leaned back in her chair feeling suddenly detached from this family party. What she would have liked better than anything was for Guy to have been here with her, enjoying the juvenile fun. Yet even as the thought went through her mind she knew that it would be anathema to him.

Lucy felt a sudden jab of fear. What would happen when they had children? Not that she intended to have a baby for years yet, but when she did . . . This lovely carefree childhood she'd enjoyed was what she would want for her kids. Was Guy going to demand something different? Why hadn't they discussed this before their marriage?

Because there simply had not been time, she answered her own question. Guy had quite literally rushed her off her feet. When the thought of one day having his children had crossed her mind, her mother's considered remark about Guy being able to afford the very best for his children – a lovely home, good schools, ponies, maybe a tennis court – had put her mind at rest. When she had thought of the future at all, it had held no fears for her.

All too soon, it was four o'clock. Joan Lyford had still not arrived or answered her telephone when, stifling her reluctance to leave the family party, Lucy stood up to go. Julia put her arms round her sister's slim waist and hugged her.

'Must you go?' she asked. 'Surely it wouldn't matter if you drove back later?'

Lucy released herself from Julia's grip and went to kiss her mother goodbye. Tears were threatening, and not daring to speak, she blew a kiss to Jemma, waved to her friends, and

hurried out of the front door. Julia and their mother came
hurrying after her.

'I suppose there's no hope of seeing you again before
Sunday,' Bridget said as Lucy got into her car. 'We all do
miss you, darling!'

And with Julia beside her, she stood waving until Lucy's
little green Golf turned out of the drive and was lost to sight.

Ten

'Late again, Beck!' Inspector Govern said with a sigh as his detective sergeant came hurrying into the room. 'Don't tell me – the fog!' He stood up and reached for his overcoat. 'Keep that dead sheep jacket of yours on. We're on our way to Seaford – been a nasty murder there.'

'I came as quickly as I could, sir,' his sergeant said, an apologetic smile on his good-looking face. 'Matter of fact I was still in bed when I got your phone call, and I didn't think you'd want me unshaven.'

Inspector Govern opened the door of his BMW and said caustically: 'You should know by now, Beck, that when I say "immediately", that's exactly what I mean. I don't think your chin, shaven or unshaven, will be of any consequence to the murder victim – an elderly lady, by the way. A robbery, according to our friend PC Plod, who was called to the scene of the crime by the milkman.'

Beck shot a glance at his boss and decided he might risk a small joke. 'I enjoyed the Noddy books, you know. It wouldn't be so bad if old Todd didn't look rather like Noddy's Mr Plod the Policeman!'

'Be quiet, Beck!' Govern replied but his mouth twitched as he covered up a smile. 'I'll update you. Victim, a Miss Joan Lyford; lives – or should I say lived – in a bungalow at the end of a cul-de-sac, on the outskirts of Seaford. The milkman noticed the back door was ajar and put his head round it see if the old girl who lived there alone was all right. Seeing no one and getting no answer when he called out to her, he sensibly telephoned the police on his mobile and they dispatched PC Plod who found the victim. That call was logged at five minutes to eight. The old lady was tied to a chair – dead of course – and the place ransacked. Plod was a bit shaken by the amount of blood everywhere but still managed to tell me with great pride that he had all but solved the crime! He suspected a burglar had been caught in the act of stealing the stuff from the display cabinet, so he bumped her off.'

'If the old girl was tied up, why kill her?'

'Exactly!' said Govern dryly. 'Moreover, it was an extremely vicious killing. The unfortunate victim had multiple stab wounds, one or more obviously fatal.'

Beck's eyebrows shot up. Accustomed though he was to violent death, he was still shocked by the unnecessary violence of such an attack as this.

'Something doesn't make sense. If he had a reason to kill her, one or two stabs would have been sufficient to bump the old girl off. Sounds nasty!'

'Obviously we'll know more *when* we get there, which *should* have been half an hour ago,' was Inspector Govern's veiled reproof.

Beck remained silent, feeling it would better for him if he did not start again trying to excuse himself for being late. He'd worked with the inspector ever since he had been promoted to detective sergeant four years ago, and had the highest regard for his superior's abilities. Not only did Govern nearly always solve whatever crime they were investigating, but he went about it in an entirely civilized way. He could be ruthless enough when it was necessary but equally he could be gentle and sympathetic with those who needed it.

As Govern drove past Seaford College and the old church with Seaford Head in the distance towards the lane leading to Miss Lyford's bungalow, Beck's mind went back to the recent mystery they had solved last year. Two teenage girls – identical twins – were involved, in a murder case on Cheyne Manor Golf Course. Both had written to the inspector after the case was closed to thank him. One of them – Beck could never tell them apart – had actually invited him and Govern to her wedding!

'Not like you to be silent!' Inspector Govern commented. 'Not half-asleep still, I hope?'

Ignoring the jibe which he knew it to be, Beck replied: 'I was just thinking about some of the murder cases we've been on together, sir. The Cheyne Manor Golf Course one, and that Millers Lane one with the batty sister. Remember?'

Govern nodded and seeing the flashing of a police car and the police doctor's unmarked Peugeot outside a bungalow, he turned into the gateway.

'Looks like this is it!' he said. 'That's Doc's car so he's beaten us to it. Come on, let go see what's what.'

Later that day, David Beck was to say to his boss that had they known what a gruesome sight awaited them, they would not have been so ready to enter the house. As it was, they hurried through the mahogany front door into the dark hallway. The police doctor, Hugh Barley, came out of the sitting room to meet them.

'Not too nice a sight in there,' he warned Govern. 'I've left everything as I found it, but I did manage to get an approximate time of death – twenty-four hours ago, I'd say. Believe it or not, there were thirty-five stab wounds. I've sent PC Todd into the kitchen. Poor fellow was feeling a bit sick. Can't say I blame him. Blood everywhere, of course. I told him to make himself a strong cup of tea so he should have recovered enough by now to answer your questions. We'll know more after the post-mortem of course. A quick wash and I'm off. Due in court this morning.'

With a murmured thank you, Govern walked past the doctor into the room. Beck, following close behind him, saw the victim at the same time. She had been secured to a dining chair with parcel tape. Her mouth and nose were similarly covered, the tape sticky with congealed blood. What now partly explained the police constable's collapse was the rest of the victim's features, such as they could be seen, for not only was her body covered with stab wounds but her eyes, too. Moreover, the front of the pink blouse she was wearing was a mass of congealed blood as was the floor around her chair. Only her cardigan on the chair by the window seemed to have escaped the murderer's attacks.

Beck turned quickly away and went across to the window, in front of which stood a green baize covered table, the surface neatly laid out for a game of bridge with two packs of cards, four scorecards and tasselled pencils. The three remaining upright chairs – the fourth was occupied by the victim – were placed in readiness for the card players. Surely it could not be one of them who had carried out such a horrible deed?

'Right, Beck, to work,' the inspector said behind him

sounding both brisk and controlled. 'Get Todd in here – see what he has to say.'

An hour later, Govern had as much information as he thought he could obtain for the moment. The fingerprint chaps had arrived, and after he had authorized the release of the unfortunate woman from her bondage, an ambulance had driven her off to the hospital in Brighton for the pathologist to carry out the post-mortem. It was now clear to him that only the sitting room and dining room had been disturbed by the intruder. Cutlery had been tipped out of the sideboard drawers, papers lay scattered on the floor beneath the victim's writing desk, several ornaments lay in fragments by the fireplace. Nothing had been touched elsewhere or in the kitchen, although objects had clearly been taken from the empty shelves of the display cabinet, and he had a gut feeling that this was no more than an amateurish attempt to make the murder look like the work of a burglar disturbed at his activities.

'Whoever did it was a vicious sadist,' Beck said as they returned to the BMW and drove back to the police station, leaving PC Todd to secure the premises. 'He would have been able to tie up an old woman of her age without much difficulty, so why kill her? And even if he wanted her dead lest she identify him at some later stage, why stab her – what did Doc say – thirty-five times? It doesn't make sense. Any ideas at all, sir?'

Govern shook his head.

'Pretty vague ones, I'm afraid. Hopefully we'll get some clues after we've interviewed the people in her address book. He'd obviously had a pretty good look round judging by the papers all over the floor. The victim's address book was amongst them.'

Later, the inspector knew, he would have a chance to look through them when SOCO, wearing gloves so as to preserve fingerprints, would bag them up and take them back to the station.

'Maybe he knew he wouldn't be in her address book if he was a stranger,' Beck said. 'It's possible he simply intended a robbery and she surprised him, so he bumped her off and beat it. Of course, we don't know yet if he took anything of value – always supposing it *was* a burglar. The cleaner would probably know if there is anything valuable missing.'

Beck had seen the cleaner's telephone number on a board in the kitchen. *'Mrs Endip Thurs, Fri. 10–12'* followed by a telephone number, and underneath *'Memo. Polish silver Thurs. Oven next week.'* She was to have been their first port of call but as she did not answer her phone and this was Wednesday, she obviously had other jobs to go to when she was not at Whitegates. This, Govern said dryly, was a pity as cleaning ladies were usually the providers of the most knowledge about their employers!

Apart from a list of Miss Lyford's bridge-playing friends and bridge clubs, Beck had found an invitation to a wedding from a Mr and Mrs George Godstow with an address near Ferrybridge. It was out of date but nevertheless it could be a useful starting point, Govern said. If Beck could manage to get himself out of bed in time in the morning, they would make the Godstows their first port of call. Meanwhile it was back to the station to see what other information about the unfortunate victim could be gleaned from interviews with Miss Lyford's friends. Within a matter of a few hours, Govern had the name and telephone number of Miss Lyford's solicitor who he arranged to meet the following day. There was little of any consequence to be had from Miss Lyford's bridge friends, all of whom were deeply shocked by her death. Inspector Govern now hoped for but did not expect, some clues to the murder from the Godstows.

The next afternoon Govern and Beck drove to Ferrybridge – a simple journey of less then twenty miles.

'Up the A259 to Lewes and then the A276 into Ferrybridge,' Beck said reading the map as Inspector Govern decided, some-what unusually, to take the wheel as they left Seaford behind them. The weather was not particularly cold for early November but it was damp and slightly foggy. When they drove over the South Downs, the fog was thicker and Beck suggested they did not stay any longer than necessary with the Godstows lest the fog worsened.

Inspector Govern's mobile rang and he told Beck to answer it.

'Details about the Godstows, sir,' Beck said, aware his boss had asked someone at the station to do some research and phone it through. He filtered through the information he was receiving.

'Married couple: Bridget, forty-nine, housewife . . . George, fifty-five, solicitor, office in Ferrybridge. Address: The Willows, Hurst Heath. Four children. Do you want him to go deeper?'

Govern shook his head.

'No need. Tell him thanks.'

He put his foot down on the accelerator as they left Ditchling behind them and headed north towards Ferrybridge.

'You know, Beck, I'm almost certain I've come across that Lyford woman's name before. I've been trying to remember. It's not all that long ago, either. Ring any bells with you?'

Beck shook his head. Past experience told him that when Govern came up with one of his 'vague' memories, nine times out of ten they led to something positive. He had a most prodigious memory. Very occasionally, he himself could help the memory process.

'We did the Brighton Race Course hold-up last month, sir; and what about that suicide in Maddison Street two months ago, but I don't suppose . . .'

'Yes, that's it!' Govern interrupted him. 'The suicide. That girl – Vanessa Lyford, wasn't she? Good for you, Beck. I might put you up for promotion yet!'

Beck grinned.

'It's not a very common surname so I suppose there could be a connection – although one thing's for sure, she can't have been the murderer.'

The inspector gave a large, exaggerated sigh.

'Bang goes that promotion if you're going to insult me with stupid information like that, Beck. And it's not funny!'

'I wasn't laughing, sir,' Beck said, but he was, albeit silently.

As they were driving through Ferrybridge, Govern decided to stop at the solicitor's office and interview Mr George Godstow. The man was obviously deeply shocked when Govern told him the reason for their visit.

'That's terrible, really terrible!' he commented as told his secretary to bring in coffee for his visitors. 'Miss Lyford was a very nice woman – not the sort you'd get close to; not quite on the same wavelength as my wife and myself, but why . . . I mean . . . why on earth would anyone want to kill her? She was absolutely harmless. She only had one interest in life, her bridge. She was an extremely good player, I believe. Who could possibly want to harm her?'

'That's what we are trying to find out, sir,' Govern said, making a mental note that this man was clearly upset and absolutely genuine. 'Is there any other information you can give us? We know very little about the victim.'

George took the cups of coffee from the tray his secretary brought in and handed them to his visitors.

Once the young woman had left the room, he said: 'Miss Joan Lyford was a spinster, as perhaps you already know. I think there was once someone – a soldier who was killed in the last war but that's all we know. She was rising eighty, but in very good health. Years ago – about twelve, I think, when Vanessa's parents died she came over from Australia to live with Miss Lyford who was her great aunt and guardian. She and my eldest daughter, Lucy, became very close friends so, of course, my wife and I had occasion to meet Miss Lyford quite often. As I say, her visits were somewhat formal so I can't tell you much more about her other than that I don't think she was very well off. Though she had an adequate pension, I believe, and I think there was a small legacy she had inherited. I didn't handle her affairs so I can't be more precise.'

Govern put down his empty coffee cup and stood up.

'There's just one more question, sir, about your daughter's friend, Vanessa Lyford.' As George Godstow nodded, he went on: 'She lived in Brighton, did she not? We became involved there briefly when she . . . er, died.'

'Oh, her suicide – it was so tragic. She was only twenty-three, you know. Same age as our Lucy – but of course, you will know that if you handled the case. Is that how you came to know of our family's connection to Miss Lyford?'

'No, sir, it was the invitation,' Govern said, nodding to Beck to hand it to the solicitor. He looked even more upset as he took it from Beck.

'It was all so very sad. We didn't know, you see, on the day of the wedding, that the poor girl had died. Her brother, that's Tom Lyford, simply told us she was ill – so the wedding could go on as planned. Lucy knew nothing about it until she came back from honeymoon and she was devastated. The girls were very close – like sisters.'

Glancing at the inspector, he said anxiously: 'Has anyone informed Tom? Miss Lyford was his great-aunt, too, although he lives in Switzerland with his godfather. I think he was flying back this morning so I would telephone him there. He'll be very upset, this coming on top of his sister's death. That hit him pretty hard. They said it was a clear case of suicide, but we all think it must have been accidental – an overdose, you understand.'

Inspector Govern nodded.

'Sometimes these young people take overdoses as a cry for help – they don't actually mean to kill themselves,' he said. 'It's tragic for their families who so often blame themselves.'

George Godstow leaned forward on his desk, his expression cheering a little,

'That's what I tell my wife. Will you be calling to see her, Inspector? If you do, try and break this news as gently as you can – as I'm sure you mean to do. It's just that she has been really down in the dumps since Vanessa . . . well, she was very attached to the girl . . . we all were. Poor Miss Lyford's death will bring everything back. Who on earth would want to kill her, Inspector? A burglary, do you think? There are some really dreadful thugs around these days. As far as I know, she didn't have anything very valuable – a few heirlooms left by her parents. She asked me once if I thought she should insure them so I told her to get them valued but I don't know if she ever did.'

Not wishing to add further distress to the solicitor, Govern forbore to give him the grisly details about Miss Lyford's murder, although the man would inevitably read all about it in the newspapers once the journalists got hold of the story. 'Thirty-five stab wounds on a lonely old pensioner' – bound to make news.

As her husband had anticipated, Bridget Godstow dissolved into tears when she heard the reason for the inspector's visit. For a short while, all she could say was: 'Poor Miss Lyford! Poor Vanessa!' over and over again. When she'd calmed down a bit, she remembered that Miss Lyford had never turned up for lunch nor rung to give an explanation for any change of plan. It was unlike the elderly spinster to be anything less than meticulous in her arrangements.

'Oh dear, Inspector!' she concluded 'All the time that poor woman was . . .' Unable to voice the word 'dead', she murmured tearfully: 'All the time she had passed away.'

She could tell them very little more than had her husband, she said finally. She knew absolutely no one who could possibly wish Miss Lyford any harm; that nearly all her friends consisted of fanatical bridge players like herself – a harmless enough occupation. According to the accounts Vanessa used to give of her guardian's home life, no one came to the house other than bridge players and people like electricity-meter readers, window cleaners and the like. Bridget did not think Miss Lyford was very rich but neither was she on the poverty line like some old age pensioners. She had inherited some money from Tom and Vanessa's father, her nephew, who had also left money in trust for both his children and a few family heirlooms.

'Is it possible Miss Lyford could have won a lot of money at bridge clubs?' Beck asked. His own mother returned home triumphant sometimes because she had won the jackpot at bingo; but the only bridge player he knew, an elderly uncle, seemed to lose most of his pension at the snooker club!

Bridget Godstow could not provide an answer. She told them that she thought it was unlikely that either her son, Jonathan or her daughters could give them any more information than she had done.

'But if you want to talk to Lucy, she and Guy are coming down for lunch on Sunday. You could come back and see her here if you wish. I'm sure she would want to be as helpful as possible.'

On the drive back to Brighton, Govern said they might well return at the weekend to have a word with Miss Lucy Godstow.'

'Mrs Guy Weaver!' Beck corrected him. 'She was on her honeymoon when we were investigating her friend's suicide, do you remember? When she returned, you and I were in Scotland investigating that body in the loch. I think it was Inspector Simpson who interviewed her – said she hadn't been able to shed any light on the suicide. At the inquest it was mooted that she was in despair at the thought of parting with her best friend – Lucy was getting married. The family thought it unlikely to cause her to be suicidal.'

'Yes, I remember now,' Inspector Govern said from the

passenger seat beside him. 'I also remember that you have some views about lesbians if I'm not mistaken. I sometimes think, Beck, my boy, that your whole life is ruled by sexual thoughts. All hormone-related. It's high time you settled down and got yourself married.'

'Would if I could, sir!' Beck replied. 'Remember those smashing twins, Rose was one of them – and Lily – no, Poppy? I'd have married either of them – or both! – if they'd fancied me. One of them was tied up with that American – and married him. Don't know what happened to the other.'

'Well, stop thinking about them,' Govern said sharply, 'and watch your driving. Speed limit here is thirty, not fifty! Slow down.'

'Bang goes my promotion,' muttered Beck under his breath, but he slowed down all the same.

Eleven

In the front of the crematorium chapel, Tom, his Great Aunt's only relative, stood alone. Behind him on the right were six of Joan Lyford's elderly bridge partners, a retired brigadier, her bank manager, three widows, a middle-aged schoolmaster and her solicitor.

Beck and Inspector Govern, seated right at the back of the chapel, were in silent agreement that none of them could be even vaguely associated with the victim's murderer. Nor, indeed, could young Tom Lyford who was clearly very distressed by his relative's death.

'She was my sister's guardian after our parents died,' he had told them whilst they had gathered in the waiting room before the last service had finished and theirs could begin. 'She was not a maternal person but she was always kind to Vanessa and did her best for her. Van . . .' His voice became husky as he mentioned her name. 'Van was fond of her. I'm glad she isn't here – that she doesn't know what happened to Aunt Joan.'

On the left side of the small chapel were the Godstow family, the two girls between their parents, the elder married daughter standing beside her husband. As the service progressed, Govern noticed that Lucy Weaver was in tears. Still emotional about her the suicide of her best friend, Vanessa's Lyford, perhaps. He mentioned this later to Beck as they went out of the door into the cold December air. It was, after all, less than three months since the family had had to attend that funeral.

They stood at a discreet distance, watching the mourners stop to look at the wreaths and bouquets on the grass outside the chapel. Tom Lyford, who had obeyed the instructions left in his Great Aunt's will that she should be cremated, had acceded to their request to be present at the ceremony.

'It sometimes happens that a murderer is drawn to the final disposal of his victim,' Govern had explained. 'We'd appreciate it if we could be there as a sort of courtesy. If any stranger did turn up, we don't want him aware we are watching for him.'

There was one spectacular arrangement of red and white roses designating the hearts, diamonds, spades and clubs in tribute to the deceased's obsession with the game of bridge.

'Must have cost an absolute packet!' Beck whispered to the Inspector. 'Wonder who that was from!'

As if Julia had overheard the remark, she turned to Beck, her expression almost a happy one.

'Isn't that perfectly beautiful!' she exclaimed. 'Guy had it sent from London. Of course, he's terribly rich so he could afford it.' The last remark was in a different tone of voice from the first, Govern noticed. It was almost disparaging. He recalled the girl's name, Julia, fourteen; youngest of the Godstows' three daughters. Was she jealous of her now wealthy sister? he asked himself. Yet somehow, he didn't think so. She was clearly avoiding the husband and had attached herself to Tom Lyford's side.

George Godstow came over to their car as they were preparing to depart.

'We thought it would be easier for everyone if we had some refreshments at our house,' he said courteously. 'Do please join us. By the way, we all appreciate you coming this afternoon. I'm sure you must be very busy.'

Govern nodded.

'Most of the time, yes, but thank you very much, sir. Sergeant Beck and I would be happy to join you for a little while.'

Beck only just managed to withhold a gasp of surprise. The very last thing Govern ever did was socialize when he was on a case.

As they drove back from the Brighton crematorium to Hurst Heath Govern was silent for part of the way and then said suddenly: 'I'm not sure what it is about that Weaver fellow. He's just a tad too smooth . . . well, maybe he has to be; wealthy company director and all that. I don't know . . .'

Beck slowed down as they drove into the small town of Ferrybridge and turned westward towards Hurst Heath.

'One of your hunches, sir?' he asked.

Govern sighed.

'I don't think you could quite call it that. One thing is for sure; he can't be that poor woman's murderer. I checked the evidence very carefully and he definitely was in Birmingham that day. Both his wife and his customer endorsed his statement. Besides, he had no motive. He barely knew Miss Lyford and he certainly didn't need to steal her silver.'

'Strange we've had no whisper from the fences!' Beck muttered. 'I suppose it's fairly early days. All the same . . .'

'Could have gone abroad,' Govern commented thoughtfully. 'We may never trace it. I'm beginning to think those DNA samples are our only hope of ever catching this maniac. He's definitely a mental case, I'd say.'

'Wants locking up and the key thrown away!' was Beck's rejoinder, only to earn the inspector's ironic reproof.

'You're forgetting "human rights", my boy. If we do get the killer put away, they'll let them out before they've finished half their sentence; or the medics would pronounce them cured if they'd sent them to Rampton. I sometimes wonder why we stay in this job.'

Govern was depressed by their failure so far to come up with a single clue as to the old lady's murderer. Moreover, it had been a particularly gruesome one and unnecessary. One or two stab wounds would have finished her off! But thirty-five . . . Surely there had to be a clue somewhere.

As they turned into the driveway of The Willows, Tom Lyford's car drew up just in front of them, followed by Guy Weaver and his pretty young wife. Waiting to park behind them, the two detectives watched as Tom jumped out of his car and hurried to open the passenger door of Weaver's TVR. They both noticed the wide smile on Lucy's face as she stepped out into his embrace, and the angry scowl of her husband.

'Jealous!' Govern muttered. 'Interesting! Older man dislikes younger rival's familiarity with his pretty young wife.'

Lucy drew back from Tom's embrace and hurried round the back of the car to link her arm through her husband's.

'I do wish it was not such an unhappy day for you, Tom,' she said. 'Come on, let's go indoors and see what Ma has cooked up for us to eat. Julia says she was up till all hours last night baking.'

Tom smiled back at her although smiling was the very last thing he felt like as he made complimentary remarks about

Bridget Godstow's culinary efforts, which he had always enjoyed when he'd stayed with the family in the past.

He was extremely concerned by Lucy's marked loss of weight. Her face was pale and there were deep shadows under her eyes, visible despite her frequent smiles which, though he couldn't explain his reasons, he suspected were put on for his and her family's benefit. Somehow, he decided as he walked with her and Guy into the house, he must try to get her alone – ask her what, if anything, was wrong.

There was no such opportunity, however, as not once did Guy leave Lucy's side. His anxiety growing, Tom resorted to questioning Julia who was, as always, following him about like an adoring puppy. He drew her out to the cloakroom where the wellingtons, umbrellas, tennis racquets and the like were stored. He knew that there he had the best hope of privacy as his late aunt's bridge friends, vicar, doctor and cleaning lady were still mingling with the family in the living room.

Delighted to be drawn aside for a private talk to her beloved Tom, Julia was only too happy to answer his questions as to Lucy's welfare.

'Mum's worried stiff about her!' she said. 'She thinks Lucy has lost far too much weight – and so do I. Lucy swears nothing's wrong but Mum thinks there is, although she wouldn't say so to me. I heard her talking to Dad. They think she might be pregnant but Lucy swore on the telephone that she wasn't. Guy doesn't want children – well, not yet anyway. But we hardly ever get to see her now. She and Guy usually have their weekends booked up for something. If it's not a theatre or dinner party or a weekend with one of Guy's clients, he says they've had a terribly busy week and need a weekend's rest to recuperate.'

Julia's voice deepened with indignation.

'They could perfectly well 'recuperate' here with us. Lucy loves being here with us and Mum waits on her hand and foot; spoils her actually. It's all Guy's fault, Tom. I think he's just jealous because Lucy loves us and he only wants her to love him.'

Tom drew a deep sigh as he looked at Julia's plump flushed cheeks. One thing was clear, Julia was not one of Guy's fans whereas her older sister, Jemma, clearly thought the world of him. Talking to her earlier, she had told him admiringly that she thought Guy suave, very much a man of the world, always beautifully turned out with handmade suits, shoes and expensive accessories. Aware that her younger sister disliked him, Jemma had often reminded Julia that he lavished presents on Lucy and gave her a far bigger allowance than she could possibly spend on herself.

'Lucy has absolutely everything in the world she wants!' Jemma had said enviously. 'Guy's taking her to the Bahamas next month when all this horrible business with the funeral and everything is over. I just hope I can find a husband like Guy! It's obvious he absolutely adores her!'

'Well, I don't!' Julia said indignantly after she had related Jemma's opinions to the listening Tom. 'And what's more, I don't think he likes me either. Not that I care but I do care about not seeing Lucy very often. I think . . . I think . . .' she reiterated. 'I think Lucy wants to see us more often, like she used to before she was married, and Guy won't let her. Can't *you* do something about it, Tom?'

Sensing she was close to tears, Tom put a comforting arm around her shoulders.

'Darling JuJu,' he said, 'you know I, of all people, can't interfere. Lucy is Guy's wife and that's all there is to it. Maybe your mum can intervene, or your dad – but I can't.' He paused briefly before deciding that he could trust Julia – and he was desperate to tell someone. The only person in the world who knew his secret was his Uncle Charles. He drew a deep breath.

'I'm going to tell you a secret, JuJu – although I think you may know it anyway. It's that I still love Lucy. I always have and I always will. I think Guy knows it and resents the fact that Lucy and I have always been so close. I'm the last person who can try to find out what, if anything, is wrong.'

'Oh, Tom!' Julia sighed, not far from tears. 'I do so very much wish it could have been you that Lucy married – even though I sort of hoped when I was younger that you might one day fall in love with me! I always had a crush on you, but I sort of knew how you felt about Lucy and I absolutely *hated it* when she went and fell in love with Guy.'

'Not half as much as I did!' Tom said with an attempt to diffuse the emotion of the moment. 'Look, Julia, I'll be going back to Geneva once I've sold Aunt Joan's house and got probate for her will and all that. I'd be so very grateful if you would write to me – keep me in touch. I'm probably being very silly to worry about Lucy, but I think you understand, don't you? I don't want you to spy on her – just keep an eye open. Not that I could do much if you did write and say she was in trouble, but at least I could try.'

Julia's eyes were shining. A secret tryst with Tom was vastly appealing and as her concern for Lucy was very real, she felt a little less worried about her sister knowing that Tom shared her concern.

As Inspector Govern and Detective Sergeant Beck moved towards the front door, Guy followed, handing Govern his over-coat and Beck his raincoat. He had insisted on seeing them off, although they had both already thanked their host and hostess and explained their early departure due to the pres-sures of work.

'Well, Inspector, it sounds very much as if the trail's gone cold,' Guy said as he opened the front door. There was the hint of a question in his voice. 'In my opinion, too many murderers get away with it these days.'

Inspector Govern smiled although not, Beck saw, with his eyes.

'It may seem that way to you, sir, but you'd be surprised – like the Mounties, we more often than not get our man – however many years it may take. There's no such thing as closing our books on an unsolved crime, especially one as abhorrent as that inflicted on Miss Lyford.'

'Well, yes, of course!' was Guy's response. 'Oh, well, good luck, Inspector. Safe journey back!'

Govern was silent as they drove back towards Brighton until they reached the South Downs. Then he turned to Beck who was driving and said suddenly: 'So Weaver isn't our murderer but I'd never trust him. Had the strangest feeling he was taunting me. Maybe I'm misjudging him and he just wanted to get across his superiority – you know? Useless police force . . . no good at our jobs whereas he . . .'

He broke off, leaving his sergeant uncertain what to say.

'He'd make a good James Bond!' he said finally, only to be met with his inspector's grunt of disapproval.

'If no other, you do have one talent, Beck – that of making

very stupid comments at inappropriate moments. Mark my words – Weaver isn't what he seems.'

He didn't speak again until they reached the station where the duty constable told him that one of the fences had reported the offer of two pieces of silver. The detective had duly paid the grass but although the tankard and the fish servers had been stolen, they did not correspond to the description given them by Miss Lyford's daily help of the objects she had polished once a month for her employer.

Their hopes dashed, Govern went into his office, closed the door and settled down to clearing some overdue paper work. Beck, he said, would do well to do the same.

Back at The Willows, Tom managed to corner Lucy on her own as she came downstairs from her old bedroom where she had left her black coat and handbag. She and Guy were just leaving, she told him. Tom did not return her smile.

'Look, Lucy, I'm not leaving England for another week or two. Can I come up to London and take you out to lunch, or something? We haven't had a chance to get together since . . . since . . . that day when we cleared the flat.'

Still standing on the stairs just above him, Lucy glanced over his shoulder. The hall was empty and she looked down into Tom's face, a huge wave of regret sweeping over her. They had had so many happy times together – Tom, Vanessa and herself. Now those carefree days were gone forever and she could hardly bear the thought. She would really love to see more of Tom before he returned to Switzerland, but she wasn't sure if it was feasible. She decided to be honest with him although she knew she would be revealing a less admirable trait of Guy's character. She put a hand on Tom's shoulder and looked into his eyes.

'It's just that Guy is terribly jealous – especially of you, darling Tombo. He knows how close you and I and Van were and that everyone thought you and I . . . well, that we might end up getting married!' She gave a shy little laugh before continuing awkwardly: 'I suppose it wasn't very tactful of Julia who blurted it all out after Van's funeral and you'd gone home. Of course, I've told him there's absolutely nothing like that between us . . . I mean, we'll always love each other – won't we? – but I'd never, ever be unfaithful to Guy, although he doesn't believe it. He says nearly all married women have affairs after they've been married some time and are bored with their husbands.'

She saw the look of surprise on Tom's face and added quickly: 'I know he has no right to stop me seeing you but . . . well, if we do meet, it would probably save a lot of worry for everyone if you didn't come to the flat. We could go out to lunch somewhere. Well, somewhere we wouldn't be seen.'

It was a spur of the moment suggestion Lucy had not intended to make, but she had been so very happy to see Tom again, albeit at the sad funeral of his aunt, that she couldn't face the thought of him going abroad again without them having time together. She badly wanted an hour or two with him when they could talk about Vanessa. She still missed her so terribly that some afternoons she would dissolve into tears simply looking at the treasured photograph she had on her dressing table. Guy had told her she was only adding to her bereavement by keeping the photograph where she could see it every time she looked in her mirror, and that she should put it away in a drawer. She had refused with an unusual determination, the more telling to Guy because she so rarely did otherwise than defer to his wishes. When she did do so, Guy's manner would change instantly. The loving, caring looks became cold, hard, even to the point where she sometimes wondered if at that moment he actually hated her. Such moments, rare though they were, frightened and distressed her.

On the day she had made her wedding vows, she had been utterly determined that theirs would never be one of the one in three marriages which ended in divorce. They would, she'd told him on the first night of their honeymoon, be like her father and mother who were still as much in love in their forties as they had been in their twenties. Guy had made no comment but his expression had been wry as if he didn't believe her. Taking her in his arms, he had hugged her so tightly that she was all but breathless as he'd said fiercely:

'Don't you ever dare leave me, Lucy.' It was almost a threat but she had been flattered by the extent of his passion and responded to him in mind and body.

Tom was regarding her quizzically.

'Lucy, wouldn't it be better to be upfront? As you say, it isn't as if there is anything wrong in our relationship. Surely Guy can't object to you having friends – male friends? Doesn't he trust you?'

Lucy glanced nervously towards the drawing room door as if afraid Guy might suddenly open it and see them murmuring together. It seemed suddenly quite unreasonable that she should concern herself with his unfounded fears and yet, oddly, she couldn't ignore them. She gave a seemingly carefree shrug and smiled.

'Maybe he's right not to do so, darling Tombo!' she said. 'You are still my favourite boyfriend – after Guy, of course!'

It was a silly, flirtatious remark, out of keeping with the trend of their conversation and Tom ignored it.

'Then at least I can come up to London and take you out to lunch. Name a day and a place, Lucy, and I'll be there.'

Looking at Tom's serious face and hearing the intensity in his voice, Lucy felt a moment of regret for agreeing to the assignation. She could not ignore the fact that she knew very well Tom was still in love with her. Was she being unfair to him by keeping him as so close a friend when there could never be any question of her loving anyone else but Guy? She did love her husband – passionately. He was a wonderful lover, considerate yet always masterful, and she sometimes wondered if the amount of time they spent in bed was overmuch, even for relative newly-weds. Guy was an experienced lover and she did not question his past although she knew he had had many affairs before he met her. But he had never wanted to marry any of those other women, of that he had left her in no doubt, and he'd sworn that from the day he had first seen her, he'd known he would never want anyone else. Very occasionally, Lucy felt his adoration to be a little overpowering; as if he wanted mentally as well as physically to devour her. That thought had immediately seemed ridiculous, yet his possessiveness was very real.

She took her hand off Tom's arm and jumped lightly down the last two stairs. 'How about that Italian restaurant near the South Kensington underground? The one you and Van and I used to go to – when we could afford it!' Her voice suddenly broke. 'Oh, Tom,' she whispered, 'I do so terribly wish Van hadn't left us. I miss her so much.'

He moved forward to take her in his arms to comfort her when the drawing room door opened. It was not Guy but Bridget Godstow carrying a large empty teapot. She smiled fondly at them.

'I think it's all gone very well, don't you? Lucy, darling, your father has just given Miss Lyford's elderly friends a generous slug of sherry and they've cheered up enormously. Her death, you know, was a terrible shock for them. At their age, they feel so vulnerable.' She turned to Tom, her face now serious as she added: 'Of course, your aunt should never have gone on living in that isolated house all on her own. These days . . .' She sighed, leaving the rest of the sentence unsaid. Then her face cleared as Tom stepped forward and put his arm round her shoulders.

'I'm afraid I've got to leave, Aunt Bridget, but I promise I'll come and see you all again soon. I don't go back to Geneva for another fortnight so I'll try and call in before I leave. Thank you a hundred times for all you've done. I don't think I could possibly have hosted a wake in a hotel in Seaford – your offer to do the honours has made a sad day far less so.'

Pleased by his praise, Bridget stood on tiptoe and kissed his cheek.

'You know you're like a second son to me, Tom. I want you always to look on this as your second home – the way Vanessa did, poor child.'

She glanced anxiously at Lucy, who was looking very pale, with gaunt cheeks and shadowed eyes. Her eyes had more sparkle in them than before though.

As Tom left the wake, he kissed both Lucy and her mother lightly on the cheek and asked them to say his goodbyes to the girls for him, before he hurried out of the house.

Unlike his sister, he had had very little contact with his great aunt and did not pretend to be personally greatly affected by her death – only by the horrific manner of it. As he was driving back through Brighton to the King George, where he had booked himself a room for the necessary weeks he was obliged to remain in England, he drove past Maddison Street and his eyes filled with tears as he recalled the few precious days he had spent there with Vanessa in the attic flat.

Would he ever be as happy again? he asked himself as he drove along the seafront, glancing briefly at the grey,

windswept skies and white-flecked waves smashing relentlessly up the pebbled beach? Uncle Charles had said time was
a great healer, but he couldn't see any time in the future when
he would not miss his sister or be part of Lucy's life again.

Twelve

It was the first week of April and Bridget Godstow told her youngest daughter that she could go up to London to spend four whole days with her sister. Lucy was having bad bouts of early morning sickness and had admitted to her mother that she was feeling very low. Needless to say, Bridget wanted to have her come home but apparently Guy would not hear of it. He was more than capable of looking after her himself, he'd said, and in any event, he thought Lucy was better staying quietly at their home. Julia had disagreed.

'It would cheer her up, Mum; me and Jemma . . .'

'Jemma and I!' Bridget broke in automatically. Julia grinned.

'It would be fun with Jemma and me and Jonnie and his friend Whatshisname! We could play It's a Deal and Monopoly and . . . well, take Lucy's mind off being sick.'

Bridget had asked her but although Lucy had sounded reluctant to miss this jolly family party, she nevertheless opted to remain in London. It was then Julia had suggested she go to see Lucy, always her favourite sister who she had adored since infancy. Jemma, on the other hand, was closer to their brother, Jonathan.

Lucy greeted Julia almost tearfully when she arrived on her doorstep.

'It's so lovely to see you, JuJu!' she exclaimed, hugging her rosy-cheeked sister. Her face clouded. 'I'm afraid it isn't going to be very exciting for you – your precious Easter holidays, too! I'd hoped to take you to a theatre and the Tate Modern but I daren't go anywhere where I can't easily throw up. Who'd have a baby, eh?'

Julia was shocked.

'You can't mean that!' she said. 'Mum said you were absolutely thrilled when the tests were positive.'

Lucy turned away and busied herself unpacking Julia's suit-case, laying the contents on the double bed she and Guy shared. Since she had told him about her pregnancy, he had opted to sleep in the spare room – so as not to disturb her, he'd said, but instinct told her that for some reason, her condition had ceased to make her sexually desirable to him. One thing he had made clear to her from that very first moment, was that he did not want a child and that he wanted her to have an abortion.

'We've only been married seven months!' he'd muttered, removing himself abruptly from the circle of her arms. 'Besides, I'd been planning to spend quite a bit of time in Spain this year. The last thing we need is a squalling baby to lug around.' He'd walked away from her towards the window before adding thoughtfully: 'I suppose we *could* afford a nanny but . . .' He had turned then to face her. 'Get rid of it, Lucy. For my sake!'

Something primitive within her had prompted Lucy to abandon the calm voice she usually used when Guy was in one of his awkward moods. Cheeks flushed, her voice raised, she had moved closer so that her face was only a few centimetres from his.

'It's *my* baby, Guy, and I will *not* even *consider* destroying it.' With a flash of insight, she added: 'You're just being selfish, wanting me all to yourself. Well, it's time you gave a bit of thought to what life is like for me. You go off to your business meetings leaving me with a whole day to fill in just waiting for you to return. You don't want me to have a job and you don't like it when I tell you I'm going home for the day. Well, a baby will give me something to think about, to do.' Close once more to tears, her voice had softened and she'd reached up to touch Guy's cheek. 'Darling, try and see my point of view. This is *our* baby. We made it loving each other the way we do. He or she will be part of us both and once it's born, you'll love it, too. I know you will!'

For a moment, his expression had remained blank. Then the colour had rushed into his cheeks and he had taken her in his arms, holding her so closely that she could scarcely breathe. His mouth had pressed fiercely down on hers, crushing her lip against her teeth. Sex was the last thing Lucy had felt like at that moment but as her husband's hands had wandered over her body, he had been able to rouse in her a half-hearted response.

Sensitive to Guy's every mood, Lucy had been shocked by the anger she'd seen in his face after he had made love to her there on the Persian rug in front of the window. He'd known somehow that she had faked her orgasm, but neither had mentioned it. That night, Guy had moved into their spare room.

Hurt by his negative attitude to her pregnancy and a little concerned, Lucy had not asked him if he would mind her young sister visiting in the Easter holidays, a courtesy she would have normally paid him. The flat was, after all, more his than hers! In one of the rare moments they actually spoke to one another, she simply announced that Julia was arriving shortly and would be sleeping with her in the double bed. Guy's only comment had been that he wished it was her other sister who was coming and not Julia who, he had declared, had a 'thing' about him originating, absurdly, from the time he'd been obliged to kill the rabbit.

Knowing he was right about Julia's sentiments, Lucy was all the more grateful to her young sister for this visit. Impulsively, she gave her a big hug.

'I'm really, really pleased to see you, JuJu!' she said. 'I never thought I'd miss the family so much. Somehow it was different when Van and I left home – we sort of had each other.'

Julia sat down on the side of the bed and nodded.

'Vanessa was like a sister, wasn't she? Sometimes when I think about her, I get all weepy. And what's more, now she isn't there for Tom to visit, he hardly ever comes to England any more.'

To lighten the moment, Lucy said teasingly: 'You always had a crush on Tom, didn't you, JuJu? I suppose in a way, we all loved him – Mum, too. I sometimes think she got on much better with him than with our Jonnie!'

Julia grinned.

'Dad once told me Mum spoilt Jonnie when he was little! Her first-born baby boy. And Jonnie has taken advantage ever since. I think he's getting better now he's left school, don't you?'

For a while, the two girls sat together in the bedroom

chatting about the family. It was to be their parents' silver wedding anniversary next Christmas and they discussed how to arrange a surprise party for them with lots of their old friends there to celebrate with them. They only stopped chattering once when Lucy had to rush off to the bathroom to be sick. When she returned, looking pale and doing her best to smile reassuringly at Julia, she lay back on the bed obviously exhausted. Julia looked at her anxiously.

'I suppose this isn't the right moment to suggest I get some lunch for us!' she said, pleased to see the smile of agreement on Lucy's face. 'Is there anything I can do for you whilst you're resting Lucy?'

Lucy lent up on one elbow.

'Actually there is, darling. I've been meaning to go up to the loft ever since I came to live here but kept putting it off. You know how I hate ladders! Guy says there's only junk up there. He's goes up there once a week – just to make sure there aren't any trapped birds or mice or anything, but I can't get him to tell me what exactly is stored there.'

Julia sprang off the bed and waved her arms excitedly.

'It's just the sort of exploring thing I love doing!' she enthused. 'I'll take a pad and pencil up there and make a list for you. It'll be fun.'

Within minutes, she had lowered the loft ladder, climbed to the top, removed the board covering the opening and disappeared with a torch, pencil and paper into the low-ceilinged roof space.

Despite the fact that she was still feeling nauseous, Lucy smiled remembering the happy expression on her sister's face as she'd gone 'exploring', as she termed it. For a few moments, she forgot how weak and washed-out she felt. She forgot, too, that Guy did not want the child she was carrying, and still wanted her to have an abortion.

It wasn't as if she had ever been particularly maternal, Lucy thought. This baby had most certainly not been planned. When she and Guy had discussed children before their wedding, they'd both agreed a family was something they might consider way into the future. She was, after all, only in her early twenties and nowadays, an even greater number of women were opting to have their babies in their thirties – even forties. Mostly because they had careers, she told herself, whereas

Guy simply refused to allow her to go back to teaching. He'd bought her the latest thing in computers so she could 'tinker about with eBay and Google' or even learn another language. But she needed the company of other people her own age and despite Guy telling her not to be so negative, she joined a cookery class specializing in haute cuisine run by an old school friend, and once a week, was able to socialize with a group of other young, married women. Some already had children or babies and were eagerly grabbing what they called 'a bit of me time'.

Until her pregnancy, Lucy was so physically in love with Guy that his obsessional needs to 'own' her had been a satisfaction rather than a restriction. She'd wanted him to want her and as soon as he'd returned back home after a day away they had made love, in bed, in the bath, on the living-room floor. Laughing, back then Lucy had teased Guy about his phenomenal stamina. But lately sex was the very last thing she needed and when Guy insisted on making love to her, he had become much more demanding, much rougher, as if he could force her to respond. Once or twice, it crossed Lucy's mind that maybe he was hoping when he thrust deep inside her that he could destroy their child, and although she quickly rejected such a shocking idea, it had remained at the back of her mind sufficiently to suppress her own sex drive.

Above her head, she could hear Julia moving around. It was not long before she climbed back down the ladder, a cobweb or two clinging to her jeans and jersey. Her cheeks were bright pink.

'It's really spooky up there,' she said fervently. 'There's an old armchair with the stuffing coming out and a few boxes with books in them which look as if the mice have enjoyed eating them. But Lucy – ' her eyes lit up with excitement – 'there's a big chest – quite new-looking with a big padlock. I tried to lift it but it was heavy. Do you think there's something valuable in it?'

Lucy smiled indulgently.

'I doubt it, darling. Guy's very meticulous about insuring things – some of the furniture and ornaments in the flat are quite valuable, I believe. When I came here to live with him, I said I thought it was a bit dangerous these days leaving such expensive things for anyone – the window cleaner or meter reader for instance – to see, but Guy says there's absolutely no point having beautiful things and hiding them away. So I can't imagine he's hidden anything interesting in that chest. Are you sure you can't open it?'

'I didn't try very hard! 'Julia admitted, her excitement abated by Lucy's comments. 'But there was a key – at least I think it might be a key for the chest. It was under an old telephone – you know, those whirly ones people used to swivel round the numbers? I tripped over it and must have knocked the key out somehow. Lucy – ' her eyes were shining again – 'shall I go back up and see if it fits?'

Lucy sat up, her nausea forgotten as she looked at Julia's expectant face. Suddenly, memories of their childhood filled her mind – midnight feasts, nipping out to the swimming pool in the garden for a forbidden swim in the moonlight, stealing baby cherry tomatoes from their father's greenhouse and eating them whilst they were still sun-warmed. There were the summer afternoons when Julia was little more than a toddler when Lucy would take her into the woods for 'an adventure', which meant searching for a bright copper coin she had hidden earlier in a hole in a tree or digging in the sand on the beach at the seaside for pirates' gold!

She laughed but shook her head.

'Better wait until Guy gets home. I shouldn't have let you go up there in the first place. He told me not to do so in case I fell through the ceiling or something!' She put her arms round her sister's shoulders and hugged her. 'Oh, it is good to see you, Juju. How's Mum? Dad? And the dogs? I wanted to get a puppy – for company, but Guy thought it would be too much of a tie – for when we go abroad. Now, with the baby coming, I'll have quite enough to do without having to exercise a dog, so he was quite right to say no.'

Julia looked at her curiously.

'Do you always let Guy boss you around?' she asked. 'I know Mum always defers to Dad but they're old-fashioned. Mum said in her parents' day, the husband was the bread-winner and therefore it was right for him to lay down the law! But it's a new century, for goodness sake! And I can remember you and Van saying that when you had husbands, you'd insist on being equals.'

For a moment, Lucy did not reply. Then she said thoughtfully:

'Sometimes it's simpler just to agree. I mean, Guy is a lot older than I am and I think he likes . . . well, taking care of me . . . a bit like Dad, really!' She gave a half-hearted laugh. 'Now I'm making him sound positively Victorian. Anyway, JuJu, I really don't mind if he wants to be in control. I'm very much in love with him, you know, and I'm happy if he's happy!'

Young though she was, Julia managed to hold her tongue. Every part of her longed to dispute Lucy's declaration.

To lighten the sudden uneasiness between herself and Lucy, she said: 'Do you realize I'll be an aunt? And Mum will be a granny! I think it's terribly exciting. Have you thought of names?'

Lucy shook her head.

'It's early days, JuJu!' She had a sudden inspiration. 'How would you like to be a godmother,' she asked, 'as well as an aunt?'

Julia's eyes shone with pleasure.

'I really love that!' she gasped, starry-eyed. Then she giggled. 'Jemma will be terribly jealous you asked me instead of her!'

For a moment, Lucy was able to enjoy Julia's happiness but within minutes, she recalled Guy's antipathy to her younger sister – a dislike he barely bothered to disguise. He might object very strongly to having Julia as a godmother to his child!

Suddenly Lucy's mouth set in a tight, determined line. This time, she would have what she wanted regardless of his wishes. If he hadn't expressed so forcefully his objection to her having this child, she would almost certainly have discussed godparents and names with him.

A wave of depression washed over her as she realized the way her thoughts had taken her. The very last thing she wanted was to be at odds with Guy. When she had made her marriage vows that day in church, it was true she had omitted the words 'serve and obey' which were in her mother's 1930 Book of Common Prayer but Guy had had to agree that they were outdated.

Julia's voice interrupted her thoughts.

'Are you feeling better, Lucy? Do you think you could eat some lunch now? I could make an omelette . . .' She giggled. 'That's about the only thing I can cook other than chips and sausages – oh, and fried eggs!'

Forgetting Guy and, indeed, the baby, Lucy laughed.

'I shall suggest to Mum that instead of swanning round the world in your gap year, you go to cookery classes like I do.' She swung her legs over the side of the bed and stood up, her nausea quite forgotten as she headed for the kitchen. 'I'll cook you a smoked salmon soufflé, JuJu,' she said. 'It's quite delicious. We'll have it with some brown bread and butter, I bought a fresh loaf yesterday.

An hour later, she and Julia were making their way to the Science Museum – a favourite haunt of Julia's. With Lucy now fully recovered, they stayed far longer than they had intended and by the time they got back to the flat, Guy was home.

With barely a glance at Julia he got up from his chair by the television and stood facing Lucy. His face was expressionless and he made no attempt to kiss her or even acknowledge Julia's presence.

'So where have you two been?' he enquired in a strangely quiet voice. 'The note you left me in the kitchen said you'd be back by five o'clock latest.' He presented Lucy with his watch face. 'It's now a quarter past six.'

As the colour flared into Lucy's cheeks, the muscles of his face relaxed slightly.

'You may disregard my concern but I am unhappily aware of the extremely unpleasant things which could have detained you – bombs on the underground, muggers, car accidents. If you are going to be later than you planned, you could at least have the forethought to telephone me. I do have a mobile, you know.'

Feeling almost as if she were a schoolgirl being reprimanded by the head teacher, Lucy was on the point of suggesting that *he* might ring *her* on her mobile whenever *he* was going to be late, but with Julia listening open-mouthed, she decided to let the moment pass. As she and Julia removed their jackets and scarves she deliberately changed the conversation.

'We've been dying to ask you, Guy. What's in the chest in the attic? JuJu said it was locked so she couldn't satisfy our curiosity, although you did find a key, didn't you, JuJu?'

Later, when she remembered that moment, Lucy was in no doubt whatsoever that Guy's normal complexion went a deathly white – with anger, she realized.

He kept his voice well under control as he said: 'If I lock things up, it's for a purpose. The chest happens to contain some important business files. If they were lost or mislaid could have disastrous consequences for my financial affairs.' His voice still ominously quiet, he turned to look directly at Lucy. 'I thought I said you should not go up there, Lucy – it isn't safe!'

Unhappy that Guy should be reprimanding her sister in such a way, Julia rushed, ill-advisedly, to her defence.

'It seemed safe enough to me!' she said indignantly. 'There are perfectly good floor boards so I was hardly likely to fall through the ceiling.'

To Lucy's total surprise, Guy ignored Julia's comment and with a completely unexpected change of mood, he suddenly linked his arm through hers.

'It's good to see you looking so much better, darling!' he told her. 'It means I can take you and Julia out to dinner. I thought we might go somewhere a little bit out of the ordinary. What do you say to the Oxo Tower, Julia? You've never been there, have you? I booked a table just in case you both felt up to it.'

Julia looked to her sister for guidance.

'I'd love to go there if you feel well enough, Lucy!' she said.

'Then that's what we'll do, darling! I'm feeling absolutely fine.' Lucy informed Guy who was now pouring himself a drink. He no longer looked angry but on the contrary, smiled down at her and put his arm round her shoulders. She felt a sudden unexpected rush of love for him. This was the Guy with whom she had fallen in love. It was wrong of her to get so annoyed when he was cross or distant. He travelled long distances to his meetings, often leaving early and not getting home until late. It was understandable if he was sometimes tired and perhaps, because of it, a little inconsiderate. She was particularly happy because knowing his feelings about Julia, he was trying, doubtless for her sake, to be especially nice to her. Julia seldom came to London and when she did, it was usually for a Christmas or birthday treat, or possibly a dental appointment. She was having to wear a brace to straighten her teeth and their mother had a 'thing' about national health dentists and insisted on paying a private dentist in Wimpole Street.

'Mum made me pack a dress,' Julia was saying. She giggled. 'She said it wasn't appropriate for me to wear jeans if we went to a posh restaurant. I'll go and have a shower and change, shall I?'

When her sister left the room, Lucy went and sat down beside Guy on the sofa and linked her arm through his.

'Love you lots, darling!' she said huskily. 'Sorry if I've been a bit – well, down in the dumps lately. I spoke to Doctor Griffiths this morning and she assured me this morning sickness will almost certainly stop in another month or so. Then I'll be back to normal and . . .' She hesitated momentarily before adding shyly 'Then we can be lovers again.'

Guy nodded but gave no reply.

When Lucy went to get changed, Guy's thoughts reflected on the thoroughly unwelcome knowledge that Julia and Lucy might probe further into what was in the chest in the attic. He would have to do something about the contents which were not papers, as he'd told them, but small silver ornaments. As far as he could judge, they were worth very little and he had not the slightest intention of trying to sell them – an act which could very well lead to his connection to the old woman's death. Nevertheless, he thought, as Lucy went off to change, he would do well to get rid of the stuff. As long as they were in his possession, they could be a serious danger.

As he finished off his drink and poured himself another, Guy decided that on his next trip to Birmingham, he would throw the lot into the River Cherwell which ran from left to right beneath the M40. If necessary, he could come off at Exit 10 and find a bank of the river where he would not be seen. Meanwhile, he must think up some activity for the two girls which would keep them out of the flat tomorrow so he could go up to the attic. The less they knew of his activities, the better it would be if that detective inspector and his side-kick came asking questions . . . not that that seemed likely after all this time.

Feeling more relaxed about Julia's foray into the loft, Guy decided it might be to his advantage to be nice to the girl despite his dislike of her – or indeed, her dislike of him! He smiled, remembering suddenly his English master's obsession with Shakespearean quotations and one in particular he would repeat from *Julius Caesar* if he caught the boys fighting. '*I had rather have such men my friends than enemies.*' It was certainly not Guy's intention that the plump, fourteen-year-old Julia might bring about his downfall.

Thirteen

It was a gloriously hot June day when Tom drove up to The Willows and was welcomed with a big hug from Bridget.

'It's really lovely to see you – must be six months or more since you were last here. Julia will be thrilled to find you when she gets back from school. You are going to stay, aren't you, Tom dear?'

'I'd love to if you're sure I'm not imposing,' Tom said as she led him into the house.

Bridget gave a playful shove to his shoulder. She was smiling broadly as she said: 'Tom, you know perfectly well that we expect you to treat this as your second home. Jonnie has gone off to New Zealand backpacking with some university friends, so you can have his room. You're looking well!'

As he followed his hostess through the hall and out into the back garden, Tom's feelings were very mixed. There were so many memories which were bitter-sweet – days spent here in the holidays with the family – with Lucy. Being here in her home brought her closer but was nevertheless too nostalgic for comfort.

Bridget drew him down beside her on the old swing seat and patted his knee, looking genuinely pleased to see him. George would be, too. They had never grown really fond of Guy. Somehow, although he was always scrupulously polite and never failed to arrive without flowers and bottles of champagne and presents for the girls, the Godstows never felt at ease with him, even though Guy would be able to give Lucy a totally secure future and a life free of financial worries – something which was so difficult these days what with debts from their universities, soaring house prices and sometimes a lack of jobs even for those who had degrees.

She turned her attention back to Tom.

'Are you just on holiday?' she asked him. 'Or are you here for a purpose?'

Tom smiled.

'Well, both really. First of all, I think I have finally got a buyer for Aunt Joan's bungalow. It's taken a while to find someone who –' his voice faltered for a moment and then he continued – 'who wasn't put off by what happened there. Of course, as the estate agent advised, we kept the price down, and now a young couple have bought it. We're exchanging contracts next week. So I came a little sooner because there are still some of my aunt's possessions there which the couple don't want. I thought I'd give them to some charity or other.'

He turned to look directly into Bridget's face.

'How's Lucy?' he asked quietly. 'Julia e-mails me every now and again, but I've heard nothing for a few weeks. Is she OK?'

Bridget's face clouded.

'Didn't Julia write and tell you, Tom? She lost the baby!'

For a moment, Tom remained silent. His first reaction was one of sympathy for Lucy, but further thoughts quickly followed. Julia had written to tell him that Guy did not want a child – anyway, not as yet. Would the baby have been a bone of contention between them? His next thought, which he tried unsuccessfully to suppress because he knew it was an entirely selfish one, was that he had secretly hated the knowledge that Lucy – his Lucy – was carrying another man's child. Doing his best to curb his reactions, he asked Bridget if there might be a chance of Lucy coming down to visit the family.

'I don't think it's very likely, Tom,' she told him. 'When it happened – the miscarriage – Lucy did come down to recuperate here but only for a week. She was very depressed but the doctor said that was only to be expected. Then Guy came to fetch her as he had organized another wonderful holiday, so she could soak up the sunshine and rest. They came home a fortnight ago.'

'And is Lucy feeling better?' Tom asked, no longer trying to hide his personal concern.

Bridget sighed.

'It's hard to tell, Tom. I went up to London to see her and she was all bright smiles and insisting she was over the depression, but every once in a while I'd look at her when she wasn't aware of it, and she seemed . . . I don't know . . . sad, maybe. Anxious. Oh, really, I think I'm being just a silly old molly-coddling mother.' She drew a deep sigh and attempted a smile. 'It isn't always easy being a mother, you know, Tom!' she said. 'We can never really quite let go. I mean Lucy is now twenty-four years old and a married woman. It's not my prerogative to look after her. Besides, Guy spoils her terribly and my interference is the very last thing he would want.'

Tom longed at that moment to ask if Bridget was still as enthusiastic about her son-in-law as she had been when Lucy first announced she was going to marry him, but he bit back the words, aware that it really was none of his business. Bridget, of course, would have been far too polite to tell him her true feelings and he had no wish to embarrass her.

'Maybe I could pop up to town and take Lucy out for a meal!' he suggested.

Bridget's plump face was once more wreathed in smiles.

'Oh, yes, do! I know she'd love to see you. She still misses Vanessa terribly and you're the closest link to those happy days when you were all children together. I miss her, too, you know.'

Tom nodded.

'I still can't come to terms with the fact that she meant to end her life,' he said. 'I'm in no doubt whatever that she over-dosed by accident.'

'George and I think so, too. Tell me, Tom, has that nice inspector found out anything more about your poor dear aunt?'

'Not much, I'm afraid!' Tom replied. 'I saw him yesterday and he told me they had been able to get a DNA sample they think must be that of the murderer, but there's no match on their computer so they can't for the moment link it to anyone. No one has reported receiving any of Aunt Joan's silver.'

A smile briefly crossed his face.

'Inspector Govern said they had had a mine of information from Aunt Joan's help. Apparently she used to clean the missing silver once a month without fail. They weren't very valuable pieces, my aunt told her, but they had belonged to her grand-mother, my great-great-grandmother, and the only family possessions she had inherited. All the rest had gone to another branch of the family. Inspector Govern said that sooner or later, Aunt Joan's silver would turn up. Could be months, even years.'

'So the investigation is on the back burner?' Bridget remarked, sighing. 'You know, Tom, I have nightmares thinking about it. It seems odd that no one saw the burglar . . . the killer.'

'No one has come forward yet,' Tom said. 'Apparently a kid reported he'd seen a Volvo – a Turbo S80 – parked in a lay-by just before you get to Pepper Lane. But he was only ten years old so the police took the sighting with a pinch of salt.'

Remembering his long conversation with the inspector and afterwards with his detective sergeant, Tom managed a smile.

'I have to say, they are being pretty tenacious. They arranged for *Crimewatch* to feature the murder in the hope that someone, somewhere would have noticed the car and been able to place it geographically.' His face clouded as he added thoughtfully: 'Even if they catch the brute that killed my aunt, it won't bring her back, will it? I suppose if they do, it will be life with only half the time to be served. If I had my way, they'd put him in a mental home and lock him up for ever.'

'Well let's hope they do catch him,' Bridget said quietly. 'It's quite frightening knowing that someone like him is roaming the streets. I may be a silly old woman but knowing there are such people about – psychopaths, do you call them? – make me anxious every time any of the children are out of the house. Julia wanted to go off on a bike ride across the Downs to Lewes with some friends but if George hadn't said she could go, I wouldn't have allowed it. George said they were to be a party of eight – four boys and four girls and provided Julia never got left behind, she'd be perfectly safe. But I didn't stop worrying until she was safely home.'

She smiled ruefully and got to her feet.

'Tea time,' she announced. 'You're in luck, Tom, I made some scones yesterday and George refused to eat them – said he was putting on far too much weight and it was time I stopped baking!'

'I'm glad you haven't!' Tom chuckled. 'I'll never forget coming to stay with you one school holiday. It was my first visit after I'd gone to live with Uncle Charles. I'd come over on the ferry and I was absolutely ravenous, and when you opened the door as I arrived, this wonderful aroma of newly baked food enveloped me!'

Bridget sighed.

'Fancy you remembering that, Tom! Well, all I can say is that I always loved your visits – not least because you were so appreciative of my home cooking. Darling Jonnie was always such a fussy eater, whereas you . . .'

'Ate everything you put in front of me!' Tom laughed.

Sensitive to his feelings for her eldest daughter, as soon as they had finished tea, Bridget offered to telephone Lucy and then passed the phone over to Tom. Lucy sounded really pleased to hear his voice and when he suggested a meeting, she immediately agreed.

'Same place – La Lizza – in South Ken as before!' she said quickly. 'Tomorrow, Tom? I can't wait to see you! I'll meet you there. One o'clock.'

Tom had arranged to meet the prospective buyers at his aunt's house at midday, but without hesitation, he decided to telephone and postpone the appointment. With Lucy so anxious to see him, he didn't care even if the sale of the house fell through, albeit that was an unlikely event.

On the following day as the fast train took him from Ferrybridge to Victoria, he recalled the last time he and Lucy had had lunch. On that occasion, too, she had asked to meet him at the restaurant rather than meet at her flat.

Was Guy still jealous of him? he asked himself as he walked to the underground to take the tube to South Kensington. The pleasure the thought momentarily gave him quickly vanished as he sat at the restaurant table and watched Lucy come through the door. Just for a moment, he actually did not recognize her. Although she'd always been petite, her weight had been in keeping with her slender figure. Now, as stood up and pulled out a chair for her and she sat down beside him, he bent to kiss her cheek, wondering if the rosy colour was from her make-up box. It was almost too pink to be natural and in no way matched the hollows beneath her cheekbones or the dark shadows under her eyes. She was, nevertheless, looking exceedingly happy.

'Tom, darling Tom! I'm so pleased to see you!' she enthused. 'It seems absolute donkey's years since you were last here. How are you? How long will you be in England? Have you sold Aunt Joan's house yet? You're staying with Mum and Dad, aren't you?'

'Hey, steady on!' Tom said smiling. 'One question at a time. But let's order our meal and then we can get down to talk, shall we?'

Lucy seemed unable to make up her mind what she wanted to choose from the moderately extensive menu. All she would say was that she did not have a very big appetite. Unsurprised seeing that she had lost so much weight, Tom ordered for them both – an avocado salad followed by spaghetti with prawns and garlic and a side salad.

'A white wine to go with it?' he asked, but Lucy shook her head.

'I've not been drinking any alcohol since – ' her voice turned suddenly husky – 'since I lost the baby. I've been given pills, you see – sleeping pills.' She looked up at Tom as if for understanding, and then added as if making an apology: 'It was only seven weeks ago, you see, and I'd wake up in the night forgetting . . . and then remembering I didn't have a baby any more and . . . well, it was difficult to sleep and so Guy made me see a Harley Street doctor when we got back from holiday and he put me on sleeping pills. It's stupid to be so spineless, isn't it? I mean, hundreds of women lose their babies and don't behave like me.'

Tom tried to keep his face expressionless as he took her hand in his and held it tightly.

'I don't think it's in the least "spineless". I read something in the Sunday supplement the other day about depression – it isn't something you can see like a measles rash but it can be just as serious – and debilitating, and that it's quite pointless for people to say, "Pull yourself together" because they can't.'

'But that's what Guy keeps telling me – that it's time I got over it and there's absolutely no reason why I can't have another baby. Not now – he doesn't want me to get pregnant again so soon, but perhaps in a year or two.'

Her eyes suddenly filled with tears and she grabbed her handbag and drew out a handkerchief. Blowing her nose, she looked up, her eyes still full of tears, and attempted a smile.

'See what I'm like?' she said. 'Cry at the drop of a pin – and this is so, so silly when I'm the happiest I've been for absolute ages – seeing you, I mean. Let's talk about you, Tom.'

They were interrupted by the arrival of their food. At least Lucy ate her avocado salad, Tom reassured himself, but she only managed half the prawn dish which was delicious; and tipped half of her own on to his plate.

She made a joke of it, saying: 'Growing lad needs nourishment. How tall are you, Tom – six three? I do believe you've grown some more since I last saw you.'

He realized that Lucy was attempting to divert the conversation from herself and because he could not bear to see her in tears again, he talked about his Uncle Charles and his work in the bank in Geneva. After Vanessa died and with Lucy married, he had asked his guardian if he could remain at the Geneva bank instead of going to England, there being little reason now for wanting to live nearer to the Godstows. This was, thankfully, a topic to interest Lucy because an investigator had managed to unearth a forgotten secret account at his uncle's bank, which was without any doubt, the property of a former Nazi. Hitler's thugs were known to rob the Jews whenever they ousted them from their homes and when possible, get the money or jewellery out of the country to a safe hiding place. To have kept it in Germany would have meant, most probably, being forced to hand it over to the Nazi party.

'Chap must have died because he's never been back for his ill-gotten gains. Records show that the account was opened nearly seventy years ago. No one at the bank had any idea who he was or what he looked like as none of them were alive at the time, and undoubtedly the man had given a false name.'

'So what happened to the contents?' Lucy asked, successfully diverted from thoughts of her lost baby.

'It was worth an enormous sum of money,' Tom told her. 'So the bank felt honour-bound to try and find if there were any relatives, or indeed, anyone who had known the man, but there wasn't a single trace of anyone; and that despite the fact that the Germans are well known to have kept their records so methodically.'

'So what happens to the ill-gotten wealth?' Lucy asked. 'Will your uncle's bank keep it?'

Tom shook his head.

'There was a board meeting with all the directors and Uncle

Charles said he really didn't want to keep money belonging to some unfortunate Jew who'd ended his life in a gas chamber. So it's to go to a Jewish charity. He hasn't decided which one yet. We're all supposed to be putting our suggestions in a box for him to consider.'

Lucy looked really happy.

'I think that's a lovely idea!' she exclaimed. 'And just like your Uncle Charles.' She gave a sudden chuckle. 'Do you know, I had a crush on him when I was in my teens – that very first time Vanessa and I were invited out to stay with you, remember? I still think he's a very attractive man.'

Tom laughed.

'So does half the female population of Geneva,' he said. 'My uncle never goes short of female company.'

Lucy looked up from the lemon sorbet Tom had ordered for her.

'And what about you, Tom?' she asked in a deliberately light tone of voice. 'Haven't you got yourself a steady girl-friend chasing you? Or are you going to fulfil Julia's dreams and wait for her to grow up so she can marry you?'

Tom laughed.

'You know how fond of her I am, Lucy. But . . . yes, I do have several girlfriends who I go skiing, dancing, ice-skating with. There's one – an Italian girl who proposes to me at least once a month! But they all know I'm not in love with any of them or ever likely to be.'

He looked down into Lucy's face, his own taut with suppressed emotion. Managing to keep his tone very casual, he said: 'I'll never be in love with anyone but you, Lucy. I think you know that and I have always known it. And don't look so . . . so anxious. I don't mind you marrying Guy just so long as you are happy. You are happy, aren't you, Lucy? Tell me honestly.'

'Of course I am!' Lucy said quickly – too quickly. She bit her lip, aware that she had sounded too emphatic. She quickly qualified her statement. 'Of course, I haven't exactly been happy lately – since the miscarriage; and I've simply got to pull myself together. Guy gets so upset when . . . when he knows I'm thinking about it.' She was silent for a few seconds and then, as if compelled to bare her soul, she said in a rush: 'He didn't want it, you see. He swears he did, but I know he was glad when . . . when I lost it. So it's all a bit . . . well, difficult at the moment.' Regretting that she had revealed so much, to Tom, of all people, she added quickly: 'Everything will be fine again once I get over this stupid depression. I don't wonder poor darling Guy gets fed up coming back every evening to a red-eyed, blotchy-faced weepy wife!'

His heart aching for her, Tom wanted nothing more than to take her in his arms and hold her. Instead, he reached for her hand and held it tightly in his own.

'Lucy, do you think Guy would consider letting you come out to Geneva for a week or two? Uncle Charles would welcome you and a complete change of scene, a different environment, might be just what you need. We could go hill walking if you felt physically up to it. If not, there are some wonderful concerts, theatres we could go to. If you wanted, Julia could come, too – a sort of chaperone!'

For one brief moment, he saw a flash of excitement in Lucy's brown eyes. It lasted no longer than a few seconds before her lashes dipped to conceal her expression.

'It's a great idea, Tom, and I'd love to come and visit you but some other time. You see, we've only just got back from Barbados and now Guy is planning for us both to go out to Spain to stay with his father as soon as he has concluded a property sale he's currently involved with. Could be in a week or two, three at most. To tell you the truth, I wasn't too keen on the idea at first – being so far from the family and having to pack and close up the flat. Then I realized I was just being negative and once we are on the way, it could be fun.'

She smiled up at Tom, her expression happier.

'Guy says we will drive out in the TVR, spend two or three days stopping at different places overnight. He says it will give me a chance to see the real Spain which I won't when we get to the south.'

She made no mention of the fact that Guy had added they would make the trip a mini-honeymoon – just the two of them discovering the countryside and exciting new places together. Instead she told Tom that Guy had said they would stay with his father who owned a large villa up in the hills.

'Guy wants to teach me to play golf,' she added. 'Did you know he is a five handicap? I'm not quite sure what that means but I do know its something special. He says the exercise will help me get really fit again.'

'Golf!' Tom heard himself repeating. 'But when your father wanted to teach you, you always said it wasn't your 'thing' and you had tennis coaching instead – you and Van. You won he junior under-fifteen tennis tournament one year, remember?'

Lucy laughed.

'Fancy you remembering that, Tom!' she said. 'And we won it the next year, too.'

I remember every little thing about you, Tom thought. Most of all I remember what a bright, carefree, happy person you were. Vanessa was the serious one – you were like a bright shaft of sunlight, lighting up everywhere you smiled and your voice touched. Now . . .

He tried to quell the deep feeling of unease inside him. Somehow, he was certain Lucy was not happy – and not just because of the lost baby. But there was nothing he could do, and that was a very difficult concept when he loved her so very much.

'What about a walk in Kensington Gardens?' he suggested. 'Nothing too strenuous. We could go and have a peek at the Peter Pan statue. Remember how Aunt Bridget took us there the day after she'd taken us to see the pantomime? She gave us all pads and pencils and we had a competition to see who could draw the statue the best.'

Lucy's face was now bright with smiles.

'Yes, and Jemma won it. She's so clever with her hands. She wants to be an illustrator when she leaves art school.'

By the time the taxi dropped Lucy off at her flat two hours later, her cheeks were glowing and the laughter hovered around her mouth as Tom did an imitation of the driver's Irish accent.

'Darling Tom, it's been such fun!' she enthused as she reached up to kiss him goodbye. 'You'll come and see me again soon, promise?'

As Tom promised and stood watching as she searched for her keys and unlocked the door to her home, he was painfully aware that she had not invited him in for tea despite her genuine pleasure in his company. It had to be that Guy was still jealous, he told himself, and Lucy had not the will to stand up to him.

Despite his pleasure in the past few hours, Tom's heart was heavy as he took the underground back to Victoria and caught his train back to Ferrybridge, where he would be staying the night at The Willows – which could never be the same happy place without her.

He was, however, a little cheered by the arrival home of Julia from school that evening. She was over the moon with pleasure at his unexpected visit. Surprisingly, in the months since Tom had last seen her, she had all but made the transition from girl to young woman. Her pale gold hair had been straightened and hung in a smooth curtain down her back, and her large brown eyes were touched with eye shadow and mascara. How old was she now? he wondered as she flung herself into his arms and he realized she had lost a great deal of her former puppy fat. Surprising him, he saw she now bore quite a likeness to Lucy.

Her bubbly manner, however, remained the same and sitting beside him on the old chintz-covered sofa in the living room, she told him proudly that she had been elected deputy head girl by her peers for the next school year; and that she had been given the lead part in the school play next term as well as being nominated captain of the school hockey team. What pleased him almost as much as her prowess was her cheerful announcement that she was madly in love with a boy at Ferrybridge Grammar School.

'He's really, really cool,' she said breathlessly, 'and guess what, Tom, he's called Tom, too!' She tucked her arm through his and hugged it. 'Of course, I'll always love *you*,' she added. matter-of-factly, 'but now I'm getting older, I can see how silly I was ever to dream you might one day stop loving Lucy and fall in love with me. I mean, there'll always be that huge age gap between us, won't there? And as Tom – my Tom – said, it was a typical schoolgirl crush, not the real thing!'

Hiding both his smile and his relief that he no longer had to worry about her adolescent feelings for him, Tom changed the subject, asking her if by any chance she could make use of a spare laptop.

'It belonged to Vanessa,' he told her. 'I had her belongings shipped out to me in a crate, I didn't realize it was among them. Maybe you have one already?'

Julia beamed.

'No, I don't and I really, really, really want one. But Pa says they cost too much and he's not buying one even for combined birthday and Christmas as he thinks it's not necessary and I only want one because Jemma has got one now she's going to art school. Lots of girls at school have got them and I'll be needing one even more next term when I'm starting A levels.'

Tom laughed, his anxiety about Lucy momentarily forgotten. 'I'll almost certainly be coming back again before the end of the summer, so I'll bring it with me then.'

Julia turned and kissed him on the cheek, her eyes sparkling with pleasure.

'I told Tom – my Tom – you were ace and I love you to bits. I just wish you and . . .'

'No, don't say it, Julia,' Tom broke in. He tried to lighten the sudden change of mood. 'I think there's a Latin quotation. About never seeking to undo that which is already done – something like that. Lucy is Guy's wife now and whatever our private feelings, we have to accept it.'

Seeing the acute look of sadness in Tom's eyes, for once Julia did not put forward an argument. Instead, she nodded, put a cheerful expression on her own face, and suggested they took the dogs for a walk in the woods before supper as it was a warm evening. She knew it was something Tom really loved to do, and that it would make him happy even if Lucy was not with them and was stuck in London with that horrible Guy.

Fourteen

Detective Sergeant David Beck looked across the desk to where his boss was sitting, one hand propping up his chin. He was obviously deep in thought. Beck knew better than to interrupt him.

After a minute or two, Govern handed some sheets of paper over to the younger man saying: 'Look at report number twenty-three, David. Green Volvo S80. Remember?'

Beck grinned. It was not easy to forget the hugely fat woman who came storming into the police station with her son after a request on the local radio for anyone to come forward who had seen a vehicle in the neighbourhood of Miss Lyford's bungalow on the day after the murder. It seemed the desk sergeant had refused to take a statement from the ten-year-old who was insisting he'd seen a green Volvo S80 in Seaford, saying that even if the boy knew the make of car, he was much too young to know one model from another. By sheer relentless persistence, the parent had finally forced her way into Inspector Govern's office and Beck had had to take down the child's statement.

The mother had not left until Beck had formally witnessed the lad's signature on an official statement which also included the number eleven as being on the car's number plate! They had laughed at the time but now Govern was pointing his finger at a report which had come in of a green Volvo S80 observed in Oxfordshire on the date of the homicide. Lacking any clues to Miss Lyford's murder after eight months of enquiries, he had decided to follow up the kid's statement, and police covering the entire south of England, including the Home Counties, had been instructed to make enquiries at garages and car dealers as to who had records of Volvo S80 owners.

Several weeks had gone by before a comprehensive list of reports from the various garages arrived on Govern's desk.

'A long shot, I know,' he said as Beck stared at the twenty-third report. It came from a police station covering one of the service stations on the M40. One of the employees at the pay counter had recalled an incident which had taken place during the last week of October. She couldn't remember which day of the week it had been, but the incident was quite clear in her mind because it had been so bizarre. The driver of a green Volvo four-door saloon had drawn up behind an old Ford estate and was waiting for it to move forward so he could get to the unleaded petrol pump. Before he could do so, the back door of the Ford opened; a child had been dragged out quickly by his father and promptly been sick over the bonnet of the Volvo.

'Must have been a bit upsetting for the owner,' Beck said grinning as he continued to read. It seemed the man had gone ballistic; stormed into the garage shop, pushed past the queue waiting to pay for their petrol and demanded that the assistant provide him with tokens for the car wash. The attendant was unable to do this, as she had no way of accounting for the equivalent money. However, the father of the unfortunate child had come in and offered to pay for the tokens so eventually, calm was restored. The employee had been quite shaken up because, she said, the Volvo owner had been so angry she'd feared he might trash the place or even hit the child's father if he didn't provide compensation. He had kept on about keeping his car immaculate and that the kid should have thrown up over his own car!'

'I suppose there's something to be said for that,' Govern said wryly. He paused briefly before adding: 'Look at this, David.' He pointed to the second paragraph of the report.

The man was tall, over six feet, aged between thirty and forty with just a hint of grey in his hair. He was possibly a businessman because he was wearing a suit and tie. When he did finally pay for his petrol, it was with an American Express card.

Beck looked nonplussed

'I know those service stations on the M40,' he said. 'That Warwick Service Area is only about thirty miles from Birmingham, in other words, a hell of a long way from the murder scene and . . .'

'But,' Govern interrupted him, 'doesn't the description of the angry man ring any bells in that thick head of yours? It does mine – that Weaver chap. What's more, he did know the old lady, however tenuous the connection might be.'

It was a minute or two before Beck replied.

'If my memory is not adrift, Guy Weaver was in Birmingham the day of the murder – his client confirmed it. Besides, he drives a TVR Sagaris, not a Volvo. Don't you remember – he drove off in it the day of Miss Lyford's funeral?'

Govern sighed.

'I hadn't forgotten that. All the same . . .'

His voice trailed away but Beck knew better than to suppose his boss rejected his sudden suspicions. He'd worked with Govern now for over five years and knew him to have an uncanny intuition. Whether it came from years of successful detective work or from a particular part of his brain, Beck had no idea; but he never ignored Govern's suspicions.

'I'll put out a general enquiry then, shall I – see if we can find the Volvo? The dealers should be able to give us a pretty good idea who they've sold that model too. There must be quite a few about but it can't be that old or the owner wouldn't have been that fussy about it!'

Govern nodded agreement, but he was frowning, his expression uneasy.

'You're right about one thing, my boy. Weaver, if he were the murderer, wouldn't have driven a car like his Sagaris to the scene of his crime. People notice new models and it would have been far too distinctive. Why do I have the feeling that the M40 fellow sounds just like him? Doesn't make sense!'

Beck knew better than to agree although it crossed his mind that there must be hundreds of men answering the description of the irate Volvo owner travelling to Birmingham or the environs that day.

'We'll see what comes up,' Govern added. 'D'you know, David, I have a feeling this could be the breakthrough we needed.'

Less than twenty-four hours later, the hoped-for break came. A regular customer at the M40 Service station, on hearing from the pay attendant that the police had been making enquiries about the Volvo S80, proudly produced the letters on the number plate. He'd been on the forecourt that day and noticed the personalized letters – V111A.

Seeing the bewildered look on the Inspector's face, Beck grinned.

'Aston Villa, sir – football club. The customer is a fan so it caught his eye. I've e-mailed Swansea and they've come through with a Jeremy Hart-Pennant, prestigious address in Chelsea, London.'

For a moment, Govern did not speak. Then he said: 'Not that far from Fulham where Weaver lives. Wonder if they know each other? On your phone, David, and see if you can get hold of the fellow. When you do, first thing I want to know is what reason he had for being on the M40 that day. Second – perhaps even more important, what does he look like? Tall? Going grey? Businessman?'

His sergeant was frowning.

'I don't see the relevance, sir. I mean this all happened on the M40 in Warwickshire. The murder was on the south coast and . . .'

'And you haven't yet worked it out, have you, my boy?' Govern interrupted. 'Remember the Seaford kid's statement? Number eleven on the number plate? The two l's in Villa? Think about it – M40 service station approximate timing, eleven thirty. Distance from Seaford about one hundred and fifty miles. A Volvo S80 in good nick averaging seventy mph – breaking some speed limits admittedly – could easily have done both journeys.' Suddenly, he smiled. 'OK, so it may sound a bit far-fetched but it would have been possible. Now see if you can locate our Mr Hart-Pennant, will you? I'm anxious to meet the chap.'

Their run of good luck came to an abrupt stop. Mr Jeremy Hart- Pennant was in Kenya on an eight-week safari. According to the porter at his block of flats, he had taken his mobile phone with him in case the porter needed to get in touch for any reason, but the fellow had tried to do so the previous week when the tenants in the basement flat had reported a damp patch on their kitchen ceiling and suspected a leak from upstairs; but there had been no signal on Hart-Pennant's phone so the porter had rung the man's office and handed the problem over to his secretary.

Inspector Govern looked far from happy.

'Eight weeks! I don't think I can wait that long. Get some more enquiries going at those Volvo dealers. It's just possible the man might have had his precious car serviced whilst he was abroad and not needing it.'

Beck looked puzzled.

'I can't see how that would help to progress the situation!' he said with a look of enquiry on his face.

Govern sighed.

'Because you don't think progressively,' he said enigmatically. Then he added: 'A dealer who services that particular Volvo would have note of the mileage between that service and the one before. It's a long shot, I know, but a businessman of Hart-Pennant's calibre almost certainly has a diary and that diary should state where he had been each day. When the Esso station finally find that till receipt, we can establish the name of the troublemaker. If it wasn't our friend, Mr Weaver, I shall be obliged to eliminate him from my suspicious mind.'

'I get the point!' Beck said. 'But do we have to bother with the dealer? I mean, why don't we just take along a photo of Mr Hart-Whatever?'

'Because, dear boy, we don't have one.' Unexpectedly, Govern smiled. 'Maybe you aren't quite as ignorant as I was beginning to suspect!' he said. 'We – that is to say you – can go back and bribe the porter. Show him your warrant card so he's not afraid he'll get the sack if he lets you into the flat. There's just a chance you can find a photo of our possible M40 driver. Give the porter a receipt for it if you do get hold of one and tell him you'll return it within forty-eight hours so Hart-Pennant isn't going to know anything about it.'

Although in the subsequent week Beck was able successfully to acquire a photo of Hart-Pennant, picturing him as best man at a society wedding, the girl at the pay desk in the M40 service station was adamant Hart-Pennant was not the same man as the one who had caused such a rumpus. The only resemblance, she said, was that they both looked about the same height and were obviously 'toffs' not 'yobbos'.

'So that's it until Hart-Pennant gets back from Africa!' Govern said frowning.

Once again, his sergeant looked nonplussed.

'I don't see how he can help with the murder when you do get to question him, sir!' he said.

'Probably not,' was Govern's reply. 'But just suppose he lent the car to a friend . . . ?'

Beck's eyebrows shot up. He looked suitably shocked as he exclaimed: 'Lent a nearly new car to another driver? It's the last thing I'd do, I can assure you. Those things cost a great deal of money, especially with all the extras that are available – direction finders, TVs – that sort of thing. Doubt there'd be much change from fifty thousand. I'd think twice about letting anyone else loose with it – unless, of course, I was so bloody rich I could simply buy another if my friend pranged it. Even then, it could take ages to get a replacement.'

Govern sighed.

'I expect you're right. You're the car buff, not me. Enough of Hart-Pennant. Let's go and have a chat with Weaver – see what he's been up to lately.'

Beck looked doubtful.

'Have we got a reason for wanting to talk to him?'

Govern grinned as he stood up and unrolling his shirtsleeves, reached for the jacket of his suit.

'Well, for one thing, we can find out if he happens to know Mr Jeremy Hart-Pennant.' Seeing the look on his sergeant's face, his smile widened. 'I'm well aware what you are thinking, David. And I'll admit that as far as we know at this moment, I don't have one single justifiable reason to suspect Weaver of stealing a lollipop, let alone committing one of the most gory murders we've had to deal with in a long time. But there is one link – however tenuous. He was one of relatively few people who knew the victim. The solicitor, George Godstow, drew up a list for me of Miss Lyford's friends, relations and acquaintances. There are a mere thirty-one – Tom Lyford, her great-nephew; the six Godstow family members, eight bridge friends, her doctor, her lawyer, her cleaner; the window cleaner, postman, the odd neighbour and so on who we can discount – all worthy, respectable citizens not given to attacking old ladies with a knife!'

Picking up his briefcase, he turned once more to look at the younger man's expectant face.

'Start eliminating, David. The nephew? No – nice, honest, decent chap.'

'But he was the old girl's beneficiary!' Beck said. 'I mean, he was the only one to benefit by her death.'

'Yes, but it wasn't a fortune and from what George Godstow told me, young Tom is an extremely wealthy godfather's proxy son and quite definitely his heir. So our Tom had no need to bump off his great-aunt. Wipe out Godstow – a magistrate, solicitor, pillar of local parish affairs; Mrs Godstow – no, I wouldn't believe it even if I caught her in the act! The girls? No way! The vicar? The doctor? The helper? And so on until we are right down to one person. Unless, of course, it really was a burglar. And that I seriously doubt.'

As Beck now followed his superior downstairs to the car, he asked Govern why he was so doubtful that the murder had been committed by a thief. He waited until Beck had started up the engine and set the car in motion before he replied.

'Even these days, David, as you know, burglars very rarely kill. If they go out on a job with a gun, then a lethal shot might be fired, but not a stabbing. Besides, the value of the stolen property was a pittance if we are to believe her helper. No! And lastly, my boy, a burglar, if such it was, would steal things he can sell. Why, then, did he ransack the old woman's writing desk? What was he looking for? It wasn't likely she'd keep cash there even if she was unwise enough to have cash lying about the house. Finally, if by some miracle it *was* a burglar, why haven't we yet had notification from any of the fences?'

Beck remained silent whilst he waited for an opportunity to pass a car carrier, which was taking up more than its fair share of the A23.

'Because the burglar realized the silver wasn't worth much after all and decided to melt it down!'

Inspector Govern sighed.

'I'll give you good marks for trying, Beck, but try and come up with something better than that. Do you honestly think most burglars have those sort of facilities?' The half smile left his face as he added in a serious tone: 'No, this was no burglar, David. He has to be a psychopath – and a very dangerous one, too. Doc Barley agrees with me – and he's seen enough stabbings in his day.'

They stopped briefly to pay a courtesy call on the Godstows. Bridget Godstow, with her usual hospitality, invited them to stay for lunch; but they explained they were on their way up to London.

'We thought we would drop in on your daughter and her husband – just to update them as well as your good self,'

Govern said casually. 'I seem to recall your daughter – Lucy, is it not? – tell us she probably knew Miss Lyford better than anyone else in the family because she used to visit her on occasion with her flatmate, Vanessa Lyford.'

'Yes, that's quite right, Inspector,' Bridget said, bending to stop Widger from biting Beck's shoelace. 'But it's no good you going all the way to London to see Lucy. She and Guy are in Spain. They went two weeks ago.'

'Ah well, we were only going to drop in on them to update them,' Govern said casually. 'In point of fact, we don't have any real progress to report. How long will your daughter and her husband be away, Mrs Godstow?'

'We don't know exactly,' Bridget said, looking uneasy. 'Guy's father lives out there, you know, and they are in business together. Mr Weaver sees to the Spanish side of the business and Guy sees to things here in England, but they do overlap, I believe.' She drew a long sigh. 'I just hope they won't stay too long this visit. It's Lucy, you see – she hasn't been too well and – ' she gave a self-deprecating smile – 'we mothers are all the same, aren't we? Never stop worrying about our babies even when they're grown up and married! George says I'll still be fussing when they get their old-age pensions – if I'm still in the land of the living myself, that is!'

'My mum's just the same, Mrs Godstow,' Beck said comfortingly. 'When I went skiing this Christmas, I had daily telephone calls from her the week before I went – had I got warm socks? Had I plenty of dry clothes to change into if I fell over and got wet? Had I got a whistle in case I was buried in an avalanche?'

They both laughed but Beck noticed that the inspector seemed to be on a different wavelength.

'I hope your daughter isn't seriously ill?' he enquired in a casual tone which did not deceive his sergeant.

Bridget hesitated.

'Between you and me, Inspector, I don't think she has fully recovered – emotionally, I mean – from losing the baby she was expecting. The doctor said it was not unusual for patients to get very depressed after a miscarriage and, of course, everyone knows these days about the baby blues, but it seems to have gone on so long. Lucy's on anti-depressants which, being as old-fashioned as I am, I really wish she didn't need. I'm against all drugs. George, my husband, says you can't put them all under the same blanket – things like drugs for painful afflictions such as arthritis, for example, are really beneficial. But I'm into alternative medicines . . . like Prince Charles!' she added with a smile.

To Beck's surprise, Govern seemed genuinely interested in Bridget Godstow's prattle.

'Tell me,' he said encouragingly, 'haven't any of your children adopted your views rather than your husband's? What about Lucy, for example? My old mother – she's dead now, God rest her – used to swear by that herb, balm, I think it was! I think it was Culpepper who recommended it in the seventeenth century for melancholia! Balm! That was the herb she insisted made even the gloomiest person merry. As a child, I used to associate that word with *God Rest Ye Merry Gentlemen* and assumed them all to be drunk as lords!'

They all laughed and, as she showed them to the door, Bridget looked a lot more cheerful.

'I know George is quite right and I worry far too much. So shall I let you know, Inspector, when Lucy and Guy are coming back? We do talk on the phone several times a week and Lucy will give me lots of warning. I like to send flowers, you see – to welcome them home. I always think it's so depressing to get back to an empty flat or house with no one there to open the door and give you a hug!'

'One really nice lady!' Beck said as they drove back to Brighton. 'Ah, well, I suppose your visit to our friend, Mr Weaver, will have to wait for a week or two. Not that there was anything much to go on, was there?'

For a moment or two, Govern did not reply. Then he said enigmatically: 'That depends what the inner man is saying to you, David.'

Familiar with this remark, Beck knew his boss was referring yet again to his uncanny instincts which had in the past so often proved well-founded.

'Oh, well, sir!' he said as they approached the narrow winding main street of the village of Ditchling. 'I can tell you what my inner man is saying – in other words, isn't it about time for some lunch?'

Govern grimaced.

'I sometimes wonder why I enjoy your company, David. Food and drink seem to take priority in your life. There's a pub on the left. Pull in there. It says home cooking!'

Beck turned into the car park and as he got out of the car and went round the passenger door to open it for the inspector, he was still smiling.

'Not just food and drink, sir!' He nodded towards a slim, leggy blonde who was unwinding her limbs out of a smart little red MG. Catching Beck's glance, she gave him a wicked come-on smile and then walked into the restaurant. As Beck turned to lock the car door and started towards the pub, Govern put a restraining hand on Beck's arm.

'No need to hurry, David. She'll still be in there even if we take our time. I'm not as young as I was, you know. Now, you can consider yourself officially off-duty for the next hour. Understand? We can always eat at separate tables if you manage to make any headway. Off you go!'

His sergeant needed no second bidding as, with a heart-felt 'thank you, sir!', he hurried into the pub in search of the pretty blonde girl.

Fifteen

Despite the blazing afternoon Spanish sunshine, it was relatively cool under the shade of the trees in the orange grove. Lucy's book lay unopened on her lap and her eyes were closed although she was not asleep. In one hand, she held a folded cloth steeped in witch hazel and crushed ice against her cheek. The bruise was causing her quite a lot of pain, but she was hardly aware of it, the bruising to her heart being so much more painful than the physical injury. In fact, her distress and anxiety had gone so deep she had been unable to cry.

How could Guy have hit her? The question tormented her mind like an angry wasp struggling against a windowpane. How could he? And so hard? It was true he had shown violence once before when they'd been invited for drinks with a neighbour soon after their arrival in Spain. She had been talking in fluent French to another of their guests, a visitor from Paris who was buying a large Andalucian property from Guy. Delighted to be able to converse in his own language, the middle-aged man had monopolized her. Later, when Guy heard she had accepted an invitation to go to his host's villa to play tennis the following day, he had unreasonably told her he suspected that they were planning an assignation. He had grabbed her by the wrist and pulled her roughly upstairs to their bedroom where he'd accused her of flirting with his client.

Lucy's assurances that in absolute truth she had not found the visitor in the least physically attractive but had merely enjoyed the opportunity to make use of her French and would love to make use of their tennis court, were finally accepted by Guy. He had then done his utmost to make amends for treating her so discourteously, as he described his behaviour. Unwilling to reignite his anger, she had bitten back her rejoinder that the word 'discourteous' did not reflect the bruises on her arms where he had held her in a vice-like grip.

When he had struck her last night, she had staggered backwards and almost fallen, so vicious had been the blow to her face. Vicious! The word itself frightened her. She could not get out of her mind the cold, white fury in Guy's eyes as he raised his arm and spat the words at her.

'Don't you ever dare speak to Carlos again. Don't think I didn't see you – smiling, flirting with him – an ignorant peasant – encouraging him to think you fancy him.' Guy's voice had been full of disgust. 'I can tell you this much, if I see him even so much as looking at you he'll get the sack, whatever my father says about him being the best gardener he has ever had.'

Whilst Lucy was still trying to recall when she had last spoken to Carlos, Guy had struck her across face. Without waiting to hear what she might have to say in her defence, he had turned and left the room and a few minutes later, she'd heard him start up the car and, sending up a shower of gravel, speed away down the drive in the direction of Marbella. He did not return until dawn when she had feigned sleep.

As Lucy lay back in the garden chair still holding the cool pack to her cheek, she attempted to make sense of what had happened. It was true she had been talking to Carlos. She had wanted him to cut some flowers for the house. La Finca de Azahar, Guy's father's house, was a lovely Andalucian villa tucked into the side of the lower slopes of the mountains overlooking the tourist town of Marbella. Although the rooms were large and attractively furnished, the house was obviously very much a bachelor establishment and lacked the softness and colour of a feminine touch. When Guy had first brought Lucy here and she had remarked upon the impression of starkness the house emanated, he had told her she could do whatever she liked to change it as she thought fit; that his father had no interest in interior décor and would not care what she did provided she did not encroach on his study. Flowers everywhere were the one small change Lucy had so far made.

So she had, as was her custom every morning after breakfast, gone down to the vegetable garden where Carlos would be watering the asparagus, tomatoes, courgettes and melons to ask him for an armful of freshly cut blooms. He was not

an old man and because he worked on the land, he was fit
and strong with, Lucy had remarked, astonishingly white teeth
in his tanned face. He always gave her a wide-smiling
welcome, pleased that she admired the things he grew with
such loving care. His manner towards her was impeccable and
in the past few weeks since she and Guy had come out to
stay with his father, Lucy liked to think they had almost become
friends. That Guy could possibly, by any stretch of the imagination, think there was anything untoward in the relationship
was beyond her understanding. How could he be so unreasonably jealous that he thought she might flirt with the
gardener, not only an employee but also a man certainly old
enough to be her father? And be so certain of her guilt that
he had actually struck her?

Tears now stung Lucy's eyes as the full impact of what
Guy had done to her now overwhelmed her. It was not so
much the physical pain, although her bruised cheek was
extremely painful. It was that her husband of only eleven
months could suspect her of finding other men attractive
enough to flirt with; that he never gave her one single moment
to defend herself against such accusations; and not least, that
he could become incensed enough to strike her.

Miserably, Lucy was forced to realize that her husband's
jealousy was getting worse. When she had first arrived at
the villa, she had reminded Guy that he had promised to
arrange some golf lessons for her at his club. Knowing they
were going to be in Spain for some time, she was anxious
to make friends whose company she could enjoy whilst Guy
was in his father's Marbella office for most of the day. She
had brought up the subject one evening at dinner when her
father-in-law mentioned a forthcoming golf tournament to
Guy.

Herbert Weaver had turned to smile at Lucy, of whom he
was becoming quite fond, saying: 'Good idea! Lots of quite
good lady golfers at our club. Got a new pro there – Angel
he's called.' He gave a loud laugh. 'Not much of an angel if
you ask me. All the women rave about him and I'm told they
are queuing up for lessons!'

'And Lucy will not be joining the queue,' Guy said sharply.
'I fully intend to teach her myself.'

But nothing had come of it and when she had asked a

second time, he'd made some excuse about the weather being too hot and that he was too busy.

Wishing she had not conjured up such worrying and depressing thoughts, Lucy tried to concentrate on the quiet, peaceful beauty of her surroundings. She watched a large purple-and-white butterfly settle on the glass tabletop beside her chair. There was a ring of water there where her glass of *limonada* had been standing and she could see the beautiful insect drinking before flying back up into the leafy shadow of the overhanging tree.

She felt a sudden overwhelming longing to be home; to feel her mother's comforting arms round her; to hear her father's voice telling her what she should do with a husband who used physical force on his wife. Was she being paranoid? she asked herself. It had only happened twice. Although, now she thought about the last few months, Guy's behaviour had been . . . Lucy hesitated, searching for a word to adequately describe Guy's moods; overbearing, she decided; dictatorial; possessive. Before leaving London, he had twice cancelled parties to which they had been invited – on the grounds that she was not yet well enough for long nights out. He had found ways, too, to keep her with him on some pretence or other every time she had arranged to go home for the day. If she did go out to lunch with a friend, or to do some shopping, when she returned home he would question her so indeterminably she finally accused him of carrying out an interrogation.

It was only when he had made passionate love to her which he now chose to do night after night despite Lucy pleading exhaustion, that she saw a different side to Guy. He was like a small boy as he clung to her swearing he loved her, needed her, that she must never, ever leave him; that barely a day – an hour – went by that he did not live in fear that she would do so. He even had nightmares during which he would think he was waking up in the middle of the night and she was not in bed beside him.

If only Van was here! Lucy thought. *I could talk to her; ask her what I should do.* Vanessa, so much more level-headed than she was herself, would probably tell her Guy was still paying the price for his mother's sudden abandonment of him when he was only twelve years old. Guy himself never spoke of those days but one evening, when he was in Marbella, Herbert Weaver had had a little too much Spanish brandy and became unusually voluble. He had then proceeded to tell Lucy how devastated his young son had been when he came home from school one day and found his mother had gone – not just for a holiday but for good. Guy, it seemed, worshipped her, and although she had never been particularly maternal, it had amused her to have her good-looking little boy running round doing everything he could to please her, particularly when her female friends commented on the child's slavish devotion.

'Thoroughly self-centred, selfish woman, my ex,' Herbert had told her, pouring himself yet another large brandy. 'Tried to take me to the cleaners but the fellow she ran away with had a bloody sight more money than I did, so when we divorced, she only got the absolute minimum from me.'

More than a little embarrassed by this description of the woman he had once, presumably, loved enough to marry, Lucy had made her excuses and had gone up to bed. Lying back in her chair, the ice pack now on the grass beside her, she recalled the conversation and tried to make sense of it. Was it possible Guy's unreasonable jealousy was connected in some way to his mother's desertion? Perhaps it was not so much that he imagined she, Lucy, might be unfaithful to him, as that she might run off and leave him. The thought was small comfort to her. A man did not have the right to strike his wife across the face no matter what the provocation. Her parents would be deeply shocked if they knew.

Once again, tears stung Lucy's eyes as another wave of homesickness engulfed her. Guy wanted to stay in Spain until the end of October, telling her the sunshine and change of scene would help her recover from her depression, but now, only three weeks into their visit, she longed to go home. Tonight, she would tell him she had decided to go back to England, if only for a week or two. Julia would be home for the summer holidays and Jonnie would be back from his travels. Hopefully Jemma, too, would be home and they could all be together.

Lucy did not see the maid, Conchita, coming across the terrace to talk to her. Herbert Weaver had thoughtfully engaged a local girl from the nearby village as an addition to his usual staff, to attend to Lucy's needs. She was a happy, dark-eyed, dark-haired pretty young woman, always smiling, and Lucy had grown quite fond of her. She spoke reasonable English having worked very briefly as a nursemaid to an English family before taking on her present job.

'Señora, the señor telephone – very busy. Not coming for *merienda*. He say tell you he coming in five hours.' She glanced momentarily at the blackening bruise on Lucy's cheek, and reached down to pick up the melting ice pack. Lucy had told her at breakfast that she had walked into an open cupboard door not looking where she was going; but Conchita had heard Guy shouting at her in their bedroom. She made no comment now and just shook her head as she gently touched Lucy's cheek. Then with a smile, she suggested Lucy might like to have her lunch on a tray under the tree rather than go alone into the dining room.

The young girl's thoughtfulness once more brought tears to Lucy's eyes and she berated herself for being so pathetic. The antidepressants she had been taking ever since her miscarriage did not seem to be having much in the way of a beneficial effect, and they made her feel slightly dizzy and lethargic. The row with Guy had done little to improve matters.

Whilst she waited for Conchita to bring her lunch, she watched Carlos far away at the bottom of the garden. He, too, was about to have his midday meal which he always took sharp at one o'clock, sitting in the shade of the olive trees which grew down by the southern boundary fence. He wore an old straw hat to further shade him from the sun. Sometimes when he had finished his meal and enjoyed a half-hour siesta, he would pick a pannier of strawberries and bring them to her to have with her tea. Now, she shrank back as far into her garden chair as possible, hoping he could not see her across the distance between them.

Realizing suddenly that she was reacting as if Guy had been justified in imagining she had been flirting with Carlos, she berated herself for even thinking she must no longer talk to the gardener. It was more than just ridiculous of Guy to put such an embargo on her and she would tell him so this evening when he returned. Marriage was a two-way partnership and her feelings and wishes should carry every bit as much weight as Guy's. Just because he was ten years older did not give him the right to dictate to her.

The fact that she was now feeling angry with Guy made it easier, somehow, to put to the back of her mind the memory of the physical force he had used so suddenly and unexpectedly. After Conchita had removed her half-eaten luncheon, she actually managed to sleep away part of the afternoon. It was only when Conchita brought her a cup of tea soon after four o'clock that she woke and saw the basket of strawberries by the side of her chair. For a moment, she felt a chill down her spine. How was she to explain the fruit to Guy without him thinking she had deliberately disobeyed him and been communicating with Carlos again?

Aware suddenly that the whole side of her face was now aching, and suspecting that the bruise was worsening, Lucy's resentment returned and she now actually looked forward to five o'clock when she intended to tell Guy that if he ever hit her again, that would be the last time and she would leave him. If that was what he feared, it should be enough for him to keep control of his unwarranted suspicions were they to arise again.

Lucy went up to her room, showered and changed into a pale yellow Amanda Wakely dress – one she had bought specifically for this visit supposing that Guy and his father would be introducing her to their friends and neighbours and also, quite possibly, their clients. It was deceptively cut with a flared skirt and shoestring shoulder straps, and enhanced her size ten slender figure. Conchita came into the bedroom and seeing how beautiful Lucy looked, asked if she might twist Lucy's long blonde hair into a chignon. The result was to add several years and a great deal of sophistication to Lucy's appearance and both young women stood admiring Lucy's reflection in the dressing table mirror.

Conchita reached for Lucy's jewel case, but Lucy shook her head.

'I like it plain,' she told the maid. 'The dress is pretty enough without any extras!'

Knowing that she was now looking nearer Guy's age than her own gave Lucy added confidence as she went downstairs to the salon where Herbert Weaver's manservant had placed a tray of drinks. Her father-in-law had not yet arrived home, but Guy was standing by the picture window, a gin and tonic in his hand. Hearing the door open, he turned to see her but just for the tiniest part of a second, he did not recognize her. When he did, colour rushed into his face.

'You are looking quite beautiful.' He took a step closer and peered at her face. She had managed almost to conceal the ugly bruise with make-up but there was still a marked swelling.

'Lucy . . .' Guy's voice was husky and he was frowning slightly as he repeated her name. 'Lucy, my darling girl, can you forgive me? I was a positive brute to you and I'm so, so sorry.' He put his glass down on a side table and made as if to take her in his arms, but Lucy shrank back, her face expressionless.

Pretending he had not noticed her withdrawal, Guy said huskily: 'Lucy, darling, I know you don't believe this but I love you so very much – far, far more than you realize, or indeed, than you love me! Can you try and understand how it is for me, loving you the way I do and aware all the time that you are so much younger than I am; that you may begin to find me unattractive, boring, inadequate? I know it's wrong to be jealous but I admit that it hurts . . . worries me even if another man is looking at you admiringly. And if I see you laughing, smiling, chatting to another man, I can't help myself – I start thinking you are falling out of love with me.' He drew a deep sigh before adding: 'I know I shouldn't let these feelings get on top of me and I swear I will do everything I possibly can to curb them.' He held out a hand towards her. 'Lucy, can you forgive me?'

Lucy's thoughts flew back over the years to her childhood. She could almost hear her father's voice – so seldom raised but in this instance, in earnest. '*People can say horrible things to each other when they quarrel, but if one of the protagonists holds out a hand and asks for forgiveness, it would be both churlish and unkind to refuse to shake it. One day it could be you who wishes to be forgiven.*'

Although Lucy could not yet bring herself to let Guy put his arms round her, she did let him take her hand and draw her towards him so that their bodies were touching.

'Let's forget it happened!' she said quietly. 'But Guy, I would like to go home – just for a week or two, to see the family. I'll come straight back of course.' Seeing the scowl on his face, she added: 'It isn't because of what happened last night. It's that I had a letter from Mummy yesterday saying Jonnie and the girls would all be home next week. We haven't all been together since our wedding and . . . well, I miss them.'

For a moment, Guy did not comment. Then he said: 'My darling, of course I see why you want to be with them all and of course I wouldn't normally raise any objections but . . . well, I suppose I should have told you although it never occurred to me you might need your passport. I noticed it was out of date and I sent it away to be renewed.'

Lucy looked at him disbelievingly.

'But Guy, Daddy checked it before the wedding, I know he did. I remember him saying: "Wouldn't do to have you going off for your honeymoon and being forced to turn round and come home at the airport!" '

Guy released her hand and picked up his drink.

'Mistakes do happen, darling – not your father's – I know how meticulous he is – but at the passport office? I think they had the expiry date for the wrong year. That fellow checking passports at Malaga airport pointed it out to me. Maybe you didn't grasp what he was saying. It was in Spanish, of course.' Seeing the look on Lucy's face, he said quickly: 'I'll make enquiries first thing tomorrow. With a bit of luck, we can get it back before you want to leave. Next week, you said?'

Lucy nodded, saying: 'So you wouldn't mind if I book a flight home – say a week from today?'

Yet again Guy hesitated before replying:

'No, of course not. It wouldn't be the end of the world if the passport hadn't yet arrived back and you couldn't use the ticket – what's a couple of hundred euros when all's said and done?' He laughed and putting down his now-empty glass, he reached in his pocket. 'Here, darling! A little "forgive me" present. I was coming home after lunch but the wretched jeweller was shut until four for siesta so I had to hang around the office until then. Anyway, I hope you like it!'

The pretty gift-wrapped parcel contained a velvet-lined box on which lay a silver pendant picked out in coloured enamels. Lucy's eyes widened in admiration.

'The jeweller told me it's an early-twentieth-century piece made in England, not Spain,' Guy said. 'Do you like it, darling?

I thought with so many coloured stones it would go with any of your outfits.'

It was, undoubtedly, very pretty and although Guy had brought her several piece of jewellery since they were married, none had been as individual or attractive as the pendant. It was, he'd admitted, a peace offering – but a very lovely one and, she could imagine, a very expensive one. Fortuitously, one of the enamel beads exactly matched her pale yellow dress. She hung the pendant round her neck and Guy stepped behind her to fasten it. As he did so, he bent his head and she could feel the pressure of his lips against the nape of her neck. He would, she realized, want to make love to her later. Would she be able to respond? It had been so difficult to match Guy's sexual demands since her miscarriage, yet she would have expected her body to be receptive to his love-making; to achieve another pregnancy to replace her lost baby. But it had not seemed to happen like that. For one thing, the idea of having a child Guy did not want seemed unfair both to him and more importantly to the baby. It was almost, she had told her sympathetic female doctor, as if without the end product of love-making, her body now considered there was no point to sex. The doctor had assured her that her libido would return and suggested she herself talk to Guy. But Guy, not un-expectedly, had refused.

As Lucy had anticipated, Guy was at his most ardent that night, although keeping his own feelings strictly in control whilst he attempted to arouse her. Eventually Lucy simulated the orgasm he intended her to have, after which he felt free to sink himself deep inside her and assuage his unremitting hunger. He stayed inside her for as long as he possibly could. When finally he withdrew, he said, in a voice devoid of emotion: 'You faked it, didn't you, Lucy?'

She pulled his face down to hers and kissed him, her voice soft but emphatic as she lied to him.

'Darling Guy, you are being paranoid. Of course I didn't fake it.'

But of course, she had.

Sixteen

In a small 1930s farmhouse, Andy Richards, the farmer's eighteen-year-old son, propped his fishing rod up against the back door and went into the kitchen for his tea. His two younger sisters were already seated at the scrubbed wooden table eating the fresh farmyard eggs laid by their own chickens. They looked up at their tall brother expectantly as he sat down at the opposite end of the table to his father.

'No more treasure trove?' one of the girls demanded hopefully.

Andy shook his head.

'No, but I landed three two-pounders. Can we have them for tea tomorrow, Mum?'

Whenever her son was not busy helping his father on the farm, he was fishing down on the River Cherwell which ran past the south border of Hollow Field. He did not, of course, have a licence to fish there but with the bank largely obscured by willows, the boy was well concealed. His father maintained it was not poaching as the good God had provided rivers for everyone and not just for a few rich landowners.

It was over a week now since Andy had returned from one of his outings with two silver objects which were in a cotton shoe bag in the river. He had miscast his line and the hook had caught in an overhanging branch of a willow tree. Unable to pull it free, he had waded in and seen the bag just underwater, caught in debris which had collected in the roots of the tree. More concerned with the problem of freeing his hook, he had not bothered to retrieve the bag until he had disentangled his line. Curiosity then prompted him to reach down and lift the bag on to the bank. Looking inside it, Andy saw the two black objects and would have thrown them back had he not failed to catch any fish that evening. Perhaps the girls would find a use for them, he'd decided, provided they could be cleaned up.

Having no silver polish in the house, the eldest girl, Wendy
bought some on her way back from school. Both she and her
sister became excited when as they started to clean them, the
objects began to shine. Knowing nothing about hallmarks,
their mother thought they were almost certainly silver plated,
and the girls were each allowed to choose one of the pieces.
Wendy chose the little silver lace-edged basket with the handle
to put on her dressing table for what she called her 'bits and
bobs'. Her sister, Debbie, said she would like the little box
with a picture of a castle on the lid.

Seeing them sparkling under the electric light, Andy was
quite pleased with himself and said if the fish weren't biting
next time he went down to the river, he would look and see
if there were any more bags lying around. It did not cross the
minds of anyone in the family that the silver objects could be
valuable. As Andy said, people did not throw expensive possessions into a river to rust and rot away, and Wendy maintained
that unwanted items these days were more often given to a
charity shop of else put in a car boot sale. Besides which, his
mother added to the discussion, people couldn't be bothered
with silver nowadays – too much trouble and time needed to
clean it. Her stainless steel cutlery didn't need cleaning, it
could go in the dishwasher, her husband's Christmas present
to her which she had only just got accustomed to using.

Nearly two months passed before the 'treasure trove' was
spoken about again. By then, the girls had ceased to clean or
even notice the objects in their rooms and once again, the air
had turned the silver a dull cloudy black. Their mother threatened to throw them back in the river if her daughters didn't
keep them in better condition. It was Wendy who brought
them sharply back to everyone's attention. It was her regular
habit to watch *Antiques Road Show* on a Sunday evening,
sometimes to her mother's annoyance if she was trying to get
the girl to sit down at the kitchen table for her tea. Wendy's
insistence that she would rather eat her food cold than miss
the programme was supported by her father, an easy-going
man who nevertheless insisted on watching football on a
Saturday regardless of what his family might prefer to see on
their only television set.

'Mum! Dad! Andy! Come quick. Look at this!' Wendy's
voice sounded urgent enough to make them look up from the

tea table. Wendy was pointing at the screen with one hand, the other waving excitedly towards them. When they remained seated, she urged them even more frantically to come and look. The valuer was holding a small, silver box chased with a castle, almost identical to the one Debbie had appropriated.

'He just said it should fetch two thousand pounds!' she gasped. 'He thinks it might have been made in the eighteenth century and if it was, it could be worth even more. He's consulting a colleague.'

It was a moment or two before Andy understood her excitement. Recalling the little silver box he had fished out of the river, he could see that there was a marked likeness.

'You don't suppose Debbie's box is . . . is . . . valuable, too, do you, Dad?' he asked. 'What do you think, Mum? I mean – thousands of pounds! Shit! That's one hell of a lot of money!'

For once his father did not reprimand him for swearing in front of his mother and sisters. He, like them, remained silent whilst the valuation of the silver box was made. They held their breath as the sum of two thousand pounds crept up to three and then four when it was established the silver was of Russian origin. After her father switched off the television, Wendy for once raised no objection.

'You girls had best go to the jewellers with Mother when you come out of school tomorrow,' he said in a quiet, serious tone. 'There's bound to be one in the High Street – look in the Yellow Pages, Andy. A jeweller should be able to give us some idea what our silver bits are worth.'

'Won't he ask where we got them?' Andy said anxiously. He gave a weak smile. 'I don't want to get done for poaching, Dad.'

'No need to say too much,' his father muttered. 'I'm not one for untruths as well you all know, but in this instance, I think you might say Andy found the bag with the stuff in it at the south end of Hollow Field by the towpath. That's near enough the truth.' He turned to look at his daughters' flushed faces. 'And don't you go saying anything to the girls at school, do you hear me? Less other people know of our business the better. Besides, it doesn't necessarily follow that what Andy found is the same as what was on the telly just because it looks like it.'

'Sometimes the man says things are only copies and not worth anything,' Wendy said knowledgeably. 'Maybe ours are copies and that's why someone threw them away.'

'Don't be a spoilsport!' Andy reproached her, thrilled with the idea that he had fished up a fortune. Four thousand pounds! Surely his father would agree to him buying that second-hand motorbike he so desperately wanted?

It was not until teatime next day that Andy's hopes were realized. According to the High Street jeweller, one of the two boxes was indeed hallmarked as Russian and although he could not give a value, it would be worth a very great deal, he had told their mother. Understandably, he was curious as to how they had come by such a remarkable piece of silver.

'I told him what you said, John,' she informed her husband, 'and he said because it was worth such a lot, I must tell the police.'

'What, and lose all that money?' Andy said, appalled at the very idea.

Mrs Richards nodded.

'Yes, but he said there would almost certainly be a big reward. He seemed to think it could have been stolen, you see, and the thief found out he couldn't sell it because it was so special, so threw it away.'

Mr Richards sat down in the big pinewood chair at the top of the table, his eyes narrowed in thought.

'I don't think we have any alternative now but to report it,' he said after a minute or two, during which no one spoke. 'The chances are the jeweller will have done so anyway. I'll go down to the police station after we've had our tea. Provided we all stick to the story that Andy found the things at the bottom of the Hollow, we won't be in any trouble and if there is a reward, we should certainly be entitled to it.'

For the remainder of the meal, Andy and his sisters speculated on the size of the reward they were hoping to receive, but as their mother reminded them, there was no guarantee a reward would be forthcoming.

Down in Brighton, Beck was regarding his boss with an expression of real pleasure.

'Looks like we've finally got a breakthrough!' he said, holding out the e-mail printout of the silver boxes. 'They tally exactly with the description Miss Lyford's cleaner gave us.'

'Seems strange Miss Lyford had no idea of the value,' Govern said in a sceptical tone. 'I mean, you would have expected the old lady to have stressed the necessity to treat them with great care because of their value had she known their worth.'

'Yes sir,' Beck agreed, 'but perhaps she thought her possessions would be less likely to be stolen if no one knew their true value. Or . . .' he added, 'perhaps Miss Lyford really didn't know herself.'

Govern nodded.

'I sometimes wonder if I misjudge you, David,' he said with a smile he concealed from his sergeant. 'Now you mention it, I remember the cleaning woman saying Miss Lyford had referred to everything in the display cabinet being heirlooms passed down from her grandparents. If she had known their present-day value, I imagine she would have insured them. We mustn't forget she belonged to a generation who on the whole placed more sentimental than monetary value on their possessions. In any case, we know Miss Lyford did not insure them. We must assume, therefore, that she didn't know what each item was worth.'

'So what now, sir?' Beck enquired. It was a moment or two before Govern replied.

'What now, Beck, my boy, is that you take yourself down to the Richards' farm, find out exactly where they, stroke who, found the silver. We have to suppose our burglar-cum-murderer threw the stuff away knowing it could incriminate him. Why Oxfordshire? Why throw it in a field where it could be found? Questions to be asked, David, and it doesn't need the two of us to ask them. The local police sergeant said the Richards were respectable country folk. We'll get more out of them if we don't intimidate them with too big a presence.'

Only too pleased to get out of the office and always happy to be behind the wheel of a car, Beck needed no second bidding. A little over two hours later, he was sitting at Mrs Richards' kitchen table being offered a large tumbler full of creamy milk fresh from the morning's milking and one of her home-made butties. She made a number of an evening, she told him, as the family always came in from working outside starving and it kept them going until their tea was ready.

Having established a good relationship with his hostess discussing the merits of the home baking of his grandmother,

Mrs Richards was happy to tell Beck that it was her son, Andrew, who had found the silver in a shoe bag down at the bottom of Hollow Field.

'Someone must have been walking along the towpath and thrown it over our fencing,' she told him. 'If you want to talk to Andrew, he'll like as not be on the tractor ploughing Greystone Meadow. That's right next to Hollow Field where he found the bag.'

Nine times out of ten, it was Inspector Govern whose instincts had been honed by years of detective work, but on this sunny August afternoon, it was Beck who had the feeling that Mrs Richards was not telling him the truth. Keeping his eyes open, he followed her out into the yard where she pointed him in the direction of the river which, she told him, ran east to west past the boundary of their farm.

Picking his way through a field of sheep, followed relentlessly by a dozen geese who clearly supposed he was going to feed them, Beck made his way over two farm gates and a stile to where he could see the tractor moving up and down a half-ploughed meadow. It was a truly rural scene and for a moment, Beck wished his visit to this pretty piece of English countryside did not have to be associated with a murder enquiry.

Andrew saw Beck coming and as the detective was expected, he climbed down off the tractor and walked over to meet him. Beck introduced himself and asked Andrew to show him exactly where he had found the bag. He knew at once that the boy was lying – not just by the hesitant tone of his voice – he was clearly not accustomed to telling falsehoods – but because Beck's eye had caught sight of a marked dip in the top strand of barbed wire marking the boundary beyond which the river was gliding past. Moreover, the grass was worn away on both sides of the fence, and on the riverbank there was every indication that the grass had been flattened by frequent usage. Nor was that the only reason Beck was quite convinced Andrew Richards had not found the silver in the field but had, most likely, fished it out of the river. He had taken note as he had knocked on the door of the farmhouse, of the fishing rod and tackle propped against the shed door. A fisherman himself, he had wondered what interest a farmer might have in the sport. Having met young Andrew, he realized it was the son and not the father who was the fisherman.

Glancing upstream where a willow dipped its branches into the water, he saw a white board nailed to a wooden post. Even from his distance away, he could read the notice: *Fishing Strictly Forbidden. Trespassers Will Be Prosecuted.*

As he turned to look at Andrew, the boy's face coloured a fiery red. Beck reached out and put a hand on his shoulder.

'Look here, Andrew,' he said. 'I'm not trying to incriminate you. The fact is, I am not the least bit interested if you have, as I suspect, been contravening that dictate.' He pointed to the notice. 'If you want my private opinion, I think the rivers and the countryside ought to belong to us all – not to any individual.'

Andrew's face lost its anxious expression and he gave a visible sigh of relief.

'That's what Mum says,' he told Beck. 'I don't take much – just the odd fish. Sometimes I put them back. It's just for the sport, you see.'

'Indeed I do!' Beck said. 'I'm a sea fisherman myself. I live in Brighton on the south coast and fish off the pier. So what's with this bag you found? Last month, I'm told?'

Reassured that he was not going to get into any trouble, Andrew relaxed.

'Actually it was eight weeks ago – the fifth of June. I remember it because it was the day before Debbie's birthday and that's on the sixth,' he elaborated. 'None of us realized there was something valuable in there. I mean, the things were all tarnished from being in the water and I was going to throw them back but the girls cleaned them up and they decided to keep them. Debbie's got a thing about castles every since she went to London on a school trip and saw Buckingham Palace. Can't say I think all that much to it myself. I mean it's not much of a home for a queen – not even got no turrets!'

Beck let him talk, satisfied now that he had all the facts he needed. Not that they would be any the wiser as to how long the silver had been in the river before Andrew hooked it out. Since the objects had been cleaned, the experts wouldn't be able to gauge the length of time either.

Having said his farewells to Andrew and Mrs Richards, he

made his way slowly back to the M40 taking note of the mileage as he did so. There was no way, he had realized, that whoever threw the silver into the river could have done so from the motorway even had they been able to slow down the car on the bridge in order to do so. Even in the slow lane, traffic was travelling at a minimum of fifty miles an hour. So even if the thief had managed it somehow and the current had carried it downstream towards the Richard's boundary, the odds were dead against it having done so. It stood to reason, therefore that whoever had thrown it into the river must have come off the motorway, probably at Junction 10, the Cherwell Service Area, and found a track leading to the towpath. In all probability, he surmised, the towpath led to the area where the boy fished. He had decided that this was as good a time as any to investigate.

It was nearly an hour before he found the track he was looking for. Although not directly opposite Hollow Field, it was within a few metres. Moreover, the track was just wide enough to take a car although the driver would have had to reverse to get it back on the tarmac road. There had been heavy rainfalls right across the Midlands and Southern part of the country during the previous month and Beck saw no hope of getting any results if the Oxfordshire forensic team was called out to look for tyre prints. Too much water had gone under the bridge, Beck had told himself grinning at the word association, in what was a minimum of two months and could be a lot longer.

Inspector Govern was clearly pleased when Beck related his day's activities to him. 'Interesting that some of Miss Lyford's silver has turned up in the Cherwell. Has it crossed your mind, Beck, that there is a bridge over that river on the M40?'

'So?' Beck asked.

'So the M40 leads us to Birmingham – and that's where our good friend Mr Guy Weaver has a client.'

Beck was sceptical.

'There must be a thousand and one other men with clients in Birmingham, not to mention hundreds and thousands of people with other reasons to go there via the M40.'

Govern's face remained impassive and Beck knew better than to question him further.

'Showed a bit of initiative, didn't you?' he commented.

'And although we may not have any new evidence to nail my suspect, I see this as yet another reason to keep him on hold. Now how about a pint, Beck? I think you deserve one and the sun is long gone.'

By no means for the first time, as he followed Inspector Govern out into the street and he strode off purposefully in the direction of their local pub, Beck thought how very lucky he had been, and still was, to be working in partnership with a man like his boss.

Seventeen

The sun was just beginning to touch the balcony outside Lucy's bedroom window when she sat down at the little wrought iron table whilst she waited for Conchita to bring her breakfast. It was Guy's habit to breakfast in the dining room with his father during which they invariably discussed the day's business, so as Lucy had no appetite for the full English meal they both enjoyed, she had asked Conchita to bring her a continental breakfast of rolls, delicious coffee and fresh fruit to her room.

She had come to love these quiet moments first thing in the morning when the air was still fresh, and from up in the hills, there was often a gentle breeze filling the air with the scent of the jasmine which grew in profusion beneath her balcony.

As always, Conchita was smiling as she walked across the bedroom and placed the tray in front of Lucy.

'*Buenos días, señora!*' she said, bending to pour a cup of coffee for Lucy. 'Is the señora feeling better?'

Lucy had been suffering some severe headaches – so severe that she had wondered if she was starting to have migraines. The bruising on her cheek had at last disappeared but the headaches persisted. Today, however, she was feeling better.

'I might go into Marbella and do some shopping,' she told the maid. 'It's my brother's birthday next month and I thought I might find him a present in that lovely leather shop you told me about.'

Conchita stood for a moment as between them they discussed the merits of a belt or a document wallet which would be useful when Jonnie went off to Asia, which he planned to do as soon as he had saved enough money.

Lucy had almost finished her breakfast and was drinking her second cup of coffee before Conchita said hesitantly: 'Señora, may I please ask if you will permit me?'

Lucy smiled encouragingly. She had grown very fond of the young girl in the weeks she had been at La Finca de Azahar and was happy to be able to grant whatever wish she might have.

'It is the *sello*,' Conchita said. 'How you say in English – for the letter?' She mimed the tiny square at the top of an envelope.

'The stamp!' Lucy said. 'But what stamp, Conchita? You have the English ones from my family.' She knew Conchita's ten-year-old brother was an avid collector and had asked her mother to try and put as many different denominations on her letters as she could.

'The *sello* from *Suiza*, señora? The *cartero* brings it this morning.'

'From Switzerland? For me?' Lucy asked stupidly. 'But why didn't you bring the letter to me, Conchita?' It could only be from Tom, she realized, and she could not wait to read it.

The maid looked uncomfortable.

'The señor has said Pepe must take all letters first to him, señor Guy,' she explained. 'He say important for business.'

Lucy frowned. Why should Guy, or indeed his father, think it necessary to have all the mail given to them on its arrival? Business letters would be addressed to them or to the firm and were not, therefore, likely to be given to anyone else; to her.

More than anxious to read Tom's letter and not a little irritated that it had been delayed in reaching her, after a quick shower, Lucy put on a pair of shorts and a thin, Indian cotton shirt and went down. Herbert Weaver was leaving as she arrived. Invariably polite and jovial with her, he greeted her warmly and told her he was flying to Barcelona for the day; that she was to ask for anything she wanted and should she wish to go sight-seeing or shopping, his chauffeur would be back with the Mercedes after he had taken him to the airport and she would be welcome to make use of his driver.

Although still a little shy with Guy's father, Lucy had come to like him, partly because he had an excellent sense of humour but also because he was unfailingly solicitous to her.

'Reckon that son of mine has done all right for himself

marrying you, m'dear,' he'd said when they first met. 'Couldn't have chosen anyone better m'self! Now, don't you let him bully you. Likes his own way, Guy does; but I can see he dotes on you so just you let him spoil you!'

After he left the house she made her way to the dining room, she wondered what he would say if he knew Guy had hit her. As it was, he had not questioned her lie that she had walked into an open wardrobe door without looking where she was going.

She forgot Herbert Weaver as Guy half-rose in his seat to greet her. He beckoned to her to sit down beside him, saying: 'Not by any chance come to breakfast with me, have you, *amor mio*?'

Although Lucy sat down in the chair next to his, she did not return his smile.

'I've come to fetch my letter,' she said glancing at the small pile of opened mail lying in front of him.

Guy's face remained blank for a minute before he replied: 'Letter? What letter, darling? Should there have been one for you?'

'The letter from Switzerland,' Lucy said. 'Conchita told me there was one.'

Guy shrugged imperceptibly as he said casually: 'Oh, that letter. It was a business letter for me from France. Conchita must have been mistaken.'

Lucy was in no doubt that he was lying. She was certain now that the letter was from Tom – and because Guy had always been jealous of Tom, he had kept it from her. Two could play at Guy's game, she thought.

'Oh, well, if that's it, can you please give me the stamp, Guy?' she said casually, without changing her expression. 'Conchita collects them for her young brother. He's a para-plegic, you see, and stamp collecting is one of the activities he can do from his wheelchair. I promised Conchita I would save any foreign stamps for him.'

Momentarily Guy looked non-plussed. Then he reached for the pile of letters in front of him and sifted through them as if searching for the one Lucy wanted.

Since it wasn't there, he turned to her saying: 'I'm dread-fully sorry, darling, but Father must have taken it with him. He likes to keep important clients' letters in the office as they can so easily get lost here in the house. It was from a bank, if my memory serves me right!'

He sounded convincing until Lucy remembered that her father-in-law had said he was going to Barcelona – not, as Guy inferred, to his office in Marbella.

She looked straight into Guy's eyes as she said quietly: 'Then I'll ask him for the stamp when he gets back this evening!'

Was she imagining it, she asked herself as she went back upstairs to her room, or had Guy's mouth tightened and his eyes narrowed when she called his bluff – if, indeed, it had been a bluff. He could have been telling the truth, she reminded herself. What was happening to her that she should suddenly become suspicious of someone she purported to love? Conchita had had a very limited education and it would not be in the least surprising if she had confused the French and Swiss stamps. Deciding that she was being more than a little unfair to Guy, Lucy forced herself to turn her thoughts elsewhere. She would do as Herbert Weaver had suggested and ask his chauffeur, Pablo, to take her shopping. He would know exactly where to find the shop where she wished to buy Jonnie's present.

Two hours later, Lucy returned to La Finca de Azahar delighted with her purchase – a dark brown cowhide belt with a particularly beautiful large silver buckle. It was, the shop-keeper told her, a great deal more valuable than the belt itself. Jonnie would love it. He had reached the age where clothes were a matter of importance to him and she knew he could never afford to buy himself such a luxury item.

She had also bought a double-sided black leather photograph frame for Guy who was always taking photographs of her and complaining that he had no frames to put them in. It was not his birthday, but during the drive down into Marbella, she had begun to feel guilty for ever having suspected Guy of hiding a letter which was rightfully hers.

It had been chilly in the town so Lucy decided on a warm shower before lunch. As she emerged from the bathroom wrapped in one of the big white fluffy bath towels so different from the somewhat thin worn ones that were in the hot cupboard at home, her eye caught the glint of silver on her bed table where the sun was streaming in through the open window on to her mobile telephone. From habit, she kept it fully charged but she seldom had occasion to use it as Guy had told her she could phone home as often as she wished from the house phones.

She sat down on the side of the bed, staring at the small object lying within her reach. She had only to pick it up and dial Tom's mobile to be in instant touch with him. She could text him a message – *wy no leter ples rite*. If he had already written, he would reply saying so. If his letter had not been lost in the post, she would know that Guy had destroyed it because he'd guessed it was from Tom.

Her heart was thudding as she picked up the little mobile and held it against her chest. It could give her the irrefutable answer, but did she want it? Did she want to know that Guy had been lying to her? Deceiving her? The thought was like a very nasty taste in her mouth. Such behaviour coming on top of his violence towards her could only add to the feeling of total estrangement from him. So did she want proof? On the other hand, Tom might text her saying he was sorry not to have written before but would do so without further delay. Then Guy would be in the clear and she could relax.

Lucy put the phone back on the bedside table and, now dry from her shower, she put on a thin skirt and T-shirt. Although it was late September, there was still considerable warmth in the sun. As she had done the previous day, Conchita brought her lunch out to the orchard. The maid was too polite to ask a second time for the Swiss stamp and Lucy thought it best not to mention it until she knew whether her father-in-law had indeed taken a business letter to Barcelona with him. Certain now that it would be right to wait until her father-in-law returned before she texted Tom, she tried first to read her book and enjoy her after lunch siesta, but unable to concentrate, she busied herself dead-heading the roses that Carlos had planted in profusion round the house when Guy's parents had moved there from the Hacienda de los Cojollos.

By teatime, she could not wait any longer. Guy could arrive back at any moment and she knew she would find it impossible to behave as if nothing were amiss. Sensitive to her every mood, he would know something was wrong and would almost certainly associate it with the missing letter. Going back to her bedroom, she reached for her mobile and texted her query to Tom. An hour later, he replied: *Rote 4 days ago. When r u home again? Will visit. luv as always xxx.*

Lucy switched off the phone and lent forward so that her arms rested on her knees. Her heart was beating furiously and she felt sick. Four days ago! That letter must surely have reached Spain by this morning and it was far too coincidental to suppose a French client had written to either Guy or his father exactly the same time as Tom had written to her. So there was little doubt left that Guy had been lying; that he had deliberately kept Tom's letter from her. Had he opened it and read it as well, she asked herself as anger replaced the nausea? Did he have so little trust in her that he could suppose she was carrying on a secret correspondence with a former lover? If he had given her the letter, she would without question have let him read it knowing Tom would never write anything that could cause trouble between herself and Guy. Tom loved her far too much ever to hurt her deliberately.

Lucy's heart jolted as she considered her unbidden thought. Yes, she had always known Tom loved her, but that love had been put by her into a different category from the love a man might feel for a woman. Without realizing it, she had pretended it was just a childhood infatuation, tied up in obscure ways with Vanessa. For the hundredth time since Vanessa had died, Lucy wept for her presence. The dilemma she was now in was so very much something she would have talked to Vanessa about – Vanessa who was always so sensible; so much more far-seeing than she was. Other daughters might consult their mothers but there was no way Lucy would put such thoughts into her mother's head. As far as both her parents were concerned, her marriage to Guy was idyllic and only the loss of her baby had marred their happiness.

What should she do now? she asked herself. Confront Guy? There was always the faint chance her father-in-law would say yes, he had taken the letter with him; that it was in his briefcase. Yet Lucy did not believe this would happen. There had been something indefinable in Guy's responses at the breakfast table that she could not explain, yet they made her certain he was lying.

Slowly she began to get her conflicting emotions under control. She must, she realized, deal with what could be a serious situation calmly – and fairly. In English law, people were innocent until they were proven guilty and she would start on that assumption with Guy. First, she would wait for his father to return. When he did so, she would question him about the letter in front of Guy. It was possible, she thought, that if his father did not have it, he would remember it being amongst the morning mail and have seen Guy take it. Then there was the possibility she must not lose sight of, that it had been lost in the post – the post was not always reliable out here in Spain any more than it was in England. And there was yet another possibility – the letter might arrive the next day, or the day after. Four days to travel from Switzerland was not all that long.

But long enough! Lucy's instincts told her. Had she not received letters from her mother written only three days previously? Yet again, she chided herself for the way her thoughts kept taking her. The last thing in the world she wanted was to find Guy guilty of being so jealous, so possessive that he would stoop to stealing from her what was her private property. It was one thing for married couples to share their lives, but there were some things which remained personal and she had been brought up to understand that, letters and diaries were but two of them.

The arrival of Conchita to turn down her bed and put fresh towels in the bathroom, temporarily halted Lucy's reflections. The maid was engaged to be married. She and her fiancé, Mario – a waiter in one of the big hotels in Marbella – were saving up for the wedding. He wanted to buy them a little house of their own or if they could not afford a house, an apartment; but Conchita did not want to leave home because of Jorge, her young wheelchair-bound brother. Her other brother and sisters had already gone else-where, one to England as an au pair, one to America and another to a bull ranch near Seville. Their mother had died and although the father was both able and caring, the boy needed Conchita to care for him as well as for more youthful company.

On the spur of the moment, Lucy said: 'Do you think your brother would like to see the house, Conchita? And, indeed, the garden? Perhaps it would be possible for him to go in the pool if we can find someone to support him.'

Conchita's face flushed with pleasure.

'*Si, si, señora!* Jorge think he has flied to *el cielo!* He say many, many times he wish only to go to the sea and lie in the water, but *mi padre* tell him is too dangerous and is best he only think it in his mind.'

'Then he shall swim in our pool!' Lucy declared, delighted with her plan. 'I will talk to the señor and we will arrange it. For the moment, don't say anything until we know exactly which day is best and then we can make it a big surprise for Jorge. Meanwhile, Conchita, please take this . . .' She handed her a twenty-Euro note. 'I want you to buy him some swimming trunks when you are next in Marbella. If he enjoys the water, we can try to make it a regular event. I feel sure the exercise will be beneficial for him.'

Before Lucy realized what Conchita intended to do, the maid had caught hold of her hand and lifted it to her lips. There were tears in her dark brown eyes as she whispered her thanks and her gratitude to Lucy.

'My friend in the village tell me no to work here when the señor ask for a maid for when you coming from England, señora,' she said shyly. 'She tell me English ladies much more like their dogs and cats than husbands and children. *Mi padre* – he tell me this – how do you say in English? – *tontería.* You are liking children, no? Soon, maybe, you and the señor will have *niños*, yes?'

So Conchita knew nothing of her lost baby, Lucy thought with a devastating pang of sadness sweeping over her to replace the happiness of a moment ago. It seemed to encompass her whole body and as the tears filled her eyes, she turned quickly away from the smiling maid. It would be a long time yet, she knew, before she could bear to talk about that loss. Perhaps she could have shared her grief with Vanessa, and, of course, she had told her doctor how deep her depression was, but she had been unable to talk about her miscarriage either to her parents or her sisters, and least of all to Guy. Maybe she would tell Conchita – but not now. She must get dressed for the evening meal which was the main event of the day and both Guy and his father changed into smart, if casual clothes in the evening. She

would wear another of her designer dresses but . . . she
thought with a tiny flicker of surprise at the way those
thoughts were taking her . . . not with the necklace Guy had
given her. It had been a request for forgiveness, but no way
was she able to forgive him if, after all, he had purloined
her letter from Tom.

Downstairs, Guy stood by the window in the salon, a glass of
whisky in his hand. His eyes were thoughtful and he was
frowning as he pondered how exactly he was going to continue
the subterfuge regarding Lucy's letter. He had, of course, opened
and read it and it was as he had suspected from Tom Lyford.
It had contained nothing untoward – nothing to make him
suspicious that there were any secret communications going
on between him and Lucy. There had, not unexpectedly, been
that element of familiarity with references to their shared past,
and, inevitably, to Vanessa.

He had acted far too precipitately, he reproached himself,
although there'd been no reason to suppose that Lucy would
ever know what had arrived in the morning mail. If Lyford
had written again and mentioned the missing letter, he could
have made out it must have been lost in the post. It was nothing
more than sheer bad luck that the maid happened to be
collecting foreign stamps and seen the mail before Pepe had
brought it to him at breakfast. From the expression on Lucy's
face when she had asked him to produce the letter, he'd known
she thought his denial of its existence was a fabrication; that
his pretence of its being a business letter from France was
also a lie.

During the day, he had combed the town of Marbella looking
for a stationers or stamp dealer from whom he could purchase
used foreign stamps. He had finally discovered one only to
find they were all hopelessly out of date. Even had Lucy not
realized it was an old stamp he had supposedly torn off the
envelope, the wretched child who collected stamps for a hobby
would have noticed it.

He went across the room to pour himself another drink, his
mouth tightening as he considered once more how his luck
had been against him. He must, he decided, be more careful
in future. With a deepening feeling of anxiety, he heard his
father's voice greeting him as he came into the room announcing

that he had pulled off yet another successful deal. Normally, he would have been interested in the details but, perturbed as he was about Lucy's well-deserved suspicions, this evening Guy could not have cared less.

Eighteen

Inspector Govern was reading the riot act to a newly qualified young constable who had failed to provide a report he'd requested as a matter of urgency the night before, when Detective Sergeant Beck came hurrying into the room. He was holding a telephone handset which he held out to Govern.

'It's Hart-Pennant, sir. I rang his mobile on the off chance. Reception isn't too good but . . .'

Govern grabbed the phone from him and having said who he was, he wasted no time asking the man if he could remember whether he had offered to lend his Volvo to anyone whilst he was abroad.

'Absolutely not!' was Hart-Pennant's emphatic reply. 'Had it serviced whilst I was away. If I remember right, it was booked in for one a week or so after I came out here. Nothing happened to it, I hope?'

'No, it's perfectly all right, sir, but we think it's just possible someone may have used it.'

'Impossible!' Hart-Pennant replied immediately. 'I'm one of the lucky ones, Inspector, as I have my own garage where I keep it locked up. Can't be precise about the service date – I remember the garage couldn't fit it in until after I'd left – somewhere round the second week of . . .'

For a full minute, the Inspector could hear nothing but static, then he heard the man's voice again, fainter but still intelligible.

'Did you catch that, Inspector? Weaver – Guy Weaver . . . friend of mine . . . play squash together. . . . old school friend and a great player. I gave him the key. Can you hear me OK?'

'Indeed I can, Mr Hart-Pennant – and thank you very much indeed for your help.' There was a sudden laugh and some voices which the Inspector could hear in the background and then: 'Too much of a mouthful. Call me H-P. You know, the sauce? Everyone does. Look, I've got to go – the jeep is just leaving. Sorry I can't be more help. I . . .'

As the line went dead, Govern said to Beck as he handed him back the phone: 'I doubt he could have been more helpful!' He was smiling broadly much to the surprise of the young constable who he now dismissed without further reproof. 'Seems Weaver had the key to Hart-Pennant's garage. I think we just could have got our man, Beck.'

Beck looked surprised.

'You think Weaver borrowed the car without telling the owner? A bit risky, don't you think?'

'Less risky than driving to the south coast in his silver Sagaris,' Govern said succinctly.

'You're convinced it's Weaver, aren't you, sir? But why? What motive could he have had for bumping the old girl off?'

Govern frowned.

'There'll be one, mark my words.' Momentarily, he looked deep in thought, then he said: 'You know, if Weaver did borrow the car and having been down to Seaford, he then drove in it to his meeting in Birmingham, that cashier should recognize him – or hopefully if too much time has not elapsed – as the man who caused the furore at the M40 service station. We know it wasn't our friend, Mr H-P, but it was a businessman about Weaver's height and build. See if you can get hold of a photograph. I know he and his wife are in Spain but the Godstows must have a wedding photo. You've got that nippy little digital camera you're so fond off. Get them to show you a wedding album and then could you take a photo of a photo?'

'Of course I could, sir!' Beck said. 'But why don't I simply ask them for a photo of our friend?'

'Because, Beck, my boy . . .' Govern shook his head 'Because I don't wish them to know at this stage that I have the slightest suspicion about their son-in-law. Just think for a moment how shocked they would be if they thought I suspected their daughter's husband of murder. Use your noddle, Beck!'

Suitably chastized, Beck made no further comment but rang for a car to take him down to Ferrybridge. He should be there in half an hour at most, he thought as he went downstairs to the car park. With luck, that excellent cook, Mrs Godstow, who had provided such delectable food for Miss Lyford's funeral wake, would almost certainly ask him to stay for one of her excellently cooked meals if he made the journey in time for lunch.

After his sergeant had left, Govern remained at his desk, twiddling his biro thoughtfully as he pondered the next step in his investigation.

He had already worked out the mileage and knew Weaver could have driven to Seaford before going to Birmingham, but the fact that the cashier had said the troublemaker at the service station was driving a Volvo had muddied the waters. Weaver could, of course, have hired one but that would have been on record and he wouldn't have wanted that lest he'd been seen in Seaford, as indeed he was if that kid's statement turned out to be valid. If Beck got hold of a decent photograph, he was reasonably certain the cashier would identify Weaver but that was still not proof that he had driven to Seaford before going to Birmingham, still less that he committed a particularly unpleasant murder. One or two stab wounds would have been enough to kill the woman. The remainder showed the man to be a very sick sadist or a mental case. Yes, the Seaford kid had sworn he saw the Volvo coming out of Pepper Lane but the DPP were not going to base a murder charge on that! There had to be a motive for the killing – and after Beck returned, finding it must be their next step.

He pulled out the file he had started on Guy. It had little in it – age, physical description, date and place of birth, English school, names of parents. There was a single paragraph stating that although the man had been born in England, he had spent the first fifteen years of his life in Spain before being sent to England to a minor public school in the Midlands. It might be interesting to get some information about his school days, he thought – if there were still any teachers there who remembered Weaver. Presumably the fellow was not indifferent to sports since his friend, Mr H-P, said he was a regular squash player and Beck had noticed an extremely large and expensive set of golf clubs in his flat. If he had distinguished himself, there was a chance someone would remember him. Glancing at his desk diary, Govern noted that it was the 18th of September – term time. He could be in Bedford where the school was located in little over an hour. Whilst Beck was in Sussex, it might be an interesting and profitable trip for him. Inspector Govern was determined to somehow to find a motive because he now had no doubt whatever that Guy Weaver was his man.

As was invariably the case, Govern's instincts were well founded.

Although the headmaster of Abbotsford School was a moderately young man in his fifties, he introduced Inspector Govern to an elderly, grey-haired teacher, who due to his advanced years had the relatively easy task of teaching mathematics to the Lower First. He was due to retire at the end of the school year but had stayed on past retiring age as the Head had had difficulty recruiting a younger man willing to board at the school. When Guy had arrived at the school as a fifteen-year-old Paul Ironside had been his housemaster. He remembered the boy very well, he told Govern, who promptly invited him to lunch at the nearby pub.

'To tell you the truth, I was a bit intimidated by Weaver,' the man said. 'It's difficult to explain, really, but there was something different about him – something I can't explain. Of course, he'd been brought up in another country – spoke Spanish fluently – so I suppose he was bound to differ from all the other boys. He was a very serious chap – didn't laugh much, but I have to say, he was quite an exceptional mathematician. He was streets above his contemporaries. The Head decided to move him up a class. He was good at sports, too – not cricket but tennis and squash – won a lot of prizes. But you know, he wasn't a popular boy. I don't think he had many friends. There was one, whose name I forget – an easy-going chap who didn't seem to mind Weaver's odd moods.'

'Would that have been a boy called Jeremy Hart-Pennant?' Govern asked as Paul Ironside paused. The man nodded.

'At my age, the old memory isn't what it was!' he said ruefully. 'That's right, Hart-Pennant – nice boy but not very brainy. I always suspected Weaver helped him with his prep! But I couldn't prove it. Weaver was too sharp. It was always difficult to prove he was behind some of the less savoury things which happened. You know the sort of thing . . . bullying of younger boys – and he had a vicious temper.' He drew a long sigh.

'I have to be fair to the boy; he did very well. Got a first at university and I seem to remember he was in his university squash team – or it may have been tennis.' He tapped his head, nearly dislodging his spectacles as he did so. His eyes were thoughtful. 'The only other memory I have – and it's a very vague one, was that after he left university, he went back to live in Spain. Yes, that's right – I remember now. His parents were divorced and his mother lived in the States – never came to see him at school. He didn't go home to his father in the holidays, either – stayed here at Abbotsford. We take in quite a few foreign boys who stay on in the holidays for extra language tuition, so Weaver had company if he wanted it. Can't think why he didn't holiday in Spain.' He gave a sudden smile. 'It's coming back to me now. The boy's father was in business out there – made a lot of money and one year, he wrote out a very handsome cheque when the Head was trying to raise funds for another hard court. It was for more than my year's salary which is why I recall it so clearly!'

'Time I ordered some lunch for us both,' Govern said. 'What do you say to scampi and chips in the garden? And another Fosters?'

Seated on one of the wooden benches in the shade of a large umbrella, Govern resumed his questioning whilst they waited for their meal to arrive.

'Were you telling me just now that Weaver was at your school for two whole years without seeing either of his parents?'

'No, I didn't mean to say that. His father used to come over for the summer and Christmas holidays – take the boy off somewhere . . . seaside, London, France, I think, but as far as I recall, he never went home – to Spain, that is.'

An hour later, as he drove back to Brighton, Govern's thoughts returned to the last piece of conversation he and Paul Ironside had had about Guy Weaver. It was odd, to say the very least, for the boy not to go back to his home at least for one or two of the school holidays, especially as he had spent all his early childhood in Spain. Was his parents' divorce relevant in some way? Did his wealthy father keep a mistress out there he didn't want to boy to know about? Or was he involved with a criminal element on the Costa del Sol? It was known these days as the 'Costa del Crime'. It could account for his affluence and he might not have wanted his young son mixing with these people.

I'm letting my imagination override logical thinking; he chided himself as he branched off the A1 on to the M25. The rush hour had not yet started and he was making good progress. Once over the Dartford Bridge, if it continued he could be back in Brighton by four. Although a careful and conscientious driver, Inspector Govern's mind continued to worry at the inconsistencies of Weaver's teenage years.

Question: how to find out *why* he didn't go home, as would have been the normal thing to do. To ask Weaver outright would be to rouse his suspicions that he was being investigated. In any event, according to Beck he and his wife were still in Spain.

By the time Govern drove into the police station car park, he had made up his mind exactly what he was going to do. He and Beck would have a little holiday in the sunshine. It would suit Beck because he would let the chap have time off for a game of golf on one of the many courses on the Costa. They would get clearance for expenses seeing that the Superintendent had been badgering him to make a long-overdue arrest for the Seaford murder, so he shouldn't quibble over a couple of budget Easyjet tickets to Malaga and a few days at three-star hotels. They would need to hire a car, of course, but that could be done for under a hundred pounds.

As he had anticipated, Beck was beaming with delight when his boss told him they were about the have a few days' holiday. A working trip, Govern reminded him.

'Will we be going to Marbella?' Beck asked, aware that the Weavers' villa was only a few kilometres out of the town. Govern shook his head.

'No, I don't want Weaver or his father to know we are out there. Besides, I've made some enquiries and it seems Herbert Weaver only bought the Finca de Azahar where they now live, ten years ago. I'm interested in the place where his son grew up – a small town inland called Arcos de la Frontera. They had a hacienda in the area.'

He took a file from his desk drawer and turned to one of the marked pages.

'The place was called "Hacienda de los Cojollos", according to my Spanish spy!' Seeing the look on Beck's face, he laughed. 'You don't know everything I get up to, Beck. As it happens,

I have made contact with an English-speaking lawyer out there – a fellow called Jose Miguel Echevarria who has been making enquiries for me. We have an appointment with him at midday the day after tomorrow.' Govern smiled. 'Seeing it hasn't stopped raining all week, I thought we could both do with a break from our English weather.'

Beck had been to Spain before, but only to Madrid, so he was unfamiliar with the tourist-ridden Andalucian coast. Landing at Malaga the following day, and accompanying Govern along the interminable passages to reach the luggage reclaim, he was surprised to find the airport vast and modern. It seemed even more crowded than the departure check-in at Gatwick on a busy weekend. The drive from Malaga along the motorway was something of a disappointment. In the back of his mind, he had half-expected scenery as it appeared in brochures – white-painted houses dripping in bougainvillea and scarlet geraniums; donkeys with pannier baskets; orchards of orange, lemon and olive trees. Instead, he could see spreading seaside towns with huge concrete blocks of flats and yet more under construction packed tightly along the edge of a blue sea teaming with boats.

'Bit like Blackpool!' he commented wryly.

'It will be different at Arcos de la Frontera where the lawyer tells me the Weavers were living before they turned the hacienda into a five-star hotel,' Govern informed him. 'It was that enterprise way back in the sixties or seventies that I suspect was the beginning of Herbert Weaver's empire building – Weaver Developement Corporation, surveying, architecture, real estate – you name it. The huge post-war boom in developing the country was only just under way and he must have been among the first to see the huge potential out there. Apparently property was really cheap and most of the population so poor down in the south, you could buy a farmhouse, for instance, for peanuts. I imagine when Weaver sold the hotel he'd built ten years later he would have made a mint. He's a very rich man, our lawyer tells me, and has a suite of offices in Marbella, another in Barcelona, not to mention the English branch which Guy Weaver manages.'

'So that explains how the son can afford to buy a Sagaris, and the flat in Chelsea!' Beck said enviously. 'No wonder the family thought the girl, Lucy, had done very well for herself. No pinching and scraping for her!'

'Maybe not,' Govern said quietly, 'but I wouldn't want to be in her shoes, Jimi Choo though they may be.'

Knowing how suspicious his boss was of Weaver, Beck let the discussion drop. When he had been to see the attendant at the M40 service station and shown her the photograph of Weaver, she had been far from certain that he was the man with the Volvo. It was a long time since the incident had happened, she said. It could be him but then it might not. There were hundreds of tall men paying for their petrol every day. She did recall that the man had grey eyes because they were quite unusual, and he'd had a very penetrating stare; also that he'd been so angry. She described him as tallish and said he talked 'posh'; but there was absolutely no way she would formally identify him. Nor could she even try to pick him out in an identity parade.

To Beck's surprise, the Inspector had not seemed too disappointed. His own trip to Bedford, he told Beck, had consolidated his suspicions.

Now following the excellent direction the hire car attendant had given him, Beck found their hotel – an unpretentious, fairly modern establishment on the sea front. As they pulled up outside, he asked Govern why since they were aiming for a town on the way to Seville, he had opted to spend the first night an hour or more's drive away. Because, Govern told him, Arcos de la Frontera lay halfway between Marbella and Seville so the length of the drive would be more or less the same whichever airport they flew to. Besides, they had the appointment with the lawyer, Señor Echevarria in the morning and he wanted to have a private little chat with the manager of the Banco Atlántico – just to get some idea of the kind of money the Weaver family had stashed out here in Spain.

'Good, honest cash?' he asked Beck. 'Or is Weaver senior tied up in some way with the Spanish crooks? He's a resident here, of course, but Guy Weaver isn't.'

Beck gave an exaggerated sigh, softened by a grin which followed.

'Sometimes I think you would suspect your own grandmother of dastardly deeds!' he said. 'It seems to me, sir, that in your mind, everyone is guilty until you have proved them innocent.'

Govern laughed.

'Maybe you're right, Beck, but you have to concede that it is not very often I am wrong when I get one of my hunches. If I was a female in the good old days, I'd probably have been designated a witch and been burnt at the stake!'

'Or drowned in the ducking pond, more likely. I suppose the poor things choked on the duckweed and . . .'

'That's enough, Beck. Get our gear out of the car and let's get ourselves checked in. Then we can go and choke to death on an ice cold gin and tonic.'

The following day, the Spanish lawyer turned out to be even more informative than Govern had hoped. Having established Herbert Weaver's previous domicile in Arcos de la Frontera, he had further discovered amongst old records in the *Juzgados de Cádiz*, details *of* a murder committed in the nineteen eighties by a British juvenile with the surname Weaver. The teenage resident had been arrested for strangling a foreign immigrant. There had been an appeal heard by the *Audiencia de Cádiz* and the case had suddenly been dropped.

'Was that because the boy was not guilty?' Govern asked.

Señor Echevarria shook his head.

'I managed to talk to a retired member of the *Guardia Civil*, as the local police were known in those days,' he told them. 'He remembered the case because there had been a lot of talk at the time about very large sums of money changing hands, and thought to be responsible for the not-guilty verdict. A strangulation could hardly be called "accidental death" but that's what the boy got away with.'

The former policeman still lived in Arcos de la Frontera and would be happy to talk to them, the lawyer said. He might well recall further details. Could he, the lawyer, suggest the inspector and his detective sergeant book them into a very attractive *Parador* situated only two kilometres from the town of Arcos de la Frontera, as his informant had told him there was an elderly English couple who lived nearby and were known to frequent the *Parador*. They had been living in the area even longer than the Weavers so might well have been acquainted with them.

As they drove back to their hotel to pay their bill and check out, Govern was smiling broadly.

'Seems we are actually getting somewhere,' he said when Beck carried their two small suitcases out to their car. 'It may well be true that lightening never strikes twice, but murderers frequently do!'

'You're determined to prove Guy Weaver guilty of Miss Lyford's murder, aren't you, sir?' Beck remarked as he turned the car northwards in the direction of Seville. Knowing his boss so well, he was no longer in any doubt that it was only a matter of time now before he did so.

Nineteen

At first, somewhat to Lucy's surprise, Guy raised no objection to Conchita's little brother using their swimming pool. He seemed particularly anxious to please her since the debacle over the missing letter. Lucy had questioned her father-in-law the moment he had arrived home the evening of the letter's arrival, and as Lucy had half-expected, he denied ever having seen an envelope with a foreign stamp on it. Obviously he'd had no time to cover up for Guy, always supposing they had been in collusion.

'Conchita must have been mistaken!' Guy repeated as they sat down to their evening meal. 'There was a letter from France. Maybe she confused the stamp on that envelope with a Swiss one.'

Lucy knew he was lying, and his suggestion that she phone Tom and ask if he had written to her made the whole thing more, not less, suspicious.

'It isn't that important,' she lied, and changed the conversation.

The following morning, she asked Guy what had happened to her passport.

'Surely it has been returned by now!' she said. 'I really do want to go home, Guy, before Jonnie leaves.'

'Of course you do, darling! I did tell you it had to go back to London, didn't I? Tell you what, I'll e-mail the passport office in London asking them to expedite it as a matter of urgency, or at very least, let me have some idea when we can expect it.' He put an arm round her shoulders and dropped a kiss on top of her hair. 'When is that poor little kid coming to swim?' he asked, changing the subject.

So she had been temporarily diverted but that evening at supper when she remembered the morning conversation and asked him if the passport office had replied to his e-mail, he shook his head.

'I sent a second one before I left the office,' he told her. 'Maybe there will be a reply when I get there in the morning.'

The next afternoon, a Wednesday, Conchita's father pushed ten-year-old Jorge in his heavy wheelchair up the hill from the village to La Finca de Azahar. It was four o'clock and although the air cooled at night, it was still hot and sunny during the day. Lucy left the shade of a lemon tree to go and meet them. At once she was captivated by the boy's huge, liquid brown eyes and long, sweeping lashes. He gave her a beaming smile and in heavily accented English, thanked her for inviting him to her pool.

His father, a pleasant-looking man in his late forties, was wearing his best Sunday suit despite the heat and was inevitably perspiring. Lucy smiled at him and invited him to remove his jacket, which he did with obvious relief.

'Conchita – she *no es possible. Lo siento.*' He suddenly gave her a broad smile almost identical to that of his young son. 'No speak *Inglés!*'

In the wheelchair, the handicapped child grinned mischievously.

'*Papá* has say my sister, Conchita, cannot bring me here today. Her *novio* wish her to go with him to speak with the *Padre*. She very sorry.'

'Well, you certainly speak good English,' Lucy said. 'Conchita told me she would be late back to work this afternoon so I quite understand. As long as you are here to enjoy the pool that is all that matters!'

However, there remained the problem of who was going to support Jorge in the water. His father seemed to think that he could lean over the side and hold the boy by his arms.

'That would be an awful strain on his shoulders and armpits!' Lucy said. 'I will go in with him!'

'*Señora no es possible!*' The man now gabbled in Spanish and when he came to a halt, Jorge translated.

'My *papá* say you very little lady. I ten years – quite big boy. He say no possible you hold. I go to . . . how you say, floor?'

Lucy smiled.

'In English we would say you might sink to the bottom!' She looked at him more carefully. Despite the fact that his legs and arms were painfully thin, his upper body seemed quite sturdy. She herself had lost a great deal of weight after her miscarriage, and even when she was fully fit, she weighed no more than eight stone. Perhaps the father was right and she could not support Jorge's weight.

Unnoticed by any of the three by the pool, Carlos, the gardener, had come to exchange greetings with Jorge's father who was his neighbour. Hearing them discussing the problem, he spoke rapidly in Spanish which young Jorge helpfully translated.

'He make for me very quick the *bastón* with – how do you say – what is on a horse. You permit, señora?'

He mimed a large pole with a harness on the end.

'He and Papa they hold the *bastón* – very good. I go in water, yes?'

As Jorge had forecast, Carlos was back within ten minutes with a hastily made harness which, when the boy removed his outer clothing, fitted neatly round his chest and under his armpits. He had no fear as the two men lifted him out of the chair and lowered him into the shallow end of the pool. A look of pure delight spread over his face, touching Lucy's heart as she saw how much this simple pleasure meant to him. For close on half an hour, he splashed laughing and singing whilst Lucy, his father and Carlos stood on the poolside watching him.

Not one of them saw the figure of Guy approaching. Partly concealed by the lemon tree, he stood looking at them, his eyes narrowed, his fists clenched. The latent anger within him as he observed the scene was, however, not visible as he joined the group. He put his arm round Lucy's shoulders.

'You seem to be having a very jolly time!' In rapid Spanish, he spoke to Jorge who repeatedly called out his thanks: '*Gracias, gracias, señor. Muchas gracias.*'

Lucy turned happily to Jorge's father.

'Perhaps he has been in long enough for a first swim,' she suggested. 'Please do bring Jorge again whenever you have the time. I am so pleased he has enjoyed it so much.'

Guy now addressed him and spoke again in Spanish, too

rapidly for Lucy to understand. The smile that had been on the man's face was no longer to be seen and as, with Carlos' help, he lifted Jorge from the water, the boy, too, looked crestfallen.

What, Lucy wondered, had Guy said to cause their expressions to alter so rapidly?

'Guy, you didn't tell them they couldn't come back . . . ?' she asked in a low voice, suddenly suspicious.

He avoided her gaze as he answered her.

'Of course not! I merely told the fellow that he must telephone first before he brings the boy here in case we have visitors. Obviously we don't want the village hoi-poloi hobnobbing with our friends.'

'What friends?' Lucy asked both shocked and furious at his snobbishness. 'You and your father have only invited clients here since I arrived – and they don't come until dinner time. I can't possibly go shopping every day so what am I to do with so much spare time? It's not as if you have given me the golf lessons you promised,' she continued angrily. 'Anyway, what possible harm can it do if Jorge and his father come here in the afternoon?'

Guy patted her arm placatingly.

'Calm down, sweetheart. I only said they must telephone first to ask if it was in order.'

Lucy's mouth tightened.

'But they don't have a telephone. Conchita told me it was too costly for the number of times they needed to use it. All their friends and family live in the village, as does Jorge's doctor.'

As she turned back to reassure the boy that there was no problem to his enjoying further afternoons in their pool, she realized that Carlos was no longer with them. Taking his pole and harness with him, he had disappeared down the hillside. It was only at that moment she remembered Guy's furious dictate – that she must never speak to Carlos again! It was ridiculous, of course, and she had assumed it was said in an isolated moment of pure jealousy; that it was too unreasonable to be considered seriously and that on reflection next day, Guy must have realized how stupid and unfair it was. When he had given her that fabulous necklace the following evening and begged her forgiveness, she had assumed that he deeply regretted his moment of insanity. Why then was she feeling so uncomfortable because Carlos had hurried away? Surely it would have been more in order for him to greet his employer with at least a *'buenas tardes, señor!'*

'Come, darling,' Guy said linking his arm in hers. 'Pepe has drinks ready for us and the ice will be melting. I'm sure the boy and his father will manage perfectly well without us.'

Jorge and his father did not reappear the next day. Lucy asked Conchita if her brother had suffered any ill effects from the unaccustomed exercise. Conchita looked embarrassed.

'No, no, señora. He very much like the water – he say he never forget so good day and you very kind lady!'

'But he will come here again, Conchita – and you must come with him next time. It was lovely to see him enjoying it so much. I'm sure they told you about the clever harness Carlos made.'

The girl nodded.

'Carlos very good man. All the people in our village have respect for him. He always help the people – very good *carpintero* – mend roof for old people; dig garden for vegetables. You understand?'

Lucy nodded, her eyes thoughtful. She did not want to believe that despite what he had told her, Guy had actually forbidden Conchita's family to bring young Jorge to the pool again.

Conchita understood exactly what had occurred because Carlos had told her on her return that evening from her visit to the Padre, that there were big differences of opinion between the señor and his wife. They had agreed that Señor Guy was not like his father for whom Carlos had worked in harmony for the past ten years. Although the father took little interest in the growing of flowers, he had been pleased with the quality and quantity of fresh vegetables Carlos produced and had even raised his salary. The son, however, showed no interest whatever in Carlos' activities until he had brought his new young wife to the villa. At first, Carlos had shrugged off the suspicion that the señor did not like him bringing flowers every morning to the señora. She had, after all, requested that he do so. But a few weeks after her arrival – the day after she had had the 'accident', as she called it, to her face, the señor had told him in future to take the cut flowers to the kitchen door and not to bother the señora with them. From then until the day young Jorge had come with his father to swim, the señora had barely spoken to him and he resented the fact that the señor must have told her it was not acceptable for her to be friendly with the gardener.

However, Conchita did not consider it correct for her to repeat Carlos's comments, any more than admit that she had overheard the señor shouting at his wife the evening of the accident, and she had no doubt he had struck her, which was how the bruising to the señora's face had occurred. In the short time she had worked for Lucy, she had grown to like and respect her while her dislike of Guy increased. Not wishing Lucy to be upset by the knowledge that Guy had, indeed, told them they must not take advantage of his wife's charitable inclinations, she now said nothing to Lucy of the visit Guy had made to their house; or, more importantly to Carlos's house. If Carlos so much as spoke to the señora again – unless it was to say good morning – he would lose his job.

Hearing of this, Conchita's father had commented: 'The señor is jealous. You are a handsome man, Carlos, with a fine physique . . . and you are younger than he is. You have no grey in your hair and you have the hips of a matador.' He had laughed as he added: 'I would not wish you to give flowers to my wife!'

They had joined in the laughter but Conchita had a deep feeling of unease. Jealousy was an ugly emotion. It could make people do ugly things. She would not want anything really unpleasant to happen to her.

Still very far from certain that Guy had not forbidden the family to return, Lucy decided to say nothing for the time being but wait and see if they did return. Then she would know for certain if she had misjudged him. Meanwhile, she had more pressing matters on her mind. When Guy returned from Marbella that evening, she asked him again if he had had a reply from London about her passport. And if not, had Guy sent yet a third e-mail?

Indeed he had, he told her. He had also tried to telephone but was put in one of the infuriating queues and after fifteen minutes, he had given it up. He would try again next day. It was then Lucy decided to telephone her father and ask him to make enquiries for her. Immediately after the meal was over, she went up to her bedroom to make the call, but no matter where she looked, she could not find her mobile phone. As a last resort, she went out into the garden to see if she could possibly have left it by her lounge chair beneath the lemon tree, but there was no sign of it.

Back in her room, Lucy sat down on the bed and tried to fight the suspicion that Guy had taken it. It seemed nonsensical that he should do so as the house telephones were available to her. On the other hand, as there were no less than three extensions, none were as private as her mobile. She stood up and walked across to the window. Conchita had drawn the curtains but she had not closed the shutters, and parting the drapes, Lucy stared down across the lawn and flowerbeds to where the water in the swimming pool glinted in the dying light of the sun. She was reminded of the poor handicapped boy's immense pleasure when his father and Carlos lowered him into the water; the beatific smile on his face as he had called out his excitement. Inevitably, she also recalled Guy's denial that he had told them not to return. Try as she might, she could not rid herself of the certainty that he had been lying. There was the matter of Carlos, too. He had not come up to the house to enquire what flowers she wanted each day but had chosen the blooms himself and deposited them at the kitchen door. Nor had he greeted her when she had come upon him down by the greenhouses but nodded, and lifting his wheelbarrow, hurried away in the opposite direction.

Feeling slightly sick at the direction her thoughts were taking her, Lucy ran a cold flannel over her face which she then proceeded to make up again before she went back downstairs. Guy would be waiting for her, watching the door, she knew. He was always watching her and she had begun to dread the knowledge that his eyes were following her every move. It was as if he didn't trust her out of his sight.

As she put the brush through her hair and added a light touch of lipstick to her mouth, Lucy braced herself to leave her room and rejoin her husband and father-in-law. It was always a comfort to have Guy's father with them in the evenings. On several occasions, he was invited to dine with clients living in the neighbourhood and then Guy would expect – and get – her undivided attention.

He is smothering me, Lucy thought as she opened the door of the salon and Guy came hurrying towards her. Involuntarily she stiffened as he took her arm and led her across to one of the two large three-seater sofas. La Finca de Azahar was old, but the furnishings were modern, in light, expensive fabrics and dark oak furniture which blended attractively with the proportions of the rooms. Herbert Weaver had told her not long after her arrival, when he had first shown her round the property, that it was worth over two million euros since they had had it refurbished and renovated. It was a lovely house, Lucy conceded, but somehow it lacked a soul. A wave of homesickness overcame her as she thought of the crowded little farmhouse where she had grown up.

I am going home, passport or no passport, she thought as Pepe handed her a cup of coffee. I'll ask Dad to meet me at Gatwick. He's a solicitor, a legal man. He can vouch for the fact that I am his daughter – that my passport is with the authorities in London. I won't tell Guy I'm going. I'll book my ticket and leave him a note. Pablo can drive me to Malaga or perhaps I'll take a taxi, else Pepe might report to Guy where I had gone and Guy might try to stop me leaving.

'Penny for them, my love. You look positively miles away!'

Guy's voice brought her back to the present. Herbert Weaver was looking at her in his usual friendly way.

'Not finding it a bit boring out here, are you, m'dear?' he asked. 'You mustn't let Guy monopolize you, you know.' He turned to grin at his son. 'Like to keep that pretty young wife of yours all to yourself, eh, boy? Can't say I blame you! All the same, mustn't keep her cooped up here all day. What say a trip to Sevilla on Monday, Lucy? I'm lunching with a particularly charming old lady who lives on what was once a bull ranch not too far from there – beautiful house. She's thinking of selling. I'm sure she wouldn't mind if I took you along.'

In any other circumstance, Lucy would have jumped at such an opportunity, but although she now told her father-in-law she would love to join him, her mind was already made up. By next week, unless she was very unlucky and could not get a ticket to England, she would be either on her

way or actually at home. The knowledge sent her heart racing
as she deliberately evoked profiles of each member of her
family – her round, chubby untidy-haired mother who would
hug her half to death; her serious, bespectacled father who
would be gently smiling with pleasure at seeing her; Jonnie,
who could always make her laugh; Jemma, too, with her
sense of humour and freckled Julia . . . Julia, who had never
quite been able to hide her dislike of Guy. It had upset her
at the time of their engagement but now, suddenly, she found
herself wondering if Julia might have had reason to doubt
Guy's character.

As she put down her coffee cup, Guy moved closer to her
on the sofa and put an arm round her shoulders.

'An early night, do you think, darling?' he said softly.

Lucy felt her body stiffen. An early night meant Guy wanted
to make love to her. When they were first married, it had been
a kind of code message between them and she had been every
bit as eager as he to find the privacy of their double bed. Now
lovemaking with Guy was the very last thing she wanted. She
pretended she had not registered the inference.

'Actually, I'm very wide awake. I fell asleep this afternoon
when I was having my siesta. I think I must have slept at least
two hours. You go up, Guy, if you're tired. I'll stay and chat
to your father.'

Turning away to look at the older man, she did not see the
expression on Guy's face as he received her rejection.

Guy was not happy. He had no doubt that Lucy was rebuffing
him – because of the so-called faulty passport which now was
locked in his office desk. He'd known he could not hide it
from her much longer and now he knew she suspected something was amiss. Well, she was not going back to England –
at least, not without him. As far as he knew, she had not been
telephoning Tom Lyford since he had removed her mobile
phone – Pepe had done as he asked and disconnected the three
extensions. The only telephone she could have used was in
his father's study and he was all but one hundred per cent
certain she would not go in there. But she might have written
to Tom – told him she intended to go home and asked him
to fly over from Switzerland to see her. The fellow worked
freelance for his guardian so he was free to come and go as

he pleased. It was an outside chance but one he did not intend to take. If Lucy went home, he would go with her whether she wished it or not.

The possibility that Lucy might not wish it struck a sudden angry core deep inside him. When he came to consider it, she had not been nearly so affectionate these past weeks. When they were first married, it had sometimes been Lucy who had initiated their loving. She would cross a room and tuck her arm in his, drawing him close so that he could feel the warmth of her body and know that she was wanting him, desiring him.

His hold on her arm tightened. His voice carefully modulated, he said: 'You don't have to go to sleep, Lucy. You can read that paperback your sister sent you – the one you started on the plane and never finished?'

He pulled her to her feet and his arm linked tightly through hers, bid his father goodnight. It was on the tip of Lucy's tongue to protest but she did not like to create a scene in front of Guy's father who was smiling benignly at them.

'Well, off you go, you two lovebirds. Don't let me detain you!'

He winked somewhat crudely at Guy whose face remained impassive. It was not until they reached their bedroom and Guy had closed the door behind them that he challenged her.

'What's up, Lucy? Have I done something to upset you? You made it perfectly clear downstairs that you don't want me to make love to you. Maybe you'd care to enlighten me as to why not?'

Lucy tried to walk past him but he barred her way. He fastened his hands round her upper arms and pushed her back against the door. His voice rose a tone as he repeated his question, his face now so close to hers she could see the flecks of brown in his pupils. She felt rather than saw his anger.

'I'm sorry, Guy,' she said in as placating a tone as she could muster. 'but I'm just not in the right mood.' She sought desperately for a reason. 'Perhaps I had too much to eat at dinner – or I've had too much sun. Or possibly . . .'

She got no further before Guy interrupted her. His voice was ice cold as he spat the words at her.

'You mean you're angry with me because I can't get your bloody passport back. You're trying to punish me, aren't you;

as if it's my fault you can't go home? Well, you can stuff that thought back where it came from. I'm your husband, Lucy, not the fucking gardener, and I've every right to make love to my wife if I want to.'

'You've no right to do so if I don't want you to,' she said defiantly. 'That's rape if you do, Guy. That's the law!'

'Not my law!' Guy rejoined and crushed his mouth against her lips. As she stiffened in denial, his grip on her tightened. It was not just his body which was now on fire, it was his mind, his memory taking him back, back, back through the years.

'I'm leaving you, honeybun. I'm really sorry as you're a good kid as kids go and we've had some fun together, haven't we, despite your stuffy old father? But I've the chance of a new life with a man who adores me. He has promised me the earth and he can afford to give it to me. So you see, sweetie, I do have to go . . .'

He could hear his own voice, still only half-broken, begging his mother to take him with her; physically trying to hold her from walking through the door. She had not hesitated.

'Sorry, I really am sorry, but my mind is made up. Let me go, Guy. And that's an order, not a request.'

The desolation as his beloved mother had walked out on him forever was bad enough, but nothing whatever in comparison with the anger that later consumed him, just as Lucy's rejection was consuming him now.

Twenty

The *parador* recommended to Inspector Govern was perched on the side of a hill half a kilometre from the little town of Arcos de la Frontera. The Spanish *paradors* were State-funded, well-run hostelries, and were not only comfortable but also renowned for good food. Having unpacked their overnight cases, showered and changed their clothes, the two men drove down to the small hillside town to meet the lawyer's informant, the former member of the Guardia Civil.

Despite his very limited command of the English language, the former policeman, seventy-five-year-old Daniel Estrada, was more than happy to pass on such memories as he had retained. Things were very different forty years ago, he said as the three of them sat down at a table on the pavement outside the one and only bar. Govern ordered a bottle of wine and the old man told them he was able to earn a little extra money in the summer driving tourists around in his ancient taxi.

'Is that the hotel the Englishman, Señor Herbert Weaver, converted from a ranch back in the seventies?' Govern asked.

Indeed it was, the former policeman informed them. There were few building regulations to speak of in those days and in any case, the English señor had quite enough in his pocket to open doors and shut mouths, as he put it. Handouts, which meant bribery, were very much the order of the day if one came upon unwelcome restrictions. That was what had taken place when the señor's son had been accused of strangling the Latvian woman.

As Govern poured him a second glass of wine, Daniel told them that the woman had frequented the bars in Marbella. To one of these, whose name he could not immediately recall, the fifteen-year-old boy had driven on the new scooter his father had given him for his birthday, and approached the woman. Apparently he had been told by a school friend, correctly as it happened, that she earned a living as a *prostituta*. She had no papers and no proof of identity so was treated as a vagrant which, of course, helped the defence's case. After his arrest, there had been a considerable number of postponements whilst discussions went on behind the scenes, during which time the fifteen-year-old boy was allowed to return with his father to live at home. People in the village thought he should have been kept in prison until a verdict was reached but . . .

The old man shrugged his shoulders and rubbed the first finger and thumb of his right hand together. Eventually, the case was passed to the *Audiencia de Cádiz*, he related, and the appeal was thrown out on the grounds of insufficient evidence.

Only just able to conceal his intense excitement at this confirmation of the lawyer's story of Weaver's juvenile crime, Govern asked his informant for further details.

'But there was evidence of the boy's guilt, wasn't there?' he persisted.

The man nodded. At the trial, two witnesses had come forward saying they saw the youngster leave the bar with the woman; a third said he had overheard the two discussing the woman's fee for her services. Most tellingly, a woman who had been on her balcony above the alley where the two had gone for privacy, heard them arguing; then the prostitute had started laughing and the boy had become very angry. As the onlooker went back into her apartment, she had heard a scream. Half an hour later, the Latvian woman was found dead in the alley. She had been strangled.

'Of course, they did not have such modern aids as DNA evidence in those days,' Govern said wryly as he and Beck made their way back to the *parador*. The inspector had given Daniel Estrada a generous donation towards repairs to his ageing taxi, and they had been waved on their way with exhortations to ask for a Señor and Señora MacGregor who were known to frequent the bar at the *parador* every evening. They had, apparently, been friendly with the Weavers in the days before the hotel had been built so might well have more information about the family. Govern and Beck must ask the bartender who spoke excellent English to point the couple out.

Beck was still finding it hard to believe that the case against the boy had been dropped.

'There must have been clues,' he said as he steered the car up the narrow dusty road leading to the *parador*.

'Probably were, such as fibres from the murderer's clothes,' Govern agreed, 'but whilst our friends at home in Forensics would have looked for such clues, I doubt the likes of Señor Daniel Estrada would have noticed or even bothered to look, since the unfortunate victim was a prostitute as well as an immigrant – probably an illegal one at that.'

It was seven in the evening when Beck and Govern reached the *parador*, and after a quick wash, they went down to the bar where the middle-aged bartender was happy to serve his first customers of the evening. He spoke excellent English as well as French, German and Italian, as he informed them proudly when they complimented him on his accent. It was necessary, he explained as many nationalities stayed there. After Govern had told the man to pour himself a drink as well, he asked him if by any chance he knew of an English family by the name of Weaver who used to live in Arcos de la Frontera some thirty or more years previously. The bartender was unable to oblige but told them if they returned to the bar after they had dined, almost certainly the Scottish Señor and Señora MacGregor would be there. They had a small villa within walking distance from the *parador*, he explained and because the señora was no longer young and she disliked cooking, they came each night to the restaurant for their evening meal, after which they enjoyed a brandy and coffee at the bar.

'They have been here many, many years,' he told them. 'They have come from Scotland, where it is always raining, to our sunshine. The señora has a problem with her bones!'

Beck noticed that Govern was unusually silent as they ate their meal and that he kept looking at the entrance doors to see if the MacGregors had arrived.

When finally they did so – an unpretentious-looking couple in their early seventies – he finally turned to Beck and said: 'We're in luck, my boy! As my lawyer said, it stands to reason they will have known the Weavers before Herbert Weaver moved himself and his business affairs to Marbella. I don't suppose thirty-odd years ago there would have been that many English speaking people living out here. On the Costa, maybe, but as I see it, this is really only a halfway stop for visitors to Seville.'

'And for golfers!' Beck said, grinning. He'd seen a brochure in the lobby extolling the excellence of an eighteen-hole course adjoining the *parador*. It had been constructed by Sevi Ballesteros in what had once been the vast acreage of land belonging to the family who had owned the former *palacio*.

It was a good moment for him to remind his boss of the promise he had made that he get a game at some time. Govern was nodding contentedly, anticipating the information he was certain he would obtain from the MacGregors. An hour later as the four of them sat in comfortable chairs round one of the tables in the bar, his patience was rewarded. The wife, Isobel MacGregor was even more voluble than her husband. A thin, grey-haired women bent painfully by arthritis, she was clearly delighted to have someone other than her dour Scottish husband to talk to. They had known the Weavers very well, she said.

'Herbert was a workaholic. He wasn't particularly rich when he brought his wife out here in the early seventies but he had certainly made a packet by the time he left. That was in the late eighties or thereabout. Helen, Herbert's bride, was years younger than her husband – about twenty, would you say Angus?'

'And in the family way. Told me once he had to make an honest woman of her – she was a debutante, you see, doing temporary secretarial work for him. One night he had a bit too much to drink and bedded her!'

'Really, Angus,' his wife reproved him. 'The inspector doesn't need to hear that sort of gossip!'

'On the contrary, anything at all you can tell me might be useful,' Govern said, his curiosity deepening. Isobel MacGregor needed no further encouragement.

'So Helen had the baby – a boy. I remember the English nurse they had at that time – when you had your prostate done, Angus – saying what a pity it was Helen wouldn't feed the baby or look after him. Herbert had to get a nanny to take care of the child. He was a beautiful little boy, huge grey eyes with dark lashes and in no time at all, had a mop of dark chestnut brown curls. That's when Isobel started to take an interest in him.'

'Doted on him, more like!' Angus MacGregor said laconically.

His wife nodded.

'Yes, well she did and she didn't. She loved showing him off to people who stopped to admire the child; and it helped that he wasn't a bit shy like some kids. He'd smile and coo and as he got older, he'd chatter away ten to the dozen and Isobel's friends would laugh and tease him.'

Angus now interrupted her.

'Wasn't all sunshine!' he said in his clipped manner of speech. 'She'd get bored with him after a bit and hand him back to the nanny and he'd yell his head off. Hated being parted from her.'

For a moment, they were both silent, remembering events of three decades ago.

'The marriage wasn't a happy one,' Isobel continued. 'Well, you couldn't expect it, could you? Herbert marrying her because he had to. He wasn't in love with her and Angus used to say he had a mistress in Seville – a Spanish woman nearer his own age. So he was often away from home, and as the boy, Guy, got older, his mother would go to parties taking him with her as her escort. You would have thought the boy would be bored but he was such a handsome, winning little fellow, everyone fell over backwards spoiling him. Not that he cared for anyone but his mother who he worshipped.'

'Bit unsavoury if you ask me!' Angus interposed.

Isobel did not disagree with him.

'Yes, well, by the time Guy was twelve, he was taller than his father. Helen was quite short and she used to hang on her son's arm and treat him like a lover. That was until Wilbur Hunter came on the scene.'

'Hudson,' her husband corrected her. 'American – came from Texas.'

'Yes, and he fell hook, line and sinker for Isobel. Next thing, without any warning to any of us, she ups and disappears with Wilbur to the States. She wrote to me once, saying she and Wilbur were married; that he was so rich she could quite literally buy anything in the world she wanted. That didn't surprise me. What did surprise me was that she never mentioned her son and as far as we know, she never went back to England or came to Spain to visit him.'

Govern's eyes were thoughtful.

'So he must have had a very nasty shock!' he commented.

'Certainly did,' Angus said nodding. 'Sent the lad clean off the rails.'

Seeing the questioning look on Govern's and Beck's faces, Isobel enlightened them.

'It was all hushed up at the time. Seems he got drunk one night and picked up this prostitute in a seedy bar down by the harbour in Marbella. Herbert maintained that what happened next was the woman's own fault. According to him, Guy had the money to pay her but whether because he was still only a youngster or for some other reason of her own, although she had agreed to the assignation and went to the secluded alley near the bar where she took all her clients, she suddenly changed her mind and told him to get lost. Maybe the boy simply wasn't man enough for the job and she laughed at him. Whatever the reason, he was stronger than she was and he went berserk and raped her. The next day she was found dead – she had been strangled.'

'Nasty business!' Angus said. 'Felt sorry for Weaver – police all over the place and the boy carted off to the police station. Chaps in the bar had identified Guy, you see, so there wasn't any doubt he'd done it.'

Isobel shook her head.

'The case against him was thrown out on appeal, Inspector!' she said. 'Herbert had a great deal of influence with the police. He'd been greasing their palms whenever he'd needed to flout the building regulations, such as they were. Herbert got hold of a damn good lawyer and next thing, the case against the boy was dropped. I seem to recall Herbert saying it was on the grounds that he was an innocent kid, vulnerable, taunted by a much older woman who thought fit to humiliate him because he was not able to do what he'd paid for. Herbert got him acquitted and packed him off to a boarding school in England. Soon after that he sold his house and the hotel and moved away – to Marbella, I think it was. We didn't keep in touch and Helen, Guy's mother, never wrote to me again. She must be getting on a bit now.'

Beck did not need to see his boss's face to know that he

was looking like the proverbial cat which had found the cream. Everything the MacGregors had told them went to confirm Govern's belief that Guy Weaver was capable of murder; had once actually committed murder.

'Tomorrow, Beck . . .' Govern said, 'I'm really sorry about the golf but I think it's time I interviewed our Mr Guy Weaver again. Seeing he is – very conveniently – only a short distance from here, it would be a pity not to take advantage of the fact; save us a trip to London when we get home, eh?'

He's like a fixated terrier with a cornered rat, Beck thought as they said goodnight to the MacGregors and went up to bed. To think it was one thing, but he took good care not to relay it to his boss.

Twenty-One

Lucy lay unmoving in the big double bed. Guy had gone into their bathroom and for a few merciful moments, she was alone. She was lying perfectly still, her whole body too bruised for any movement to be comfortable. Most of all, she would have liked a bath but after he had flung her down on the bed, he had gone into the shower and shut the door behind him. But it was not just her body he had violated, he had also destroyed her love for him. After what had just transpired, she knew she could never, ever trust him again.

It was as if Guy was two separate people, she thought, unaware that tears were running slowly down her cheeks. In place of the tenderness, the devoted care that had been such an important part of his loving, was a cruel, remorseless brute who had not cared how much he hurt or humiliated her.

She was weeping freely now, crying for the horrible way in which her marriage was ending, as end it must now that Guy had revealed the ugly side of his character. It had happened once before when he had struck her the last time, but that blow was insignificant set against the vicious way he had just abused her body. She would go home – but how could she be sure of getting there safely without her passport? Perhaps if Guy were repentant in the morning as he had been after hitting her, she should pretend to forgive him so that he did not realize she was about to leave him and would hand over her passport when it was returned from London.

The bathroom door opened and quickly she closed her eyes, feigning sleep. She could neither bear Guy's apologies nor, as he had done not long since, his threats to harm her if she stopped loving him. At the time, frightened although she had been, his words had made little sense. Love was not something a person could turn on and off.

To her intense relief, Guy made no move to touch or kiss

her, or even to speak. He lay facing away from her, his body not touching hers. Making every effort to control her breathing, Lucy lay rigid beside him until, ten minutes later, she knew he was asleep. Taking the utmost care, she slid out of bed and crept into the bathroom. Using only a flannel for fear the sound of water running would wake Guy, she washed herself and put on the towelling dressing gown hanging on the back of the door. More than anything in the world, she wanted to leave the room, leave the house, go out into the cool night air where she need have no fear Guy could reach out and touch her.

Moving silently on bare feet, Lucy crept past the bed and made her way to the bedroom door. She turned the handle but the door did not open. She tried a second time before realizing that Guy must have locked it when he'd come into the room. In the semi-darkness, she reached for the door key but it was no longer there. She knew Guy must have done this deliberately.

As if on cue, she heard his voice, not loud but harsh: 'Thinking of leaving me, Lucy?'

She choked back the fear that his voice evoked.

'Of course not. I couldn't sleep so I was going down to the kitchen to make myself a cup of tea!'

'Well, you'd better think again because you aren't going anywhere, and the sooner you realize that the easier life will be for you.'

It was on the tip of Lucy's tongue to ask if he was threatening her, but knowing the answer, she decided to stay as calm as she could and not to be controversial. Guy was obviously not in his right mind and in the morning, she would ask his father to telephone their family doctor. The more thought she gave to the matter, the more likely this seemed – his crazy assumption that she might be attracted to the gardener, Carlos; his unexplained reluctance to introduce her to their friends and neighbours; the theft of her letter from Tom – and she was in no doubt now that he had taken it.

Keeping as far away from Guy's recumbent form as she could, Lucy returned to her side of the bed and tried not to give way to the fear that was threatening to overcome her. She recalled an incident when she and Vanessa had been at the language school when one of the Malay students had suddenly for no obvious reason, produced a *crease* and stabbed the Turkish student sitting next to him with the Malayan sword. He had been quickly overpowered by the other students and the Turkish boy had survived the attack. Nevertheless, they had all been very shaken by the incident, not least because it had come without reason or warning; and they had been told much later that the student was in a psychiatric hospital where he might remain indefinitely as he was not responding to treatment.

Was Guy mad? Lucy asked herself. Was the Guy she had seen tonight the real man or was the real one the devoted husband she had married; the generous, caring lover who was to have been her partner for life?

She was still pondering the question when she fell into an uneasy sleep. She awoke to hear Guy once more in the bathroom and feigned sleep again as he came back into the room and dressed. He did not approach the bed and as he shut the door behind him, Lucy let out her breath which she had not been aware she was holding. Her whole body ached and as memory flooded back of the brutal way in which Guy had raped her, she lay back on her pillow and wept. More than anything in the world, she wanted her mother. She needed to go home. Once again, she made the decision to ignore the loss of her passport, telephone her father and fly home, today if she could book a flight. Surely, she comforted herself, one of the many aeroplanes returning to England would have one spare seat?

She glanced at her bedside clock. It was eight o'clock. Guy would be downstairs now having breakfast with his father. At any moment, Conchita would arrive with her breakfast. She would be up and dressed by then and could ask the maid to go down to the village post office and use their telephone to book a taxi to take her to the airport at ten o'clock. Guy and his father never left for the office as late as that. If, by any chance, Guy was still at home and the taxi arrived, she would say it was to take her into Marbella to the hairdresser.

It took Lucy less than five minutes to put on a clean dress, brush her hair and make up her face. This done, she opened her dressing table drawers and took out a minimum of clothing that would fit into her big, raffia shopping bag which was all she intended to take with her. Her heart beating furiously as her excitement rose in proportion to her fear that Guy might come upstairs and guess what she was about to do, Lucy forced herself to consider the problems she might meet trying to get back into her home country without identification. She remembered her driving licence still tucked into the back flap of her wallet. There were, too, all her credit cards; the pink one from Boots, the chemist; the vivid blue one from the Co-op where her mother liked to do her big weekend shop; the silver MasterCard. Surely they must prove she was indeed who she professed to be and not an illegal immigrant?

There was a knock on the door and Lucy called, 'Enter.'

Conchita knocked again and Lucy hurried to the door to open it for her. Her heart lurched as the door remained firmly closed and she realized that Guy must have locked it again when he went downstairs. For a few seconds, she was uncertain how to deal with this new situation. Presumably Guy did not intend her to go without any breakfast even if it was his plan to keep her a prisoner in her room. Quite possibly, he would come upstairs presently and bring the tray in with him. He would expect her to be angry, upset, accusing; but, she decided, she would busy herself at her dressing table and pretend she had not known the door was locked.

'Just leave the tray outside, will you please, Conchita!' she called out in as normal a voice as possible. 'You can come up and collect it later.'

'But, señora, your coffee will become cold. *Momentito!* I bring it to you.'

She put the tray down on the landing and tried to open the door. Astonished to find it locked, for such a thing had never happened before, she called out again.

'Señora, if you will unlock the door . . .'

Biting her lip, Lucy forced herself to speak sharply.

'Just do as I say and leave it on the landing. I don't want my breakfast yet.'

Hearing the maid's footsteps receding down the marble staircase, Lucy drew a breath of relief. It was now nearly half past eight and if Guy were coming to see her before he went to work, he would be up at any moment. She went over to her dressing table and deliberately tipped over a bottle of suntan lotion. With a box of tissues nearby, she had every reason to be engrossed when he finally unlocked the door and came into the room. She looked as casually as she could over her shoulder.

'Clumsy me, I've tipped suntan lotion over absolutely everything . . . dreadful mess,' she muttered. Behind her, Guy crossed the room and put her breakfast tray on the table by the window. He seemed taken aback by the casual, uncritical tone of her voice.

'Your coffee will be getting cold!' he said finally. 'I'm leaving for the office now, Lucy. I'll try to be back for lunch. I'm sorry if you are going to be bored but that's your own fault, not mine. I'll take you down to the pool after lunch. Meanwhile, here's an English paper – yesterday's, I'm afraid. But it will give you something to look at.'

'Thanks for the paper but I think after I have had my breakfast, I might go back to bed,' Lucy said, keeping to her preconceived plan. 'I have a terrible headache – too much sun yesterday, I suppose. I was stupid enough not to wear a hat.'

Momentarily, Guy looked confused.

'Then you won't mind if I lock the door. You won't want the servants coming in and bothering you.'

He seemed to be waiting for her look of surprise or her objections but there were none. He stood watching her mopping ineffectually at the mess on the top of her dressing table, seemingly quite relaxed despite what he had done to her.

'Lucy!' he said suddenly. 'Do you still love me?'

Her hesitation was so brief, she saw that he had hardly noticed. She turned her head and gave him a gentle smile.

'But of course I do, Guy. Whatever makes you think I might not?' She turned back to her dressing table so that he could not look into her face. 'If you are worrying about last night, forget it, Guy. I'm your wife and I had no right to refuse you. Let's forget it, shall we?'

Guy looked awkward and for a moment Lucy worried he did not believe what she was saying. He moved towards her but then obviously decided against kissing her.

'So I'll be on my way,' he said casually. 'Take care of yourself.'

Lucy's face was filled with bitterness as she repeated Guy's words to herself when she heard the key turn in the lock. Take care of herself she most certainly would – and it would be far, far away from this stranger who she no longer recognized as the man she had loved so much. But had it been love – real love? she asked herself as she poured out the now cooling coffee? There was no doubt she had been physically in love – wanting Guy every bit as much as he had wanted her. Although she had had the occasional fling with one or other of the students at university, none had been more than a brief affair without deep emotional attachment. With Guy it had all been so different, so intense, so magical as he had taught her how to know and use and get pleasure from her body. To give pleasure, too. Her honeymoon had been unforgettably magical. Memories of those weeks in the Seychelles had been marred only by the terrible news of poor darling Vanessa's death the day they had returned home.

Oh, Van, wherever you are now, help me to get away, she prayed silently. I shan't feel safe until I'm out of Gatwick airport. When I tell Dad what has happened, he won't let Guy into the house if he does try to follow me.

Conchita knocking once more on her door interrupted her thoughts. She hurried to it and asked: 'Have the señores left the house yet, Conchita?'

'*Si, si, señora!*' the maid said, adding anxiously: 'Why do you not permit me to enter, señora? I have come to collect your tray. Are you not well?'

Lucy realized that if she was to embroil Conchita in her plan to get to the airport, she must tell her at least part of the truth.

'I am well enough, Conchita,' she told the maid. 'But the señor and I have had a disagreement. I wish to go home to see my family and he does not wish me to leave him. Do you understand what I am saying?'

As Conchita had waited downstairs behind the heavy oak hatstand in the hallway for Lucy to call her back to take in her breakfast, she had seen Guy hurrying upstairs; heard him unlock the bedroom door from the outside..

'I think the señor may have taken the bedroom key with him by mistake. Do you think you can possibly find another one? Maybe Pepe has a spare key – in case of fire or some-thing? I feel sure there is more than one for each room.'

'*Encontrará la llave,*' Conchita said at once, forgetting her English in her excitement, certain as she was that Pepe would indeed have duplicate keys for all the rooms. If the señora was running away from her husband, she, Conchita, would do whatever she could to assist her, even if she did lose her job. In any case, she would not want to work at the Finca de Azahar if the señora was no longer there.

Pepe was reluctant at first to part with his duplicate room key, but he was quickly won over by Conchita's smile. Were it not for the fact that she already had a fiancé, he would have been tempted to set his cap at her albeit she was so much younger than himself.

Returning to the señora's bedroom, Conchita unlocked the door, thinking as she did so how much she disliked the señor ever since he had told her father that if he didn't want a summons for trespass, he had better not show his face in the garden again; that he and his father were not a charity for deformed children such as Jorge and he'd had no right whatever to take advantage of the señora's charitable offering.

Deformed children! That had been said in front of poor Jorge and hurt him most dreadfully. No, she would offer the señora whatever assistance she could.

'I will give you some money for the telephone,' Lucy said when she had explained to Conchita she must not use the instrument in the study lest Guy had had it linked in some way to his office phone. She went over to her bedside table where she kept her wallet. For a moment, she did not believe that it had disappeared, and jostled the letters from her family which she kept there, certain that the wallet must be beneath them. Her heart sinking when it failed to reveal itself, she went to her dressing table and searched through the drawers, knowing in her heart that she would not find it. She was in no doubt that Guy had taken it – perhaps whilst she had been in the bathroom; or last night whilst she was asleep.

The realization hit her that it was not just a telephone call or indeed, a taxi ride she could not now pay for, but that her credit card was missing and therefore she would have no means of buying her air ticket without it. Without money she was truly Guy's prisoner. Would her father-in-law collude with Guy? He had never yet failed to be friendly and well-mannered towards her. On the contrary, he had seemed delighted to see his son so happily married. On the other hand, she could not be certain he would stand up to Guy and if he did not, or even debated the matter, Guy would be aware of her intention to escape back to England – for that is how she now thought of it. Escape! But how, without a credit card or money? Close to tears, she looked helplessly at Conchita.

'I cannot leave after all!' she said. 'I have lost my wallet.' Seeing the girl did not understand, she translated as best she could.

Conchita looked at first shocked and then stepped forward and put her arms round Lucy.

'Please not to cry, señora. Is possible you go. I will talk with *mi padre*. He have many euros in the bank in Marbella – he save for better wheelchair for Jorge. This cost many, many euros but soon he have enough and Jorge can ride to Marbella, see the sea and the shops.'

Lucy was deeply touched but despite her desperate need for money, she did not feel she could accept Conchita's suggestion of using the savings for Jorge's electric wheelchair. She would, of course, send money immediately from England, but suppose she never reached home and Guy caught up with her after she had purchased a ticket? The money would be lost and she would have no way to repay it.

Suddenly, she remembered her jewellery. Had Guy hidden that, too? It would be security for Conchita's father should anything happen to her. It came as no surprise to find that the jewel case, too, was missing. She was on the point of despair when she remembered that although last night Guy had torn the dress from her shoulders, he had not touched the enamelled pendant round her neck. She had only become aware of it when she was in bed after he had raped her. She had removed it as quickly as she could, feeling irrationally as if it was Guy's hands round her neck, and pushed it under her pillow.

Hurrying now to the bed, she lifted the pillow and saw that the pendant was still there. Scooping it up, she crossed the room to the wide-eyed maid and showed it to the girl.

'I will give this to your father. I am reasonably certain it will be worth no less than five hundred Euros. If . . . if anything happens . . . if for some reason I could not replace the money you say your father can lend me, he must sell this. I could not bear it if I thought Jorge had to wait longer for his chair because of me.'

At first Conchita protested that this security was unnecessary but when Lucy made it clear she would not otherwise accept a loan, she put it in her pocket. Her eyes were thoughtful when Lucy asked her once more to telephone for a taxi.

'Pepe and Pablo will know if the taxi is coming here for you, señora,' she said. 'The señor will ask them, no? Then he may think you have driven to Malaga to the airport. He has telled Pablo he will be returning for the lunch today. Perhaps he go anyway to the airport.'

She is almost certainly right, Lucy thought, dismayed. There was no certainty she would be given an early flight and if she was still at the airport . . .

'Señora, I have good plan. You stay in my house. Maybe tomorrow you go . . . or the day follows tomorrow. By this time, *mi padre* have the euros for you. Our house is not *grande* but it is clean. The señor will not think to look for you there.'

Lucy was once more close to tears. Conchita's suggestion was indeed an excellent one and as the morning had progressed, she had begun to feel the repercussions of the night before. Her whole body ached and she knew she was badly bruised both internally and externally and that it hurt her even to cross the room. A long, anxious journey home, even if she was lucky enough to get an early ticket would in itself be an ordeal.

Conchita was beaming happily.

'You will come to my house, yes?' she said. 'I have thinked how you go. I go home for siesta in two hours. Do you think it possible you go on the bicycle, señora? I give you my clothes and when you go on the bicycle, Pablo will think you are me. If I go without he see me down the hill by the path, I will be home to greet you.'

As she and Conchita exchanged clothes, Lucy knew she was too tired, too overwrought, too frightened to think of a better way to escape from this nightmare. The tears now running freely down her cheeks, she took a last look round the room where she and Guy had shared both the most loving and most horrible moments of her life, and followed Conchita downstairs.

Twenty-Two

It was not yet midday when Guy decided to return to the Finca. All morning he had sat at his desk unable to concentrate on the work awaiting his attention. He could not believe how utterly thoughtless he had been locking Lucy into their bedroom. What, he asked himself over and over again, could he have been thinking of when he turned the key in the lock and put it in his pocket? Clearly he could not keep her a prisoner indefinitely. His father would want to know where she was; the servants would suppose she was ill until her maid, Conchita, told them otherwise. Her parents would want to know why she had not telephoned them; written to them. It was even possible that persistent young former boyfriend, Tom Lyford, would come looking for her.

For an hour or two he had tried to think up some other way to prevent Lucy from running away – leaving him just as his mother had done all those years ago. He must have been out of his mind, he told himself, to have raped her the night before. No one knew better than he did how it had been his love which had captivated her; his passion, too, but not rapacious sex. As his love for her had grown, so too had his possessiveness, and with that, so had his fear grown that she might leave him.

As the morning wore on and he was able to think more objectively, he realized that his actions must be quickly reversed. He must go home, unlock the door and talk to Lucy calmly; explain his fears; reiterate his love for her; beg her to forgive him. Somehow he must convince her she could trust him. He would promise to return her passport, the contents of her wallet, her own key to the bedroom door to keep. If that were insufficient to win her forgiveness, he would offer to book them both air tickets home so she could see her family.

At last, cheered by such thoughts, of bringing about a new

start to their relationship, he drove quickly up the hill to the
Finca and without stopping to inform Pablo of his return, he
took the stairs two at a time and halted breathless in front of
the bedroom door. As he was about to put the key in the lock,
he saw that the door was very slightly ajar. His heart jolted
as he edged the door open with his foot. There was no sign
of Lucy in the room. The bed had been neatly made, the
dressing-table glass cleaned and shining in a shaft of sunlight
from the uncurtained window. Lucy's negligee lay on the dark
wood chest at the foot of the double bed, her feather mules
side by side beneath it.

His heart thudding painfully, Guy strode forward and opened
the bathroom door. This room also had been cleaned, tidied,
polished – towels hanging neatly on the holders, chrome
fittings gleaming; bottles of bath essence standing in neat rows
on the tiled shelves. In the spotless mirror, Guy suddenly saw
his own reflection, his face distorted by mixed emotions –
fear, anger, distress, disbelief. How was it possible that Lucy
was not where he had left her? Who had opened the door and
let her out?

Anger was now uppermost as he raced downstairs to
confront Pablo. The servant was the only person other than
himself to possess a key. Not a little frightened by the look
on his employer's face, Pablo explained that not long after
the señor had left the house, Conchita had come to tell him
the señora had locked herself into her room and could not
find her key. Of course, he had lent her his duplicate knowing
the señor would not wish him to do otherwise than assist his
wife.

Guy released his hold of the man, aware his reasoning was
both truthful and reasonable. Where, he demanded, was the
señora now? And where was her maid, Conchita?

Pablo tried not to show his surprise as he replied. Conchita
always went home at midday. Her duties were resumed when
she returned to the Finca at four o'clock to give the señora
her afternoon tea. Later, she would turn down the beds, draw
the curtains, put fresh water by the bedsides and help the
señora change for *la cena*.

But the señora? Guy asked. Where was she?

Still truthful, the servant replied that he had no idea.
According to Conchita, she had left the señora drinking coffee

under the lemon tree by the swimming pool. Perhaps Carlos
would have seen her leave?

Swearing under his breath, Guy strode out of the house into
the garden. He found Carlos skimming the surface of the pool
water. He, too, had seen the señora in her chair earlier that
morning but after Conchita had brought her coffee, she had
gone back into the house. Conchita had told him the señora
would not be back in her chair as she was going for a walk,
so he could go ahead and clean the pool without fear of
disturbing her.

His concern now deepening, Guy strode back into the house,
his eyes thoughtful. Could Lucy have decided to leave him
having gained her freedom from her room? Where had she
gone? Had she taken any of her clothes? She had no money
because he had emptied her wallet and removed her jewel
case, so she could not have taken a taxi to the airport and
bought herself a ticket home.

Suddenly Guy halted in his tracks as he realized Lucy could
have done exactly that. He had thought to have covered all
eventualities when he took her passport and, this morning, her
money, credit cards and jewel case, but, he now realized, he
had forgotten the pendant she had been wearing when he raped
her last night. Of all the people in the world, none knew better
than he how much money it would fetch if Lucy tried to sell
it. More than enough to buy a ticket to England – and still
pay for a taxi to the airport.

Within minutes, Guy had reached their bedroom, pulled out
the dressing table drawer and found it empty. His heart plum-
meted. He was no longer in any doubt whatever that Lucy
had finally left him; was probably already at Malaga airport
awaiting a plane to take her home. But it might not be too
late to stop her. In the Sagaris, he could reach the airport in
twenty minutes. Pablo would have known had Lucy ordered
a taxi to collect her. He could assume, therefore that she walked
down to the village and ordered a taxi to pick her up there.
Then she would have used up more time finding a *joyero* to
buy her pendant. She had not left the house until after she'd
had coffee at eleven o'clock, so there was every chance he
could catch up with her.

A quarter of an hour later, Guy was on the motorway behind
the wheel of his Sagaris. He was not aware of it but he had

bitten through his bottom lip and a trickle of blood ran down his chin. His face, white beneath his tan, was taut with nervous tension. His knuckles, too, showed white as his grip tightened on the leather covering of the steering wheel. He swore both in English and Spanish as a large coach pulled out on to the fast lane forcing him to slow his speed. He hooted furiously but the driver made no move to return to the middle lane. He drove as near as he dared to the back of the coach where he knew the driver must see him but still to no avail. For the third time, he pressed determinedly on the horn, this time keeping it pressed down. Only then did the coach swing back into the middle lane.

As Guy raced past, he was vaguely aware of the gaping stares of the coach passengers – tourists on a day trip to Seville, judging by the sticker in the back window. Such was the tension in Guy's body he could not have cared less if the whole coachload had gone over the side of a cliff and killed the lot of them, including the driver. He put his foot harder down on the accelerator and paid no attention to the speedometer as it crept up to a hundred and twenty miles an hour. He was past the turn offs to Fuengirola and Benalmadena and was soon passing the sight of Torremolinos far below him on his right. His heartbeat now quickened yet again as his thoughts turned from the coach driver to the reason he was making this journey.

If Lucy had already gone through into the departure lounge, he might have to bribe his way past the check-in desks. He might even have to buy a ticket in order to get into the departure lounge. But first he'd have to find a gap amongst the coaches and cars outside Departures where he could leave the Sagaris. There was no parking allowed there and doubtless he'd be heavily fined. He didn't care. Nothing mattered but the need to prevent Lucy leaving him. They'd been so happy at first. Surely they could be as happy again? How could their marriage have gone so wrong? He loved her; he had never stopped loving her. Was it his fault Lucy had stopped loving him? Whatever he had done, he would make it up to her. He'd drive her back to the Finca, take her up to their room and make love to her as ardently as he had on their honeymoon. He would take her on another honeymoon – to India; to Australia; to wherever she wanted to go. He would agree they should have another baby if that was what he must do to make her love him again the way she used to do.

Guy's face softened and his body relaxed as he thought of those magical days and nights when all Lucy had wanted was to be in his arms. He glanced at his watch. In another ten minutes he would be at the airport. The amount of traffic had increased and it was only with difficulty he could keep up his speed. Quite far ahead of him, he could see a blue sports Peugeot waiting to pull out on to his lane. If he slowed a little, there might just be time for it to do so but he had no intention of slowing. The Peugot driver could not know it but every second counted if he, Guy, was to prevent Lucy deserting him. His foot hit the floorboard as the speedometer reached a hundred and thirty miles as hour.

The Frenchman in the waiting Peugot saw the Sagaris coming. He knew the car was travelling fast but with no idea of its excessive speed, reckoned he just had time to squeeze his way out in front of it. He was meeting his wife on an incoming plane from Paris and was running late, so he, too, needed to get to the airport fast.

Unable to believe what he was seeing, Guy watched the Peugeot as it inched out of the approach road. The middle and slow lanes were both nose to tail with vehicles. Even before it happened, he knew a collision was unavoidable. There was no hope whatever that he could brake in time to prevent it but he had a faint glimmer or hope that the driver of the Peugeot would appreciate the danger in time and stop his car before it was fully on to the fast lane. With luck, he might just squeeze past if he was quick enough . . .

'Go faster, faster,' Guy whispered to himself as the distance between him and the car in front diminished. 'Don't hit it! Watch what you are doing! You can't have an accident! You have to get to the airport . . . stop Lucy leaving . . . Lucy . . . Lucy . . .'

Her name was on his lips as he died.

Lucy was sitting in the tiny back yard of Jorge's home teaching him how to play clock patience. She had been made more than welcome by Conchita's father who had not seemed in the least put out by her unexpected arrival. As for Jorge, he was beaming with pleasure at the thought of spending a whole afternoon and evening with the pretty English señora. With no sign of Guy appearing in the village to search for her, Lucy began to relax and managed to eat some of the spaghetti bolognese Conchita had cooked for their lunch.

She had barely finished eating when Carlos came hurrying down the hill. Perspiring freely from his exertions, he burst into the house. She could hear voice, deeply agitated, but speaking too rapidly for her to translate despite carrying clearly through the open kitchen window. The boy, too, was listening and Lucy heard him gasp as he turned to look at her, a shocked expression on his young face.

'What is it, Jorge?' Lucy asked. 'What are they saying? What has happened?'

Somewhere deep inside her, she knew whatever bad news there was somehow involved Guy. A cold shaft of fear shot through her body. Had he discovered where she was and was on his way to fetch her?

Conchita came out of the house, her face taut with agitation. She went past her young brother without speaking to him and knelt down in front of Lucy. Taking both her mistress's hands in hers, she said:

'Carlos has brought us news – bad news, señora!' She swallowed as if finding it hard to speak. '*La policia* have come to the villa. They look for you.' Seeing the expression on Lucy's face, she added quickly: 'No, señora, not because the señor has asked it . . .' She broke off and only with difficulty managed to continue: 'The señor has been in a *accidente*. He was driving many times more quick than is permitted and *la policia* were following him. He have left the motorway and is on the big road not far from the *aeropuerto* when a French car comes to the road from the side before him. He is going too quick and there was a *accidente*. It is very bad. Carlos hear *la policia* telling to Pablo.' She gripped Lucy's hands more tightly. 'Señora, all the people are . . . *muerto*.' She made the sign of the cross, as indeed did Jorge.

Lucy looked at her uncomprehendingly.

'You mean the people in the French car who collided with my husband have been killed?'

Conchita shook her head.

'*Si, si, señora*. Also the señor. He is taken to the hospital but for no good. She crossed herself again as she whispered:

'*Señor* – he is dead! When Carlos is coming to tell you, *la policia* are talking to the señor's father. He is at home from his office for the siesta. They have ask where are you, señora, and no person do not know. My father say it is best now you go home. We go together, yes? We say you have made the visit with Jorge if it is not best for you to tell true why you leave. I give you back your clothes and shoes, yes?'

Lucy took in only half what Conchita was saying. One fact took prominence over all others – Guy had been in a car accident and was dead. Death was not something she would have wished for him, frightened although she had been of his inexplicable change of character; his violence when he'd raped her. It was almost as if he hated her even whilst he was planning to keep her with him at any cost. She would never know now what plans he had for the future. He must have realized if he'd thought about it at all, that her parents would have insisted upon seeing her sooner or later; that he could not have kept her locked in her room in the villa like a character in a Brontë novel. If no one else, the servants would have talked. And what of Guy's father? It was inconceivable he would have allowed such a thing.

Only now did Lucy realize suddenly that she had no further need to fear the future. Her married life was over. She would never see Guy again. A wave of sadness suddenly engulfed her. She had once loved him and he had loved her – a jealous, possessive love, perhaps, but his adoration was unquestionable. They had been so happy at first – and could have continued as such had Guy not suddenly changed. Was it the advent of the baby, the miscarriage which had somehow altered their relationship? Could they have been happy forever after despite the fact that Guy had not wanted children? He had never admitted such feelings before their wedding – not even when she had spoken of buying a house in the country one day when they had children and needed a garden rather than a London flat.

'Señora!' Conchita's voice dragged her out of such random thoughts. 'It is soon four o'clock. If I am to stay in the employ at the Villa, it is time I am again on my duties. I think it good thing if I do not leave my work and can take care of you.'

Lucy lent forward and embraced the girl . . . who had of her own free will, offered her friendship and now her protection. Whatever happened in the future, she would never forget

Conchita or how much her moral support meant at this moment. She was still wearing her clothes and in the girl's small but spotless bedroom, she changed back into her own sundress. Staring at her reflection in the small dressing table mirror, she saw that there were dark shadows under her eyes and an ugly bruise on one bare shoulder. Conchita, too, had seen it and going to a drawer, withdrew a thin, tasselled shawl. Draping it around Lucy's shoulders, she said:

'This I wear for fiesta. Today we say you buy in Marbella for England. I do not think the good *cura* will punish me when I go to confession for the lie.' She attempted a smile as together they went back downstairs. Carlos had already left but Conchita's father was waiting for them. He took both of Lucy's hands in his and spoke rapidly in Spanish.

'He wish to tell you he very sorry so bad the accident but we must never forget that what happens to us is God's will – and even death must therefore be for the good. He wish you go safely to your family, señora, and to say he has not forget your kindness to Jorge.'

'Nor will I forget you and your family's kindness to me,' Lucy said. She drew the pendant from her pocket and pressed it into the man's hand. 'Please tell him that I have no wish to keep it – it has bad memories for me. I would like him to sell it if he can and use the money towards a really good electric chair – one Jorge can drive himself.' Seeing that the father was about to refuse the jewel, she closed her fingers over his and turned to the maid.

'Tell him, Conchita, that this is not a gift for him so he does not have to be too proud to take it. It is a present for Jorge who I think is a very brave boy and more than deserves it.'

When Conchita had translated, the man's expression changed and he nodded vigorously, smiling as he said over and over again: '*Si, si*. Jorge *bravo niño* – like a matador!'

The interlude, unrelated as it was to the dreadful news they had just received, made it easier for Lucy to say her good-byes and hurry back up the hill with Conchita who now pushed her bicycle. The sun had disappeared and there was a chilly autumnal breeze stirring the branches of the fruit trees as they reached the orchards of La Finca de Alcazar. They could now see Carlos picking grapes in the greenhouse. He waved to them and called out in Spanish to Conchita. She turned quickly to Lucy.

'Carlos tell me more people now come to talk to Señor Weaver. They in Spanish car but he say they clothed like English people. He is not near to hear they speaking. We go into the house and I find who comes, señora.'

There was no need for Conchita to do any investigations. As she disappeared round the back of the house to go in by the kitchen door, Herbert Weaver came out of the front door to meet Lucy. His face was a mask of grief.

'Lucy, my dear girl!' he said in a choked voice. 'I don't know how to tell you this but Guy . . .' His voice broke and it was a full minute before he continued huskily, 'Guy has been in a car accident. He was driving his Sagaris on that six-lane carriageway going to Malaga, and a car came out of a side turning. I don't know how to tell you this, but Guy . . . my son . . . he was killed, Lucy.'

His grief was obviously so genuine Lucy felt only the deepest pity for him. Her own feelings seemed strangely numb – almost as if she was no longer capable of feeling anything. Perhaps she was in shock, she thought as Guy's father wept on her shoulder. How long they stood there, Lucy could not be sure but she became aware that someone was now standing in the doorway looking at her. It was, she realized, one of the Englishmen that Carlos had spoken about. After a second look, she gently removed herself from her father-in-law's grasp and held out her hand. She had recognized the man but was beyond surprise at his sudden appearance, not just in Spain but here at the Finca.

'It's Inspector Govern, isn't it?' she said as he stepped forward to shake her hand. 'We last met at my home in Ferrybridge. You'd been to Miss Lyford's funeral and came back to tea with us. I'm really pleased to see you but . . . but can I ask how you come to be here? Do you know that my husband has just been killed in a car accident?'

'So Mr Weaver has been telling me,' Govern said quietly, hearing the slight note of hysteria in her voice. 'Perhaps you would like to come indoors where we can talk,' he added gently. 'I think you know my detective sergeant, David Beck. He's in your salon trying to translate what the Spanish police are telling him. He'll be as pleased to see you as I am. You see, nobody knew where you were and we had started to worry lest you had been in the car with your husband and wandered off in a dazed state after the accident.'

'I was in the village,' Lucy said, deliberately vague lest her father-in-law, who was now clinging to her arm, was aware that Guy had disapproved of her wish to befriend her maid's little brother.

'I think I'll go and lie down for a bit, Lucy,' he said as they went indoors. 'It's been such a dreadful shock.' His voice broke as the tears threatened once more. 'Lucy, my dear, will you look after the inspector? Now if you'll excuse me.'

He disappeared up the wide, marble staircase looking like an old man. Lucy beckoned Govern into the salon where Pablo had put a tray of drinks. He looked anxiously at Lucy.

'Are you all right, Mrs Weaver? Would you like to go and lie down for a little while? The Spanish police have been waiting to explain the procedure out here when there is a fatality, but I could relay this information to you later if you don't feel up to hearing the formalities at this moment.'

Lucy shook her head.

'No, I'd rather stay here,' she said. 'I was making plans to go home to visit my family but . . . but my passport is missing and now . . .' Suddenly close to tears, the words died in her throat. As Govern helped her into a chair, she became aware of the two Spanish policemen standing by the window with the second Englishman. He came forward to greet her and then enquired if she felt up to hearing what the Spaniards had to say. When she nodded her head Beck apologized for the fact that the information he had deduced might not be entirely accurate as his knowledge of the Spanish language was not even as good as the Spanish policeman's English.

'Your husband has been taken to a *tanatorio*,' he told her. 'As far as I could make out, this is the equivalent to a chapel of rest. The policemen are waiting to take your father-in-law or yourself to make a formal identification.'

The detective sergeant could see from the expression on Lucy's face that even the thought of such a thing horrified her. Aware that he was about to suggest Guy's father should carry out this formality, she asked if there was not some other person to carry out the task. Guy must have sustained some terrible injuries in the accident and knowing how devoted

Herbert Weaver was to his son, she was prepared at worst to go herself rather than subject him to such an ordeal.

At this juncture, Inspector Govern intervened.

'I believe I would be right in thinking that Mr Weaver's lawyer can make the identification. As I understand it, a business card was found in your husband's wallet after the accident and contact was made with his office who provided the police with the lawyer's name. Apparently he has the documentation required by Spanish law to make the identification if that is what you and Mr Herbert Weaver wish.'

Beck continued to explain the current situation to Lucy. Unless she or her father-in-law wished her husband's body to be flown back to England, he told her, burial here in Spain must take place within seventy-two hours. As he, Beck, had understood the legalities, for the former option to take place, many formalities would be required. Their lawyer would, of course, make such arrangements for them as inevitably there would be a great deal of paperwork.

'I'll go and talk to my father-in-law at once,' Lucy said, rising swiftly to her feet. 'I don't think he would want Guy taken back to England – he has lived out here in Spain for so long and he only goes to England very occasionally.'

When she left the room Beck closed the door behind her, and returned to Govern's side.

'I think that poor girl is genuinely very shocked,' he said in a low voice, 'but grief-stricken, no way. She hasn't even been married a whole year. She seemed more concerned about her father-in-law's feelings than her own.'

Inspector Govern's face was thoughtful.

'Wish I could speak the lingo!' he said as much to himself as to Beck. 'I think I might give my good friend Señor Jóse Miguel Echevarria a ring – see if he will come out here tomorrow and do a bit of questioning for me. That manservant, Pablo – he knows more than he admitted when he was asked if he knew why Guy Weaver had left his lunch uneaten and raced off to Malaga at a moment's notice. And where was Miss Lucy Locket? With her maid? I'll wager that girl, too, could tell us a thing of two about her mistress. Yes, David, I think Señor Echevarria might be quite useful.'

Beck regarded his superior quizzically.

'Not sure if I quite understand your motive, sir? I mean,

you can't accuse a dead man of murder, can you? Suicide maybe, but not a murder committed twenty years ago.'

'Maybe not!' Govern agreed, 'but I'd rest easier if I could at least prove it to myself. That's what we came out here to do, Beck, remember? So we learned Weaver was more than capable of murder; learned it was rejection or rebuttal by females that triggered his rages; we've learnt that he had the time, means, ability and will to attack the old lady so savagely. But what we don't have, David, my boy, is a motive. Why? It certainly wasn't because she caught him about to pinch her silver – not even her helper knew its value and our murderer was rich enough not to need to risk his life petty thieving. No, David, I shall not be able to sleep easy in my bed at night until I know *why* a respectable, wealthy, middle-aged, middle-class Englishman suddenly takes it into his head to murder a harmless pensioner virtually unknown to him. Guy Weaver killed her – I know it and one day, I'll find out why. Now David, find that Pablo fellow and get him to show you how to use the house phone. Here's the lawyer's card with his number. Tell Señor Echevarria I'd like him to be here just as soon as he can.

Twenty-Three

Although it was mid winter, the sun was sparkling on the snow outside the house. Indoors in the salon a fire was burning brightly in the fireplace when Tom returned from Geneva in search of his guardian. Charles Rowan was standing by the window watching the boats on the lake which was a slate-blue grey. Some were sailing, some fishing and the occasional passenger steamer plied to and fro. He turned to look at the young man he had come to think of after all these years as his adopted son.

'All spick and span?' he enquired, aware Tom had taken his car down to the garage for a full service. Tom had decided to sell it and buy a newer model so needed it to be in top condition.

He nodded, his mind elsewhere as he held out his hand. In it was a small silver memory stick.

'The man who was cleaning the inside of my car found this under the back of the driver's seat,' he said, his expression uneasy. 'It isn't mine. I think . . . I think it may be Van's.'

The older man looked puzzled.

'Surely not, Tom. I thought you said the police took charge of your sister's computer along with her papers and suchlike.'

Tom nodded.

'Yes, but no one could find the memory stick although I knew for a fact Van had one.' His voice faltered for a moment before he continued. 'After she died, I tried to remember when she had last used her laptop but I suppose I wasn't thinking too clearly and it wasn't until weeks later that I recalled her taking it to the Godstows the day of the wedding rehearsal. She had all her recipes on it and she had volunteered to cook the meal that evening.'

'And Vanessa left it there?'

'No! I remember her putting it on the back seat of my car. We were driving back to Brighton after the meal. I remember carrying the laptop into the flat for her but I can't recall if the memory stick was with it. It may have fallen off.'

'Where is her laptop now?' Charles asked.

'I gave it to young Julia when the police returned it. I'd wiped it clean, of course, but . . . I suppose I should plug this into my computer, just in case there's anything on it I should know about.'

Tom's guardian was sufficiently sensitive to realize that Tom half-expected to find a suicide letter on the memory stick. No explanation had ever been found for his sister's death and the boy had found it hard to accept that Vanessa had chosen to do such a horrific thing as kill herself whilst he was staying with her and would be the one to find her body. He preferred to think she had accidentally overdosed on her diabetic medicine.

Concerned for Tom, he waited anxiously for him to return from the study they both used as an office. When eventually Tom did so, he looked quite devastated and all but fell into one of the armchairs opposite his guardian. He held out a sheet of paper.

'I printed off a copy!' he said dully. 'Oh, Uncle Charles, I just wish I hadn't found that damn stick . . .' He broke off, clearly unable to continue. His voice trailed into silence as he handed the printout to his guardian.

The older man regarded him anxiously as he ran his eyes quickly down the text.

> Dear Tom,
>
> If I should have an accident or die or anyone else I know and care about is hurt or killed, I want you to know the truth about Guy Weaver. On Friday, 13th July he came to the flat and raped me. I cannot tell Lucy or anyone else because he has sworn to harm them if I do and although I have thought about it, I am in no doubt he is ruthless enough to do as he threatens. He is an evil man and I cannot bear the thought that Lucy is going to marry him. I have to say that if I were not such a coward, I would kill him rather than let Lucy marry him. I know I can't do that, not because of what would happen to me

but because of how Aunt Joan and Tom and Lucy and all the family would feel if I was imprisoned for life. That is why I have decided to put a stop to the wedding in a less drastic way.

I have offered to cook the evening meal on the day of the wedding rehearsal. I recalled the warning the doctor had given me about the effects if I had too much or too little sugar in my blood. Too little and I would become dizzy, disorientated, unsteady on my feet. People might think I was drunk.

It was then the idea came to me that I can give Guy some of Aunt Joan's diabetic tablets that keep her blood sugar levels lower. People will assume Guy is drunk or ill and if he loses consciousness, he'll be taken to hospital. Unaware he has taken the pills, they're unlikely to use a stomach pump on him. I presume they'll test him for alcohol levels since they have no reason to suspect he is suffering from low blood sugar. Hopefully on the following day, he will still be too unwell to attend the wedding.

I realize this plan is not foolproof but I can't think of anything better so it will have to suffice for the time being. I can crush the tablets and I've suggested a curry supper so the pills aren't detected. I've just *got* to stop the wedding somehow. If anything should happen to me or to the family, then this letter is to go to the police so they know who is responsible. Tom, if you find this message and anything has happened to me, please take whatever action is necessary to stop Guy hurting anyone else. He is truly an evil man . . .

'So Van didn't kill herself,' Tom murmured as his guardian returned the letter to him. 'All she wanted was to stop the wedding taking place – she must have taken the tablets she meant for Guy by mistake. Maybe it affected her own blood sugar levels.'

Man of the world though he was, Charles was shocked by the revelation. Seeing that Tom was on the brink of tears, he tried to keep his voice matter of fact.

'Have to let the police know about this,' he said. 'Daresay they'll inform the coroner, but between you and me, I doubt there will be another inquest – not now. As for Weaver – got his just desserts, didn't he?'

Tom's expression hardened.

'I think with a quick death in a car accident, he got off lightly! My God, Uncle Charles, to think Lucy was married to that man! Thank God he's dead or knowing what I know now, I might personally have killed him. I suppose Lucy will have to be told about this!'

'That's for you to decide, old chap. There's one thing I don't understand, if Vanessa meant Weaver to have that drug, how come she took it herself? It's pretty obvious she didn't mean to.'

'No, it was meant for Guy but young Julia switched the plates. She told us after Van died that she'd done so. She thought it was from food poisoning, you see, so she was horrified to think she was responsible for killing Van albeit by mistake.' A faint smile momentarily crossed his face as he added: 'I have a lot of time for JuJu; she was more perceptive than any of us; she never liked Guy – told me once there was something creepy about him.'

The older man nodded.

'It can happen like that – kids and dogs sensing things we're too preoccupied as we get older to notice. You'd better take some time off, Tom, and have a word with that detective – you said he was a decent sort of fellow. Not a good idea to drive, perhaps. Get yourself a ticket to Gatwick and fly over. I'll deal with whatever is outstanding at the bank.'

Tom booked his ticket on the internet and telephoned the Godstows to ask if he might stay with them for a few nights, by which time he had made up his mind to say nothing to the Godstows about Vanessa's letter until after he had spoken to Inspector Govern. One of the questions he wanted answered was whether he was morally or indeed legally obliged to reveal what he now knew to Lucy.

When he had visited the Godstows at New Year, he'd found Lucy very subdued. It was, of course, three months since Guy's funeral in Spain where she had remained a further two weeks supporting her grief-stricken father-in-law, so he was not particularly surprised that she had still been in shock. Nevertheless, he had hoped that the seasonal Christmas

festivities, always so warm-hearted at the Godstows, would
have cheered her up. At least by the time he was due to return
to Switzerland he had managed to persuade Lucy to join him
on a skiing holiday with her sisters and Jonnie at Easter.

Since then, Julia had kept her word to write to him.

According to Julia when Lucy had first arrived home she
had been quite ill; crying and not eating properly and having
nightmares. They were so bad that their mother had moved
into her room so she was there to reassure Lucy when she
woke from one of her horrible dreams. Personally, Julia could
not think of a reason why Lucy should be so disturbed. In the
daytime, she never mentioned Guy but talked a great deal
about the paralysed boy and his sister and the father's plan
to buy him an expensive battery-operated wheelchair so the
child was not confined to the house. Lucy had even asked her
mother if she might invite the boy, Jorge, and his sister,
Conchita, for a summer holiday. Neither had ever been out
of their own country. There was no worry about money to
pay for such a holiday – or, indeed, for anything else. Guy
had not left a will so everything he owned would go to his
widow, so their father had said, and Guy had been a wealthy
man. Julia doubted if anyone could possibly spend so much
money as he was thought to have. Lucy, Julia wrote, planned
to give most of it away, saying she was going to pay for
Jemma's and her university fees, a car for Jonnie and a new
top-of-the-range cooker for Mum. She related that their dad
had said he didn't want anything but Lucy was going to buy
him a hut to put up in the garden with all the newest DIY
tools ready for when he retired. He loved mending things and
carpentry was his main hobby.

Her most recent letter told him Lucy was really looking
forward to the skiing trip; that she had at last begun to laugh
and joke again. Moreover, she had put back some of the weight
she had lost and looked more like her old self again.

He tried now to imagine how Lucy would feel knowing the
husband she had adored was a cruel rapist; that Vanessa, her
dearest friend, had died trying to protect her from marriage
to such a man.

Twenty-four hours after he had booked his flight, Tom sat
opposite Inspector Govern in his office in Brighton Police

Station. When Govern had finished reading the print-out of Vanessa's letter which Tom had handed to him, he did not hesitate replying to Tom's question as to whether Lucy need be told about it.

'It's never a good idea to hide the truth, however unpalatable!' he said. 'If you want my honest opinion, I'm none too sure if she will even be very surprised. When my detective sergeant and I went to Spain and met Mrs Weaver – or should I say Miss Godstow as I understand she now prefers to be called – we found her shocked but not, I would say, grief stricken, by her husband's sudden death. I shouldn't really be mentioning this but we questioned her maid who told us that he had twice physically abused her and that she was on the point of leaving him. Furthermore, the manservant was under the impression she had already left the house and that her husband was racing to the airport in Malaga to prevent her escaping to England. He had hidden her passport. The father-in-law found it in his son's desk. It is all in my report of course, but his wife was anxious her parents should know nothing about it. She maintained that seeing her husband was well and truly dead, his past behaviour did not matter and that knowledge of his true character could only cause them distress.'

But it mattered to him, Tom thought. He had tried desperately hard not to be jealous of Weaver or to feel bitter about Lucy's adoration of the man; not to resent the radiant look on her face when she had returned from her honeymoon. Maybe in the future there might now be a chance for him. Even if Lucy only cared half as much for him as he loved her, it would be enough.

Having established from Govern that he would give Vanessa's letter to the Coroner and having been told there was nothing more he need do, Tom took the train to Ferrybridge and made his way to the Godstows' house. Julia and Lucy had just returned from a walk with the dogs. They were both muffled against the cold. Julia saw him first and like a large boisterous puppy, she raced across the lawn and flung herself into his arms.

'Mum said you'd be here in time for tea!' she said. 'We were coming to fetch you from the station. Did you get a taxi? Did I write and tell you Widger's going to have puppies in March? And Mum says we can keep one . . .'

She was still chattering as Tom looked beyond her as Lucy joined them. He noticed at once how much better she looked as she smiled up at him – a warm, intimate smile.

'Of all the people in the whole world, I can't think of anyone I would rather see than you, Tombo!' she said as they followed Julia and the dogs into the house. Removing their coats, they went into the sitting room. Lucy pulled Tom down beside her on the sofa. Looking at the two of them, Julia drew a long sigh.

'I suppose you two are going to start talking about the old days when you did this, that and the other together and wouldn't let me join in. Oh, well, I know when I'm not wanted. I'll go and make some tea.'

'They were good days, weren't they, Tom?' Lucy said as he took her hand in his. 'In many ways, I think they were the happiest days of my life.'

Tom smiled down at her, his heart full.

'If I have my way, there'll be many, many more,' he said. He was in no doubt now that this was not the time to burden Lucy with the knowledge that Vanessa's death had resulted from a misplaced plan to protect her. That could happen in the future when hopefully, memories of the terrible events of the past year had diminished with time. Meanwhile, he wanted nothing more then to see her continue to smile so happily again.

Back at the police station, Govern was showing the print-out of Vanessa's letter to Beck.

'Have you put two and two together yet, Beck? I'll bet you a hundred pounds to a penny the information in Vanessa Lyford's letter will turn out to be the motive for the Seaford murder.'

Beck's expression was nonplussed.

'Can't say I see the connection, sir.'

'Think about it. Weaver rapes the Lyford girl . . . gets cold feet afterwards as he realizes she can spill the beans and bust up the coming marriage. Threatens to harm the people who she cares about, so that she keeps mum. But how does he know she hasn't told at least one member of the family? No one has said anything but the girl has now killed herself. Did she leave a suicide note saying she'd been raped by him? What were the police going to discover?'

There was a look of quiet satisfaction on his face as he tapped the top of a bundle of files in his out tray.

'I had another look through the Lyford girl's file,' he said watching his sergeant's expression change as he spoke. 'I then realized – with hindsight, of course – that the statement made by the batty old girl in the flat below should not have been disregarded. In case you have forgotten, Beck, when she was questioned after the suicide, she kept reiterating that the girl in the flat had had a friend to stay – a secret lover who she took up to her flat when her nice young flatmate was away. That coincides with the date the Godstow family were on their summer holiday so it could very well have been the night of the rape that she saw the so-called lover.'

'And the description of the visitor fitted Weaver!' Beck concluded wryly.

Govern nodded.

'So what with one thing and another, Weaver must have been in a cold sweat waiting to see if anyone knew what he'd done. Follow me so far? But no one has behaved strangely towards him so he begins to relax. His wife still loves him. The Lyford girl is dead and apparently we, the police, have found nothing. Then something suddenly turns up. Here's where the elderly Miss Lyford comes in. She lets him know – or he finds out somehow – that she knows he raped her niece. She is on the point of exposing him; or maybe he just thinks it – guilty conscience and all that! Anyway, he tries to get the info from her, she refuses to hand it over and wham – he stabs her.'

'Again and again and again!' Beck reminded him dryly.

'So, the man is a psychopath. Remember the MacGregors in Spain, Beck? Remember the story of the boy's mother clearing off at a moment's notice leaving the pampered kid high and dry? Guy Weaver had every reason to feel hate, to mistrust women, to know they had the power to hurt him. He fits my picture frame, Beck, and dead or not, I'll not rest until I've proved him guilty.'

Beck glanced quickly at the rigid set of his boss's jaw. He knew that look – and the tone of voice.

'But, sir, what good will it do? Weaver's dead – well and truly buried in a foreign grave! Lest we forget!'

Govern scowled.

'I'm not in the mood for jokes, David. As for graves, what about poor Miss Lyford in her English grave? She deserves to have the police find out who ended her life so savagely – and, if I can, why.'

It was Lucy who finally produced the missing piece of the puzzle. A week later, as she and Tom sat round the kitchen table with Inspector Govern going once again through the minutiae of the weeks before Aunt Joan's death, she described how she and Tom had cleared the flat in Brighton after Vanessa's death. It had to be emptied because they were reletting it, she explained. That was when she had found an unposted letter addressed to Vanessa's great aunt. She explained why she had taken it back to the flat in order to hand it over next day to Miss Lyford but in the end, Guy had offered to post it. She had never seen it again.

'But he almost certainly did see it,' Govern said wryly, 'and fearing her niece had spilled the beans, he knew he could be in big, big trouble.'

'So he went down to Seaford and bumped her off,' Beck muttered.

Govern nodded.

'That's about it. He borrowed Hart-Pennant's Volvo, which, unfortunately for him, was recognized by the small boy. Ran out of time so had to drive it to Birmingham where he had a lunch date, which was his watertight alibi. Lost his temper at the service station so once again, the Volvo was noticed – his second big mistake. Drives back to London, returns Hart-Pennant's car and thinks he has got away with it until . . .'

He paused whilst he turned over some pages in the file in front of him.

'Until that young farm lad found some of Miss Lyford's silver in the river just off the M40, which happens to be Weaver's route to Birmingham where he had a client. That tied in with the fracas at the service station when an identical Volvo to Hart-Pennant's was involved. Then there is H-P's statement saying Weaver had the key to his garage, so we know he could have borrowed the Volvo which the kid saw in Seaford. It's all there, Beck – circumstantial evidence, but I reckon enough to convict him had he lived even without witnesses or forensic confirmation.'

'Got off lightly, didn't he?' Beck commented. 'Chap like that deserves hanging – or committing if he really was mad.'

'Mad enough to kill someone he thought could lose him the woman he loved!' the older man commented.

'Loved?' Beck's tone was one of disbelief. 'Yet according to the Spanish maid, he hit his wife so badly she was bruised for several days.'

Govern closed the file with a sigh.

'Let's turn our thoughts to happier things, such as the tenner you owe me. Are you willing to admit now that my hunch about Weaver was a hundred per cent on-target?'

Beck nodded, grinning.

'Willing to have another bet, Beck? Lucy Godstow has probably had one of the worst shocks a young girl can have but mark my words, well before the year's out, it's my bet she will have married again; if not married, then she'll be engaged. That young fellow, Tom Lyford, worships the ground she treads on and I'll hazard a guess she will realize he's just the right sort of husband for her.'

Beck snorted.

'Anyone would be better than Weaver. All the same, my old Granny used to say: "Marry in haste and repent at leisure", and as far as the Weaver girl goes, how right my Granny was.'

Govern smiled.

'There's also one about not wasting time when you find your true love! So what's your answer, Beck? Deal or no deal as Noel Edmunds might say?'

'No deal!' said Beck. 'Although I would like to know when you qualified as an agony aunt, sir?'

'That's enough cheek from you, my boy,' Govern said as he pocketed the ten-pound note Beck was offering him. But he was smiling as he added: 'Come on, treat you to a drink at the Greyhound.'

He was still smiling for some time later, knowing that he had been right about Weaver all along.